The Digest Enthusiast
Book Fourteen

I0682854

Peter Enfantino

John Kuharik

Michael Neno

Vince Nowell, Sr.

Jack Seabrook

Robert Snashall

Bob Vojtko

Ward Smith

Edited by Richard Krauss

The Digest Enthusiast (TDE) Book Fourteen
Published twice a year by Larque Press LLC

Editor/Designer: Richard Krauss
Cover: Creature from *20 Million Miles to Earth*, as seen in the classic Columbia Pictures film, photo colorized by Richard Krauss.
Cartoons: Bob Vojtko (pages 46, 47, 53, 76, and 128)

Printed on demand from June 2021 in the United States of America
and other countries.

Larque Press LLC
4130 SE 162nd Court
Vancouver, WA 98683

Visit <larquepress.com> for news about current digest magazines and vintage digest covers. Join our mailing list for exclusive updates on *The Digest Enthusiast* and other Larque Press projects. Sign up at <larquepress.com>

Back Cover Images
Manhunt Detective Story Monthly August 1955
Ed McBain's Mystery Book No. 3 1961
The Haunt of Horror No. 2 August 1973
Vanguard Science Fiction No. 1 June 1958
Terror Detective Story Magazine No. 3 Feb. 1957
Startling Mystery Stories No. 1 Summer 1966

Our thanks to our contributors for some of the cover images that appear in this edition. Cover images are retouched to remove defects from the original source material. When reference material is not available, retouched areas are "best guess." In some cases text may be reset in a font similar to the original work.

Opposite:
Ellery Queen Mystery Magazine May/June 2021. Cover by Jeff Lee Johnson.
Fantasy & Science Fiction March/April 2021. Cover by Mondolithic Studios.

The Digest Enthusiast
ISSN 2637-448X (print)
ISSN 2637-4498 (digital)
ISBN 978-1-7344548-7-1 (14C color interior)
ISBN 978-1-7344548-6-4 (14B greyscale interior)

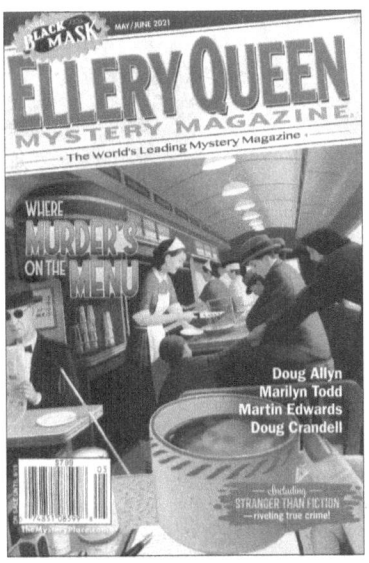

4

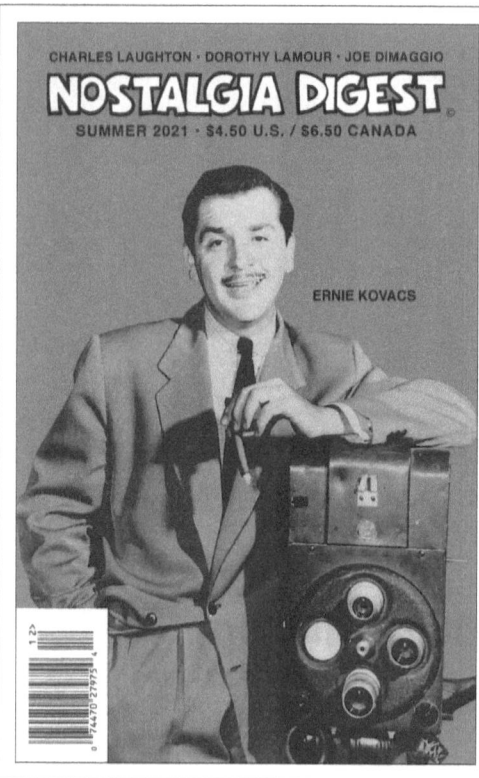

Steve Darnall: Nostalgia Digest

"The Summer issue of *Nostalgia Digest* includes a cover story about how **Ernie Kovacs** transformed television, as well as articles about movie monsters of the 1950s, the remarkable career of **Charles Laughton**, **Joe DiMaggio's** famous hitting streak, the history of Republic Pictures, how the story of a wounded GI led to the creation of a legendary radio show and more—including the schedule for our *Those Were the Days* radio show, broadcast from Chicago every Saturday 1–5 PM (CST) on WDCB 90.9 FM and online on <wdcb.org>."

News Digest

Startling Stories Vol. 34 No. 1

The long awaited return of *Startling Stories* from Wildside Press debuted in February 2021. Weighing in at 252 pages, this pulp-size trade paperback includes two dozen tales of startling science fiction and includes favorite authors like **Adrian Cole**, **Franklyn Searight**, **Robert Silverberg**, and **Cynthia Ward** to name just a few. Like *Weirdbook*, the magazine is edited by **Doug Draa**.

Rusty Barnes: Tough Crime

"Stay tuned for *Tough* 3 and 4, that'll collect stories from the ToughCrime blog. Timing remains tentative—you know aside from time, life, money, and technology it's no big whoop putting this stuff together."

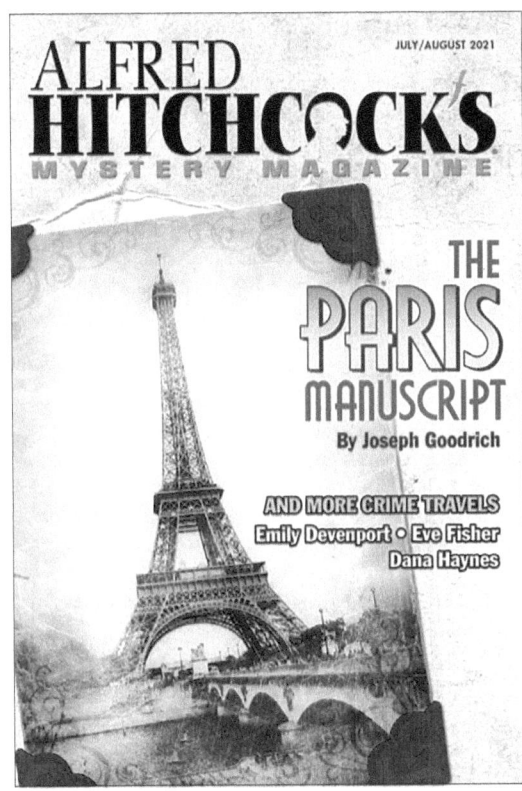

Jackie Sherbow: Alfred Hitchcock's Mystery Magazine

"*AHMM*'s July/August 2021 issue presents its Black Orchid Novella Award winner, a police procedural set in Ecuador by **Tom Larsen**, and tales by **Eve Fisher**, **Bob Tippee**, and more.

"The September/October issue features award-winning authors **John Boland**, **Michael Bracken**, **Barb Goffman**, **Robert Lopresti**, and **Mark Thielman**.

"November/December issue will ring out the year with a holiday tale and work by **Loren Estleman**, **Larry Light**, **Sharon Hunt**, and others."

Updates from the Editors, Writers, and Artists of today's newsstand and indie digest magazines.

Doug Draa: Weirdbook

"The Zombie themed annual will be the next *Weirdbook* issued after the recently published *Weirdbook* No. 44. To follow will be issues No. 45 and 46, already filled and ready for production."

Fate Magazine

Subscriptions to *Fate Magazine* will include a bonus of a classic May 1949 original

in mint condition as long as they last. Submit a recording of your "Strange Encounter" inspired by a favorite article from a past issue of *Fate* and it may be featured on their *True Accounts* podcast.

J.D. Graves: EconoClash Review

"I am currently working on several long pieces. A splatter western novel for Death's Head Press called *Mayhem Sam*, A noir/crime novella for an agent called The PAWNbroker, another round of Cheap Thrills (easy readers for Adults) Editing issue 8 of *ECR* and prepping for our first Neo-Pulp Extravaganza! It's a video event that goes above and beyond your average everday Zoom author reading.

"Lucky Number Seven of *EconoClash Review* presents nine quality cheap thrills of neo-pulp lunacy that will push the envelope of genre limitations. Themes of hard luck and ill fate weave throughout this fresh anthology featuring: time slipping lovers, day-drunk step-dads, fantastically stoned fairies, brawny tavern heroes, haunted beauty queens, underestimated female lawmen, blown-cover spies, smack fiend postmen, and even honest to God cowboys. All of them fighting to survive worlds they unwittingly created themselves. Whether you find top notch schadenfreude to be your guilty pleasure or anonymous up-vote, the seventh issue of *ECR* is your lucky ticket to a world of quality cheap thrills. Read original stories by **Simon Broder, J. Travis Grundon, Angelique Fawns, Matthew X. Gomez, Willow Croft, Russell W. Johnson, Scott Forbes Crawford, Kevin M. Folliard,** and **Mack Moyer** only in *EconoClash Review* No. 7 from Down & Out Books."

ECR Neo-Pulp Reading Extravaganza.

Are you tired of boring Zoom readings? Does life have you down? Is there something living underneath your bed? Have no fear Thrill Seekers for <EconoClash.com> is going to unleash something ten times greater than the hype. We've got a solid roster of the best up and coming indie authors performing quality cheap thrills while existing inside the phantasmagoria of the EconoClash universe. Their stories will include crime, noir, fantasy, horror, Sci-Fi, weird, humor and other words for uplifting gormandizers. **Chandler Morrison**, **V. Castro**, **Shane Hawk**, **Renee Asher Pickup**, **A.B. Patterson**, **Stephen J. Golds**, **Roy Christopher**, **Gabriel Hart**, **Elizabeth V. Aldrich**, **Matthew X Gomez**, and the one and only indie curmudgeon **Alec Cizak**. It promises to be a neo-pulp psychedelic freak-out the likes of which the literary world has never seen before. World Premiere June 1st, 2021 and leaving this world May 31st 2022.

Mini Mysteries

From the publisher of *Women's World*, *Mini Mysteries* is a new digest magzine featuring 40 two-page mystery story puzzles of increasing difficulty. "From murder to sabotage, theft to kidnapping, each enthralling case contains a secret clue. When you think you've cracked it, simply turn to the next page to reveal whodunnit." Authors include **Marti Attoun**, **Richard Ciciarelli**, **Shelley Cooper**, **Janice Curran**, **Michael D'Angona**, **Joan Dayton**, **Gary Delafield**, **Lizibeth Fischer**, **John M. Floyd**, **Michelle Giles**, **Tracie Rae Griffith**, **Rosemary Hayes**, **Amy Hueston**, **Anna Kittrell**, **Robin Kristin**, **Joyce Laird**, **Loretta Martin**, **Kathy L. Matisko**, **Michele Bazan Reed**, **Ginny Swart**, **Yvonne Weers**, **Stacy Woodson**, and **Kendra Yoder**. No indication if this is a one-shot or the beginning of a new series.

Mystery Crime and Mayhem No.6

The sixth issue of *MCM* is built on passionate crimes. "Adultery. Theft. Even dog-napping. All of these can cause tempers to rise, judgement to snap, and bad things to happen. Come explore the more criminal side of passion, along with all the feelings that get engendered."

Tales of the Magician's Skull No. 5

Published by Goodman Games and edited by **Howard Andrew Jones**, *TOTMS* includes authors **James Enge**, **Adrian Simmons**, **John C. Hocking**, **Violette Malan**, **Adrian Cole**, **C.L. Werner**, and **Terry Olson**.

Occult Detective Magazine No. 8

Editor **John Linwood Grant** announced the contents for *ODM8* on March 30. Its authors include **Brandon Barrows**, **Melanie Atherton Allen**, **Paul St. John Mackintosh**, **Uche Nwaka**, **Rhys Hughes**, **Robert Guffey**, **Rebecca Buchanan**, **D G Laredoute**, **C L Raven**, **Carsten Schmitt**, **Christina L White**, and **I.A. Watson**. It's scheduled for release in May 2021, and Grant vows No. 9 will come later this year.

Chris Rhatigan: All Due Respect

The next print collection of stories from the All Due Respect website is planned for a December release—the 2021 edition. Watch this space for more details in our January 2022 edition.

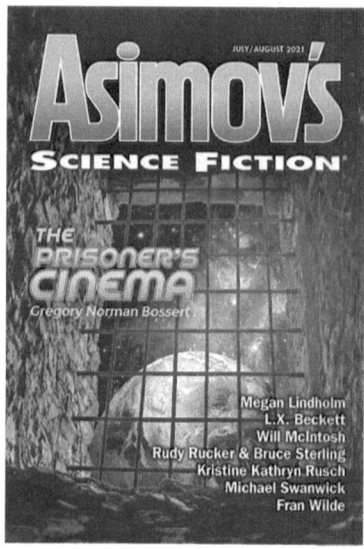

Emily Hockaday: Analog Science Fiction & Fact

Analog is introducing an exciting new award: The Analog Award for Emerging Black Writers. This award will be given to emerging Black authors and will include a year of mentorship as well as publication in the magazine. Our judges for 2021 are **Steven Barnes**, **Nisi Shawl**, **Kim-Mei Kirtland**, **Trevor Quachri**, and **Emily Hockaday**. *Analog* looks forward to the Jul/Aug issue, which features an extra long novella from **Marie Vibbert**, as well as alternate history from **Rosemary Claire Smith**, and a slew of other fiction from **C. Stuart Hardwick**, **James C. Glass**, **Audrey Ference**, **Raymond Eich**, **Brenda Kalt**, **Tom Jolly**, **Joe McDermott** & others! Sep/Oct will include the first part of **Jay Werkheiser's** new serialized novel *Kepler's Laws*, along with writing from **Marissa Lingen**, **J.T. Sharrah**, **Bianca Sayan**, **Robert Scherrer**, **Adam-Troy Castro**, **Holly Schofield** & more!

Asimov's has fiction from **Megan Lindholm**, **Will McIntosh**, **Kristine Kathryn Rusch**, **Fran Wilde**, **Michael Swanwick**, **L.X. Beckett**, and a collaboration from **Rudy Rucker** & **Bruce Sterling**, plus more, in the upcoming Jul/Aug issue. In Sep/Oct and on, we have work from **Elizabeth Bear**, **Rick Wilber**, **Mercurio D. Rivera**, **Jason Sanford**, **S. Qiouyi Lu**, **Michele Laframboise** & more! Our Sep/Oct and Nov/Dec issues will both feature beautiful commissioned covers.

The Dark City April 2021

In this issue of *The Dark City* a meth dealer's girlfriend doesn't like his new career, and a big fan of novelist Elliott Harbinger wants to know more about his idol. In another part of town a fat man doesn't like his wife losing so much weight, while a man on a fishing trip is about to be thrown into the drink. Finally, the good son of a recently deceased mother considers taking revenge on her neighbors. Authors include **Barbara DeMarco-Barrett**, **Anthony Regolino**, **Sharon Hart Addy**, **Evan Clarry**, and **A.M. Porter**.

The *Analog* Award for Emerging Black Voices

Analog Science Fiction and Fact
analogsf@dellmagazines.com

Eligibility Any writer over 18 years of age who customarily identifies as Black, has not published nor is under contract for a book, and has three or less paid fiction publications is eligible.

Logistics Submissions will be open from May 14th – July 23rd to works of hard science fiction of greater than 1,000 words but not over 5,000. Finalists and the winning author will be announced at and in partnership with the Annual City Tech Symposium on Science Fiction.

Judging A diverse committee of science fiction professionals will judge. The panel for 2021 is: Steven Barnes (*Lion's Blood*), Nisi Shawl (*Writing the Other*), Kim-Mei Kirtland (Howard Morhaim Literary Agency, Inc.), Trevor Quachri (*Analog Science Fiction and Fact*), and Emily Hockaday (*Analog Science Fiction and Fact, Asimov's Science Fiction*). Finalists will be chosen and awarded one mentorship session with *Analog* editors including a critique of their submission and a chance to ask questions about the field.

Award Winner With editorial guidance, *Analog* editors commit to purchasing and publishing the winning story in *Analog Science Fiction and Fact*, with the intent of creating a lasting relationship, including one year of monthly mentorship sessions. These sessions will be opportunities to discuss new writing, story ideas, the industry, and to receive general support from the *Analog* editors and award judges.

Submit Submissions will be read blind. Please remove all identifying information from the document before sending it. The file name should be the title of the story. Submissions should be .doc files and follow standard manuscript format. In the body of your email, please include a short cover letter with your contact information, address, the name of your entry, and a statement of interest describing eligibility. Stories can be submitted here: AnalogAward@gmail.com.

Steve Davidson: Amazing Stories

A recent notice on Kickstarter advises: ". . . boiled down to its essentials, means that we have to place the magazine in temporary hiatus, owing to the non-receipt of contracted funds. All existing subscriptions will be honored once we resume publication." Read the full press release on the <amazingstories.com> website.

Steve's most recently published book is the fourth *Amazing Selects* volume, featuring **Allen Steele's** new Captain Future original: "1,500 Light Years from Home." The digest-sized original novel is available now.

Jackie Sherbow: Ellery Queen's Mystery Magazine

EQMM continues its eightieth anniversary celebration with its July/August, September/October, and November/December 2021 issues. July/August is dedicated to the classical mystery and contains whodunits by **Gigi Pandian, Awaska Tsumao, Elvie Simons, G.M. Malliet, Dave Zeltserman,** and **Jon L. Breen**, plus a short thriller by **Joyce Carol Oates**. September/October—the anniversary issue!—contains a classic Black Mask reprint by **Frances Beck** and tales by luminaries such as **Jerome Charyn, Hilary Davidson, Bill Pronzini,** and **Kristine Kathryn Rusch**. Highlights of November/December, which will finish up *EQMM*'s anniversary year, are several holiday mysteries and a newly discovered story by **Elizabeth Peters** (MWA Grand Master and bestselling author of the Amelia Peabody series and other bestselling novels.).

Chuck Carter: Mystery Weekly Magazine

Chuck and **Kelly Carter** are adding hardcover anthologies to their efforts to support indie crime fiction. Their first edition will be *Die Laughing: An Anthology of Humorous Mysteries*. Watch for it this summer.

Gary Lovisi: Gyphon Books

Paperback Parade No. 110, from editor **Gary Lovisi** (Feb. 2021) features Beadles Frontier dime novels, Masked Rider and Lone Ranger, Ballantine Bal-hi SF pbs, Boys Wonder Library UK slim pbs, James Bama covers, Canadian White Circle, and tributes to **Richard A. Lupoff** and **Earl Kemp**.

Gary reports, "*Paperback Parade* No. 111 is out now with a long article on the sleaze fetish paperbacks of After Hours Books, and much more. I have two new books coming out soon, one a Sherlock Holmes novel, and the other a collection of my Griff & Fats hard-boiled crime stories set in the early 1960s."

Sherlock Holmes Mystery Magazine

It's been over a year, but the new *SHMM*—No. 28—became available just as final prep on this News Digest was being finalized. Editor **Marvin Kaye** shares his introduction with the good Dr. Watson, and highlights tales from **Rochelle Campbell**, **Laird Long**, Sanford Zane Meschkow, Victoria Weisfeld, Michael Hemmingson, Marc Bilgrey, Gary Lovisi, Dan Andriacco, **Michael Penncavage**, and **Lee Enderlin**.

Publisher **John Betancourt** also provided info on the nonfiction pieces: "Three 'Bucket' Mysteries," by **Eugene D. Goodwin** and "Three Cheers for Dr. Watson" by **Janice Law**. Cover artwork by **Chery Holmes**, and a cartoon by **Marc Bilgrey**.

And good news, the next issue, No. 29, is just a few months away.

Jennnifer Landels: Pulp Literature No. 30 Spring 2021

"In the futuristic landscape of **Wei-wei Xu's** Superbloom we find retro SF from **Robert Silverberg** and **Leo X Robertson** growing alongside ghostly thanes and ghostly peppers from **PG Streeter** and **Michelle F Goddard**. Celebrate the sights, scents, and sounds, of birth, life, and death with **Adrienne Gruber**, **Paige Elizabeth Wajda**, and **Claire Lawrence**. Toinette strolls the gardens of Versailles and Frankie Ray digs herself deeper in "The Shepherdess" by **JM Landels** and "The Extra" by **Mel Anastasiou**, while the dark wings of the Raven contest winners soar overhead." Content for No. 29 Winter 2021: **Kris Sayer's** mischievous cover goat leads us into lands of myth and mystery with short fiction from **Shashi Bhat**, **SL Leong**, **Brandon Crilly**, **Mike Gillis**, **Erin Wagner**, and **KT Wagner**. The winners of the Hummingbird contest alight, Allaigna returns with **JM Landels**, and Frankie Ray's troubles deepen under **Mel Anastasiou's** pen. Plus a new instalment of "Blue Skies over Nine Isles" by **Joseph Stilwell** and **Hugh Henderson**, and poetry of place from **Abner Porzio** and **Michael Penny**.

John Scoleri & Peter Enfantino: Cimarron Press

Coming in bare•bones No. 6:

- The Annotated Guide to *Web Terror Stories* by **Peter Enfantino**
- **Don D'Ammassa** on the Hammer Horror Film Omnibus Novelizations
- **Matthew R. Bradley** on Moon of the Wolf on Page and Screen
- Horror Anthology Series in Britain by **David A. Sutton**
- *The Outer Limits* on Home Video by **Craig Beam**
- Film and TV Adaptations from Gold Key by **William Schoell**
- **Caroline Munro** and the Lamb's Navy Rum Campaign by **John Scoleri**
- **Richard Krauss** on *Private Eye* digest
- Ten Quick Takes from **S. Craig Zahler**
- **Peter Enfantino's** Sleaze Alley
- **David J. Schow's** R&D on *Rod Serling's Twilight Zone Magazine*

Peter advises, "In addition to *bare•bones* 6, 7 and 8, bare•bones—*the best of*—is now available in an affordable hardback edition, and readers can look forward to revised and updated editions of **David J. Schow's** collections *Seeing Red*, *Eye*, and *Black Leather Required*, as well as a new edition of **Richard Christian Matheson's** short story collection, *Zoopraxis*."

Michael Neno Productions

"Two new public domain-sourced tiny mashup microcomics available for purchase: *Betty Bailey and Her Aeroplane of Doom!* a short but deadly spin on childrens' contests and world domination; and *Spaces*, a trippy, mind-twisting journey distilled into a tiny 20-page art object."

Betty Bailey is $3 ppd. *Spaces* is $4 ppd—or both for $6 ppd. Contact Michael for the bundled deal at <mneno@columbus.rr.com> or mail check or cash to:

M.R. Neno Productions
P.O. Box 307675
Gahanna, OH 43230

Josh Pachter Anthologies

"Two very recent releases: *The Great Filling Station Holdup: Crime Fiction Inspired by the Songs of Jimmy Buffett* (Down and Out Books, Feb. '21) and *Only the Good Die Young: Crime Fiction Inspired by the Songs of Billy Joel* (Untreed Reads, April '21). I edited the books and wrote the title story for each of them.

"Coming up this fall: *Monkey Business: Crime Fiction Inspired by the Films of the Marx Brothers* (Untreed Reads)."

Art Taylor

"I've been fortunate to be a finalist for a couple of awards recently: "The Boy Detective & The Summer of '74," from *AHMM*'s January/February 2020 issue, was named a finalist for the Agatha Award for Best Short Story (Malice Domestic is coming up in July) and winner of the Derringer Award for Best Novelette (from the Short Mystery Fiction Society).

"And I wrote the essay "The Short Mystery" for the new collection *How To Write a Mystery: A Handbook from Mystery Writers of America*, edited by **Lee Child** with **Laurie R. King**, from Scribner."

Alec Cizak: Uncle B Publications

"Uncle B. Publications will be celebrating ten years of *Pulp Modern* beginning with the summer issue, which features stories dealing in some way with the year 2011, the year *Pulp Modern* was born. In addition, Uncle B. Publications will be publishing a wide variety of other books, including: the collected adventures of Jack Laramie, *The Drifter Detective*; *Now There Was a Story!*, a collection of crime fiction stories based on the songs on the classic **Johnny Cash** record, *Now There Was a Song!*; *L.A. Stories*, a trilogy of gruesome novellas taking place in Hollywood during the late 1970s and early 1980s; Uncle B. will also be publishing several first novels from a diverse range of writers; finally, Uncle B. will be publishing several poetry chapbooks. Look for all these exciting publications wherever good books are sold!"

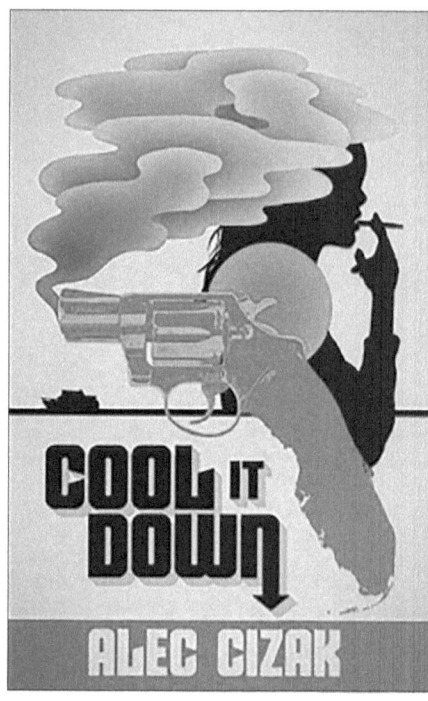

Alec's latest novel, *Cool It Down*, will be released soon from ABC Documentation, an imprint of Down & Out Books.

Weird Tales No. 364

The latest issue of "the magazine that never dies" is now available from select booksellers and the publisher.

This issue's cover is by **Lynne Hansen**. Lynne's work can be seen on covers for Cemetery Dance Publications, Thunderstorm Books, and Raw Dog Screaming Press.

In addition to the print and digital editions, audio versions of *Weird Tales* No. 363 and 364 are also available. Edited by **Jonathan Maberry**, No. 364's authors and poets include **Seanan McGuire, Gregory Frost, Marie Whittaker, Marguerite Reed, Rena Mason, Tim Waggoner, Linda Addison, Darce Stoker** and **Leverett Butts, Weston Ochse, Joe R. Lansdale, Gabrielle Faust, Lee Murray,** and **Alessandro Manzetti**.

Scotch Rutherford: Switchblade Magazine

No news on the magazine's front, but **Scotch** sent the cover he designed for Uncle B's upcoming *The Drifter Detective*.

Grandson of lawman Cash Laramie, private detective Jack Laramie travels the byways of Texas in search of work in the post WWII era. He drives a classic DeSoto along with his lodging, a horse trailer, hitching a ride.

The volume includes yarns by **Garnett Elliott**, **Wayne D. Dundee**, and **Alec Cizak**, with an introduction by **Kevin Tipple**.

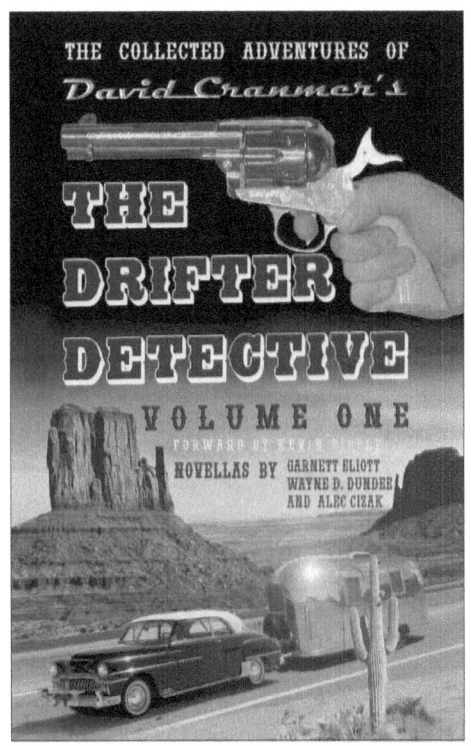

Michael Bracken: Black Cat Mystery Magazine

Since our last issue, Wildside's eighth editon of *BCMM* was released, as were the print editions of Down & Out Books' *Guns + Tacos* Vol. 3 and 4. All three volumes are edited by **Michael Bracken**, the latter with co-editor **Trey R. Barker**.

Guns + Tacos Vol. 3 includes stories by **Eric Beetner** (36 pages), **Michael Bracken** & **Trey R. Barker** (56 pages), and **Alex Cizak** (40 pages). Vol. 4 includes **Ann Aptaker** (43 pages), **Ryan Sayles** (48 pages), **Mark Troy** (49 pages), and a 10-page bonus story for subscribers only by **Trey R. Barker**.

Down & Out: The Magazine

The latest issue of **Rick Ollerman's** crime fiction digest (Vol. 2 No. 2) is out from Down & Out Books. It features an introduction by Ollerman, and fiction by **Don Stoll**, **Michael Cahlin**, **Arthur Klepchukov** & **Kyle Stout**, **John M. Floyd**, **Josh Pachter**, **James O. Born**, **Ken Luer**, **Steven Nester**, **Jeff Vorzimmer**, and **John Shepphird**. The classic reprint this time is by **Stephen Marlowe**, introduced by **Jeff Vorzimmer**. The nonfiction feature is an exchange of emails between **Walter Satterthwait** (who provided continuity where needed) and **Bill Crider** (now both deceased). No word on whether this will be the final issue . . .

Stark House Press

The Manhunt Companion by **Peter Enfantino** and **Jeff Vorzimmer** is now available. This 410-page trade paperback includes Peter's synopsis of every story as well as Jeff's origin and history of the magazine's remarkable 114-issue run. Indices include issues, authors, stories, series, and television episodes based on *Manhunt* stories.

4:20 Noir

A collection of smokin' crime fiction edited by **J. Travis Grundon**, who also designed the cover. Authors include **Alec Cizak**, **Stephen J. Golds**, **Curtis Ippolito**, **Serena Jayne**, **B.F. Jones**, **R. Daniel Lester**, **J. Rohr**, **J.B. Stevens**, **Don Stoll**, **Patrick Whitehurst**, **Rex Weiner**, and **Josh Workman**. Look for it in print and Kindle in June 2021, from Uncle B. Publications.

Justin Marriott: Battling Britons

Over two hundred capsule reviews of British war comics from the 1960s thru 2000s including *Action*, *Air Ace Picture Library*, *Battle Picture Library*, *Battle Picture Weekly*, *Commando*, *Valiant*, *Victor*, *War Picture Library* and *Warlord*. Edited and co-written by **Justin Marriott**, with contributions from **Jim O'Brien**, **Steve Myall** and **James Reasoner**. Foreword from award-winning journalist and war comics expert **Paul Trimble**. Afterword from *Commando* scripter **Gary Martin Dobbs**.

Gordon Van Gelder: Fantasy & Science Fiction

"New *F&SF* editor **Sheree Renee Thomas** continues her first year at the helm. The Sep/Oct issue of *F&SF* features a novella by **Nuzo Onoh** and novelets by **Matthew Hughes** and **Brian Trent**.

"The Nov/Dec issue of *F&SF* will have a novella by **Natalia Theodoridou** and shorter works by **Eleanor Arnason** and **Megan Lindholm**."

Mike Chomko: PulpFest/The Pulpster

PulpFest returns to the DoubleTree by Hilton Hotel Pittsburgh—Cranberry in 2021. The convention is planned for August 19 through 21 in the town of Mars, just north of Pittsburgh. At this writing, the wearing of masks will be required. However, with Covid-19 restrictions evolving, that requirement may change. It's recommended that attendees be vaccinated against the coronavirus.

"Love in the Shadows" is the theme of PulpFest 2021. The convention will salute the centennial of Street & Smith's *Love Story Magazine*—the best-selling pulp of all time—and the 90th anniversary of *The Shadow*—the magazine that launched the hero pulp explosion of the 1930s.

One of the highlights of the convention will be a panel on Shadow creator **Walter B. Gibson**. Moderated by **Ed Hulse**—the author of *The Art of Pulp Fiction*—the panel will feature writer **Will Murray**, artist **Jim Steranko**, and publisher **Anthony Tollin**. All three panelists knew Gibson.

PulpFest will also honor *Weird Tales* artist **Margaret Brundage**, writer **Edgar Rice Burroughs**—creator of Tarzan, John Carter, Pellucidar, and many other fantastic worlds and characters—and the great women editors of the pulps.

All this, plus an expansive dealers' room packed with pulp magazines and related materials, vintage paperbacks, digests, men's adventure and true crime magazines, contemporary genre fiction, first-edition hardcovers, series books, dime novels, original art, Big Little Books, Golden and Silver Age comic books, old-time-radio shows, gaming materials, and film serials, B-movies and related collectibles, and more!

Some of the digest magazines that find their way into the PulpFest dealers' room are *Amazing Stories, Analog, Ellery Queen's Mystery Magazine, Fantastic, If, Fantasy & Science Fiction, Manhunt, The Saint*, and many others. In addition to a great time, all PulpFest members will receive a complimentary copy of the convention's program book, *The Pulpster*. Cherished by pop culture fans, the magazine's 30th issue will be released at PulpFest 2021.

To learn more about PulpFest 2021—including how to register for the convention and book a room at the hotel, the 2021 programming schedule, the Munsey Award, and more, please visit the convention's homepage at <pulpfest. com>. You can also learn about PulpFest on its Facebook page, Twitter feed, or via Instagram.

Stark House Press

THE BEST IN MYSTERY AND NOIR FICTION

LIONEL WHITE
Steal Big/ The Big Caper

"White's writing is brilliant throughout and just pure noir, stripped to the basics and filled with tight detail."—Brian Greene, *Criminal Element*. New introduction by Nicholas Litchfield; afterword by Cullen Gallagher. May 2021.

ARNOLD HANO
Slade/Manhunter

"A superb example of how the characteristics of noir - usually associated with crime fiction and mysteries - can be used in a Western novel."—Alan Cranis, *Bookgasm*. "Fast-paced with strong characters in troubled waters way over their heads."—*Midwest Book Review*. New introduction by Paul Bishop. May 2021.

LORENZ HELLER
Crime Cop/ Body of the Crime

"A young detective is promoted to chief of homicide, and he's greeted with four baffling crimes almost immediately. How he solves them, and how he learns executive capacity are well told." —*The Miami News*. June 2021.

STARK HOUSE PRESS

1315 H Street, Eureka, CA 95501
707-498-3135 www.StarkHousePress.com
Available from your local bookstore, or direct from the publisher.

Stark House Press presents . . .

Staccato Crime is a new series that will offer affordable paperback editions of difficult-to-find noir fiction and true crime from the Jazz Age, 1899-1939. Our first edition brings P. J. Wolfson's *Bodies Are Dust* back into print for the first time in over 60 years with a new introduction by David Rachels!

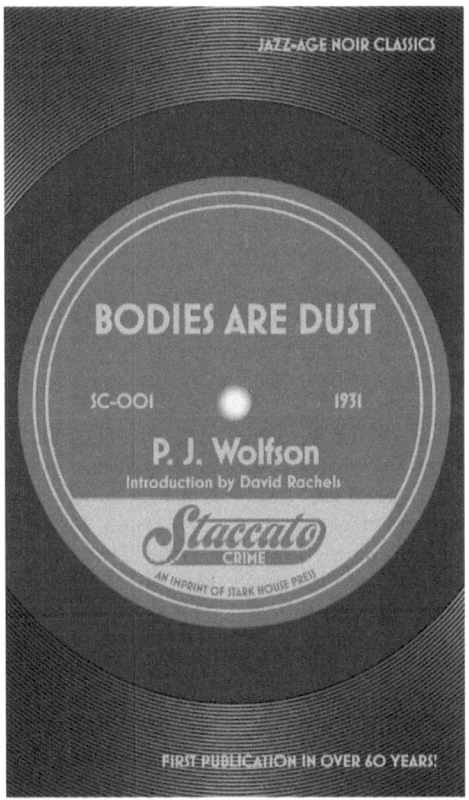

STARK HOUSE PRESS

1315 H Street, Eureka, CA 95501
(707) 498-3135 www.StarkHousePress.com
Available from your local bookstore, or direct from the publisher.

Ed McBain's Mystery Book No. 3
Article by Jack Seabrook

"In 1960, with the [87th Precinct] series selling like wildfire, Pocket books decided to enter the mystery magazine market by capitalizing on the McBain name and success."

–Francis M. Nevins, Jr. *Mystery, Detective, and Espionage Magazines* Greenwood Press, 1983

I have owned a copy of the 1961 digest, *Ed McBain's Mystery Book* No. 3, for decades, but I never thought to look at it as anything other than the place where a Fredric Brown "novelette" (more about that later) was published until recently, when I decided to inspect it more closely. To my surprise, I found that this issue, the last in the short run of the series, was an intriguing mix of fiction and non-fiction by authors born over a century ago and one author still living today. In fact, four of the writers featured in this issue went on to become Grand Masters of the Mystery Writers of America!

Ed McBain's Mystery Magazine is a standard-sized digest (5-1/4" x 7-5/8"),
with color front and back covers and black and white interiors. It was published by Pocket Books in New York and ran only three issues. The first two are dated 1960, while the third is dated 1961. The information in issue number three says it was published bi-monthly, so perhaps the first two issues came out in late 1960 and the third in early 1961. Issue three runs 148 pages, including covers. Ed McBain is listed as the editor and Robert Goodney is listed as the managing editor, so it may be the case that McBain was a figurehead and Goodney put the magazine together.

Under the letter "c" on the cover is a small circle with the number "87" inside; this symbol is also used inside

Ed McBain's Mystery Book No. 3 1961. Cover by Harry Bennett. A previous Johnny Liddell story by Frank Kane appeared in the debut issue of *The Saint Detective Magazine* in Spring 1953, that shares the title, "Dead Drunk," with the adventure in this issue of *McBain's*. But they are different stories, so the claim on this cover of "every story new!" is accurate.

the magazine to mark the end of each story or article and is intended to remind the reader of McBain's by-then popular series of mysteries about the 87th Precinct. The series had begun in 1956 with *Cop Hater* and, by 1961, McBain had written over a dozen novels about these characters. In fact, this digest seems to have ended prematurely, because a television show based on the 87th Precinct books premiered on NBC in September of that year, though it only lasted one season, till April 1962.

The cover of issue number three is a painting by Harry Bennett (1919–2012), who had also painted the covers of the first two issues. Bennett had begun drawing book covers in the mid-1950s and completed the covers for over 3000 books over his thirty-year career, which ended when he retired in 1986. Although the painting is accompanied by a blurb advertising "the first ED and AM HUNTER novelette by Fredric Brown," the scene pictured does not match any scene from the story. Perhaps the digest editor thought an eye-catching painting by a top book cover illustrator would help with sales;

it also suggests that Pocket Books was trying to position this digest to compete with paperbacks on the stands rather than with other digests.

Opening the magazine, the inside front cover features the "Squadroom," which consists of mini-bios of four of the writers whose work appears in this issue: Frank Kane, Irving Shulman, Fredric Brown, and Stuart Palmer. It's possible the bios were provided by the authors themselves; they are accompanied by line drawings of the authors' faces. The Brown mini-bio states that the diminutive author "worked for the Pinkerton Detective Agency before he became disillusioned with the lack of glamour in real-life detective work."

Brief summaries of the stories and articles in this issue follow, along with comments about the authors. (The word counts are my estimates.)

Sounds & Smells by Fletcher Flora (2500 words) ★★★

Rector Goodhue sees his neighbor Charlie Treadwell sitting on the front porch steps of his house and joins him for a chat he'd probably rather forget.

Flora creates a mood of quiet despair in suburbia in a short space, using an understated tone to describe a terrible situation.

Fletcher Flora (1914–1968) wrote mystery short stories and novels from 1950 to 1970, including three books as Ellery Queen.

The Mourners at the Bedside by Hampton Stone (11,000 words) ★★

Old William Bardon will die soon and plans to leave his fortune to his children and grandchildren, but the family thinks granddaughter Sara's husband will murder her as soon as she gets her share of the money. Assistant D.A. Jeremiah X. Gibson is asked to help the family protect the

SQUADROOM

FRANK KANE (Dead Drunk) is licensed to practice law, the result of his young wife's insistence that he secure a law degree as a safeguard in the event that he failed to earn enough at his typewriter to support them. Kane hurried through a law course, passed his bar examination and then—having gotten *that* over with—promptly broke into radio and became one of the highest-paid writers in the business, doing scores of scripts for such shows as "Gangbusters," "The Shadow" and "Nick Carter." Later, he became even more successful as the writer of the Johnny Liddell mystery novels, which have sold millions of copies and been translated into a dozen languages.

IRVING SHULMAN (Because We're Friends) began his career as a novelist with the publication of *The Amboy Dukes*, a harsh, compelling story of street gangs in Brooklyn. The book became a nationwide best seller and today is used in many colleges as a text-book and sociological classic. Since then, Shulman has written many other best sellers, including *Cry Tough!* and *The Big Brokers*. He lives in Hollywood and also writes screenplays; among his credits is *Rebel Without a Cause*, which starred the late James Dean.

FREDRIC BROWN (Before She Kills) worked for the Pinkerton Detective Agency before he became dis-illusioned with the lack of glamour in real-life detective work. He turned to writing in the early 1940's and his first book, *The Fabulous Clipjoint*, which intro-duced Ed and Am Hunter, won the Mystery Writers of America's Edgar award. Brown is one of the world's best writers of suspense novels, the latest of which is *Knock Three-One-Two*.

STUART PALMER (Cure for a Headache) is the creator of the famous spinster-schoolteacher-detective Hildegarde Withers. The attention he gained from the Withers books sent him West to write for the movies—often working on scripts with his good friend Craig Rice. Currently writing for TV in Holly-wood and working on a novel, Palmer has also written a great deal in the field of nonfiction crime, and for many years has been a student of classic murder cases.

PRINTED IN U.S.A.

young woman. He discovers that the husband had a prior wife who died of natural causes—or did she? When he drinks whisky laced with cyanide, the expected murderer becomes a victim. But who killed him, and why?

Plenty of twists and turns in this one, with an engaging narrator who never reveals his name.

Hampton Stone was a pseudonym for Aaron Marc Stein (1906–1985), the first of this issue's MWA Grand Masters. He was better known under another pseudonym, George Bagby, and he wrote over 100 novels. Gibson, featured in this issue's story, starred in

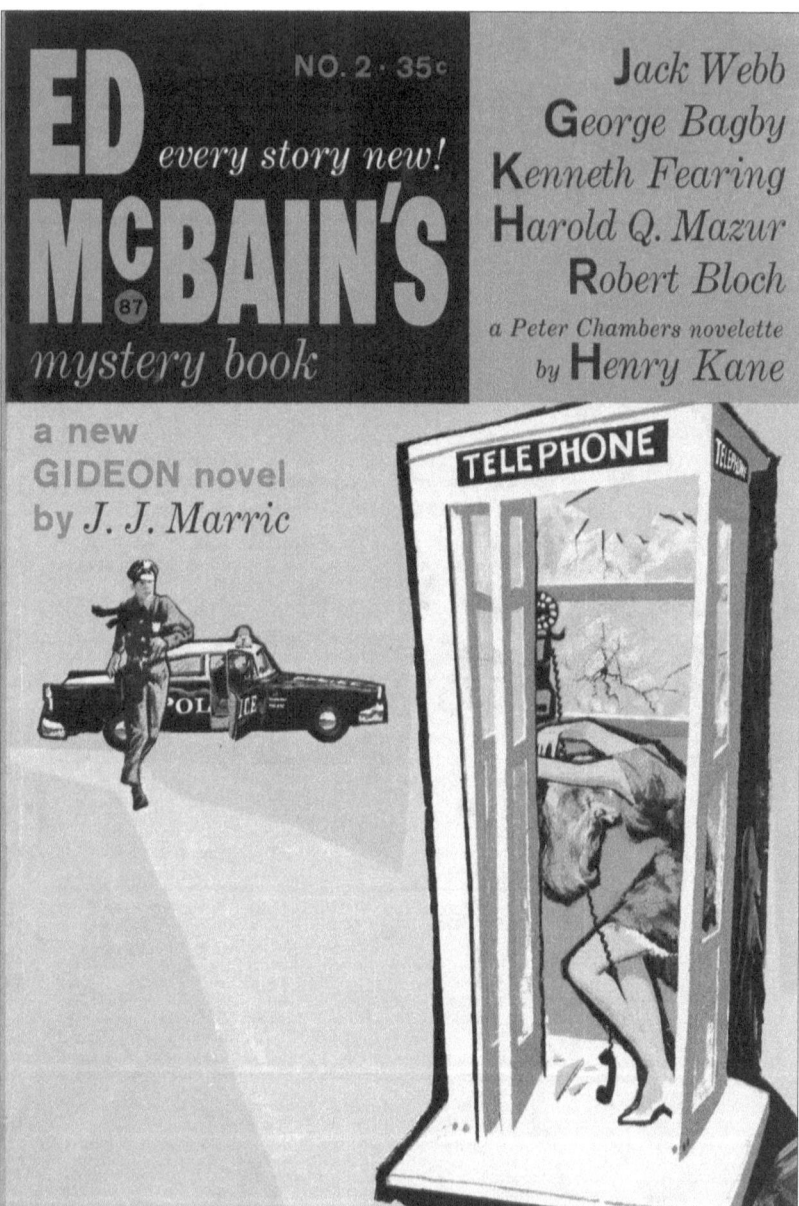

Ed McBain's Mystery Book No. 2 with one of George Bagby's Inspector Schmidt stories, "A Few Dead Birds." Cover by Harry Bennett.

a series of novels from 1948 to 1971. Stein had a story under the Bagby name in the prior issue of *Ed McBain's Mystery Book*.

Sacrifice by Warren Frost (5600 words) ★★½

Newly arrived from Boston in the Old West town of Dobert, a padre must contend with an unfriendly sheriff and a mob seeking vengeance for the murder of an old-timer.

Frost's tale has a powerful ending, but I can't find a lick of information about the author and the FictionMags Index lists just this one story under his name! Perhaps it's a pseudonym?

Incidents on B Street
by Paul W. Fairman (1300 words) ★★

A broken man chases teens out of a dangerous spot in the city and pays a price.

This is a short but effective piece by Paul W. Fairman (1909–1977), who wrote mystery and science fiction stories from 1938 to 1966, novels from 1951 to 1973, and served as editor of *Amazing Stories*, *Fantastic*, and *If* in the 1950s.

Cure for a Headache
by Stuart Palmer (5000 words) ★★★

A true crime story, set at the end of the Gay Nineties, about Roland Molineux, who was tried for two murders by poison. This is an entry in a section titled "The Crime is Murder" that was probably featured in each issue.

Stuart Palmer (1905–1968) was active from the late twenties to the late sixties and is best-remembered for his novels featuring female sleuth Hildegarde Withers. He also wrote non-fiction and scripts for TV and movies, sometimes with fellow crime writer Craig Rice.

Dead Drunk
by Frank Kane (6200 words) ★★½

Rich old Abner Kyner was boozed up when he crashed his car and died, but he wasn't known to be a big drinker. The life insurance company hires private detective Johnny Liddell to look into the death, leading to complications involving Kyner's beautiful wife, his pretty, young secretary, and a sleazy

private eye named Tim Davis.

A fast-moving, traditional private eye story with the usual stock characters.

Frank Kane (1912–1968) was licensed to practice law but chose to be a writer. He succeeded in writing for radio and then wrote nearly 40 novels from the 1940s to the 1960s. Most of his novels and short stories featured Johnny Liddell, and the books sold millions of copies.

BREAK-OUT

Break-Out by Donald E. Westlake
(4400 words) ★★

A survey of escapes through the years from seemingly inescapable prisons yields a sobering conclusion: convicts rarely put as much thought into how to live outside as they do into how to get outside.

Another non-fiction section that looks like a regular feature; this is called a "special report" from the 87th Precinct.

Donald Westlake (1933–2008) is this issue's second MWA Grand Master. He wrote short stories and over 100 books between 1954 and his death.

Service Call by Bruno Fischer
(4800 words) ★★★

When sexy Norma Hamilton is killed one day in her quiet suburban home, the TV repairman is the prime suspect, but what does nosy neighbor Margaret McKay have to do with it?

Well-written with a surprise ending, this smooth bit of work is narrated by Margaret's husband, a mild-mannered dentist.

Bruno Fischer (1908–1992) was a re-

Eve was a perfect wife. That's why Ollie's life was in danger....

BEFORE SHE KILLS
FREDRIC BROWN

THE DOOR WAS THAT OF AN OFFICE IN an old building on State Street near Chicago Avenue, on the near north side, and the lettering on it read HUNTER & HUNTER DETECTIVE AGEN-CY. I opened it and went in. Why not? I'm one of the Hunters; my name is Ed. The other Hunter is my uncle, Ambrose Hunter.

The door to the inner office was open and I could see Uncle Am play-ing solitaire at his desk in there. He's shortish, fattish and smartish, with a straggly brown mustache. I waved at him and headed for my desk in the outer office. I'd had my lunch—we take turns—and he'd be leaving now. Except that he wasn't. He swept

the cards together and stacked them but he said, "Come on in, Ed. Some-thing to talk over with you."

I went in and pulled up a chair. It was a hot day and two big flies were droning in circles around the room. I reached for the fly swatter and held it, waiting for one or both of them to light somewhere. "We ought to get a bomb," I said.

"Huh? Who do we want to blow up?"

"A bug bomb," I said. "One of these aerosol deals, so we can get flies on the wing."

"Not sporting, kid. Like shooting a sitting duck, only the opposite. Got to give the flies a chance."

AN ED AND AM HUNTER NOVELETTE

ED McBAIN'S MYSTERY BOOK / 94

---

porter who ran for office in New York before becoming a pulp fiction writer. He wrote over 25 novels and 300 short stories from 1933 to 1973. "Service Call" was one of his last story credits.

Cops and Robbers (750 words) ★

Humorous, short snippets about un-usual crimes.

Another non-fiction section that is a regular feature, penned by Vincent Gaddis (1913–1977), a newspaper re-porter and public relations man who wrote many stories about paranormal phenomena and who is credited with coining the term, "Bermuda Triangle."

Before She Kills by Fredric Brown (12,000 words) ★★½

Ollie Bookman thinks his wife Eve is trying to kill him, so he hires Ed and Am Hunter to find the truth. Bookman has a heart condition and Ed pretends to be Ed Cartwright, the young half-brother Bookman hasn't seen in years, in order to get a good look from the inside. Eve is a former stripper who

stopped sleeping with Ollie soon after their wedding; he fell in love with an-other woman and she bore him a son, but Eve refuses to grant a divorce. Who is really to blame when Ollie suddenly collapses?

Ed and Am Hunter are likeable de-tectives and this story is anything but hardboiled, but it's fun to encounter them in this setting. Ed does all of the investigating and the mystery comes to a climax quickly. It's awfully short to be called a novelette!

Fredric Brown (1906–1972) wrote seven novels and two "novelettes" fea-turing Ed and Am Hunter. These were among his many mystery and science fiction short stories and novels from 1936 to 1965. His mini-bio on the in-side front cover refers to him as one of the world's best suspense novelists and his initial book won an Edgar Award for best first novel.

Because We're Friends by Irving Shulman (4500 words) ★★★★

When he arrived in Hollywood, TV

star Tucson Cross (formerly known as Sam Slocum) had no intention of becoming an actor. But when a waitress named Rhoda took him in, it was the start of his meteoric rise to fame. Now Rhoda is back, having broken into his apartment, wanting to know what he can do for her.

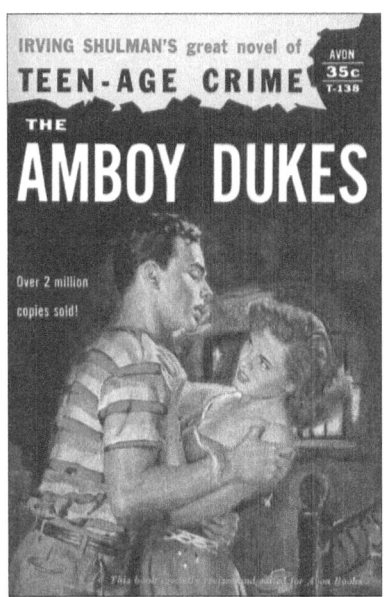

Humor and suspense mix in a terrific satire with a shattering finish!

Irving Shulman (1913–1995) was known for his novels depicting urban life. Among his best-sellers was *The Amboy Dukes*. He lived in Hollywood and wrote screenplays as of this issue's publication. This is only one of two short story credits listed in the Fiction-Mags Index.

Game by Herbert D. Kastle
(3500 words) ★★★

Ed Gaines drives south through Texas, running away from his wife and his responsibilities. On the highway, he witnesses a Cadillac intentionally run over several animals. When he meets the car's inhabitants, things quickly turn violent.

Short but effective, with an ending that becomes obvious as it approaches but is still chilling.

Herbert D. Kastle (1924–1987) started out writing mystery and science fiction stories and novels, then sold countless books when he became a Sidney Sheldon-type of novelist. He was active from 1955 to 1982.

Package Deal by Lawrence Block
(2250 words) ★★★

A hired killer named Castle is retained by the elders of Arlington, Ohio, to murder four criminals who have taken over the town. He does the job in one night but has an unexpected motive.

An excellent short piece by Block with tough and violent imagery: "The bullet went into Baron's mouth and

came out of the back of his head. The bullet had a soft nose and there was a bigger hole on the way out than on the way in."

Lawrence Block (1938–) is this issue's third MWA Grand Master and the only author still living. He started out writing soft-core porn novels in the late 1950s and began writing mystery novels in 1961, the same year this issue was published. He has written over 100 short stories and over 50 novels in his long career.

The decision to cancel *Ed McBain's Mystery Book* after the third issue must have been unexpected, since this edition includes the "Future File," with highlights of the contents of next issue:

"The Guilty Party" by Richard S. Prather, a Shell Scott story that would end up being published in the paperback anthology, *Come Seven, Come Death* (1965).

"J" by Ed McBain, an 87th Precinct novel that was soon published in the May 1961 issue of *Argosy*.

"Heat in Haiti" by Stephen Marlowe, a Chester Drum story that I can't find anywhere.

"That Night" by Steve Frazee, another story I can't find.

"House—With Ghost" by August Derleth, which was published in his collection, *Lonesome Places* (1962) and later adapted for *Night Gallery*.

Also promised are new entries in the sections titled The Crime is Murder, Cops and Robbers, and a Special Report by William S. Burroughs titled "Fix."

This issue includes a subscription form, offering six issues for $2. Anyone who cut it out and sent it in would have been disappointed, since this was the last issue!

That's only three MWA Grand Masters, you say? The fourth is Ed McBain (1926–2005) himself! Born Salvatore Lombino in New York City, he changed his name to Evan Hunter in 1952 and began writing as Ed McBain in 1956.

Ed McBain's Mystery Book No. 3 is a fun digest with a fine cross-section of mystery writers from the classic era alongside several who were at or near the start of their careers. It is worth a read, even sixty years later!

Jack Seabrook is the author of *Martians and Misplaced Clues* (1993), about Fredric Brown, *Images of America: Hopewell Valley* (2000) about New Jersey history, and *Stealing Through Time: On the Writings of Jack Finney* (2006). He writes about comic books and Alfred Hitchcock TV shows for the blog <barebonesez.blogspot.com>, has had numerous works published in various books, and appears on a DVD of *Invasion of the Body Snatchers* discussing Jack Finney.

Ed and Am Hunter Stories

Novellas

☐ "Dead Man's Indemnity"
  Mystery Book Magazine Apr. 1946;
  condensed from *The Fabulous Clipjoint*
☐ "The Dead Ringer"
  Mystery Book Magazine Spring 1948;
  lightly edited version of *The Dead Ringer*
☐ "The Bloody Moonlight" *Two Detective Mystery Novels*, Nov. 1949; lightly edited version of *The Bloody Moonlight*
☐ "Compliments of a Fiend" *Two Complete Mystery Books*, Mar. 1951; condensed from *Compliments of a Fiend*
☐ "The Late Lamented" *The Saint Mystery Magazine* Feb. 1959; condensed from *The Late Lamented*

Novelettes

☐ "Before She Kills" *Ed McBain's Mystery Book* No. 3 1961
☐ "The Missing Actor" *The Saint Mystery Magazine* Nov. 1963 (*TDE11* p86)

Novels

☐ *The Fabulous Clipjoint* (Dutton, 1947)
☐ *The Dead Ringer* (Dutton, 1948)
☐ *The Bloody Moonlight* (Dutton, 1949)
☐ *Compliments of a Fiend* (Dutton, 1950)
☐ *Death Has Many Doors* (Dutton, 1951)
☐ *The Late Lamented* (Dutton, 1959)
☐ *Mrs. Murphy's Underpants* (Dutton, 1963)

Assisted Dying

Crime fiction by Jack Seabrook

"It never gets easy," he told me. "I guess this is your first time. Unfortunately, I saw a lot of dead bodies in my day."

1

I tried to visit my grandfather once a month at the nursing home where he lived, but I didn't always make it. This time, however, I had an incentive: it was Carnival Day, a Saturday afternoon spectacular that included popcorn, cotton candy, and some mild acts—nothing too exciting or dangerous. The nurse at the front desk recognized me. She was a cute young girl, probably still in nursing school, maybe working weekends to see how she liked emptying bedpans and delivering dinners at five o'clock.

"I'm here to see Mr. Hunter," I smiled, and she brightened when she saw me.

"Right on time, aren't you? The carnival starts in a few minutes!" She filled out her nurse's uniform in all the right places, and her blue eyes twinkled as she spoke. "You know the way by now."

"I sure do," I said, "and thanks." I headed to the right, around the nurse's station and down a hallway lined on both sides with open doors. The old folks sat in their rooms or in wheelchairs out in the hall. Some were dozing while others watched me walk by or just sat there, looking at nothing in particular. I reached my grandfather's room, gave a perfunctory knock, and stepped in. He was asleep, but his roommate was wide awake.

"Ed! Good to see you." Mr. Murphy was a few years younger than my grandfather, and he was always happy to see a young face enter the room they shared. "Hunter! Wake up! Your grandson is here." My grandfather stirred, and I walked over to his bedside and took a seat in the chair. His eyes opened, but he didn't know where he was right away, so I waited quietly while he acclimated himself to his surroundings.

After a minute, he looked at me and said, "Ed! What are you doing here?" I was named after my grandfather, so I always felt like we had a common bond.

"It's Carnival Day, grandpa! Remember? I'm here for the popcorn and the trained monkeys!"

"Did I ever tell you about the time I spent working in a carnival?" he asked me with a smile. Of course he had, many times, but I knew his memory was fading so I didn't embarrass him.

"I always like to hear your stories of the old days, but we have to get ourselves down the hall and out the door so we don't miss any of the fun!" I stood up and provided a steadying hand as he slowly swung his legs over the side of the bed and stood up. He slipped on

We passed the nurse's station . . .

his shoes, I handed him his cane, and off we went. Mr. Murphy, in the next bed, said that he would be along soon. I wasn't sure if he meant it or not. It was late spring and a beautiful, warm day outside, so my grandfather had no real need for a jacket, but he insisted that I grab a light one anyway since he was often cold.

As we shuffled down the hall of the nursing home, I noticed that about half the residents seemed to be joining us on the way outside, while the other half carried on with their usual day's business, as little as it was. We passed the nurse's station and Amber, the young nurse at the front desk, smiled at both of us—tenderly, at my grandfather, and more impishly at me. "Go right out the doors and into the courtyard, Ed," she told me, though my grandfather thought she was speaking to him. "They're about to get started!"

Outside, the carnival had already begun. There were a couple of dozen old folks sitting in a makeshift audience space, some in wheelchairs and others in folding chairs that had been set up for the occasion. Volunteers were making popcorn and cotton candy at small, portable booths and bringing treats to the residents, though I had to wonder about the wisdom of serving spun sugar to people with dentures.

Smiles were shared and, very soon, my grandfather and I had found a couple of empty seats on the side of the group. We sat waiting expectantly, and my grandfather spoke.

"Ed, this is a far cry from the setup we had when I was a kid. My uncle and I worked a ball game in a traveling show going from town to town in the Midwest back in the late forties, but it was never as comfortable as this!"

Just then, the host came out and introduced the first act. He was a middle-aged man, tall and slender, wearing a top hat and a black cape with red lining. "Ladies and gentlemen!" he bellowed, "Welcome to the show!" A smattering of applause greeted him from the old folks gathered in the audience and I decided I liked this ringmaster, whose enthusiasm seemed genuine even though this was probably one of the smallest venues he'd ever played. He introduced each of the acts in turn: the juggler, the strongman, the magic act.

"I guess there's no posing show with this carnival," my grandfather whispered to me in a conspiratorial voice, and we both smiled. A posing show was something he had told me about from the old days, where pretty young women would stand like statues, re-enacting a famous scene from history with very little clothing on. The magician wasn't half-bad. He did some card tricks and some mentalist patter, nothing too complicated, but the old folks seemed to enjoy it. After a while, the show came to an end and everyone began to make their way back inside the building. My grandfather and I joined the crowd and milled about as people peeled off into their own rooms along the hallway. Finally, we reached his room, walked through the door, and saw Mr. Murphy, still in his bed.

There was something about the way he was lying that didn't look right to me so, as my grandfather sat down on the edge of his own mattress, I walked over to the neighboring bed and looked down at my grandfather's roommate. "Mr. Murphy," I said softly, not wanting to startle him, then I reached out and gave his shoulder a gentle shake. His head lolled to one side, and I began to get worried. "Mr Murphy," I said, a little louder this time. "Grandpa," I said, "I think you'd better have a look." He turned to face me and saw Mr. Murphy, and his face got serious very fast. He stood back up and slowly walked over to the bed where Mr. Murphy lay.

"Frank," said my grandfather, and gave a more vigorous shake of the man's shoulder than I had done. "Frank." No reply. "Ed, you had better go get the nurse. I think our friend Mr. Murphy is dead."

2

I rushed out into the hall and down to the nurse's station, where Amber sat looking at a computer screen. "Nurse," I said, "I think you'd better come quick."

"What's the matter, Ed?" she said, turning to face me. Even in the midst of an emergency I couldn't help noticing how well her uniform fit.

"It's Mr. Murphy, my grandfather's roommate. I don't think he's breathing." She leapt out of her chair and brushed past me. I followed her down the hall and into my grandfather's room, where he was still standing over the lifeless form of Frank Murphy.

"Mr. Hunter, please," said Amber, and my grandfather backed away as she approached the bed and took hold of the dead man's wrist to check for a pulse. She held it for a moment, then gently placed it back on his chest. She put a hand to his forehead, then turned to me and said, "Ed, I'm afraid Mr. Murphy is dead. I have to call the head nurse." Amber rushed out of the room, leaving me and my grandfather alone with the corpse. I had never seen a dead body before and stared at it in amazement.

I felt my grandfather's hand on my shoulder. "Come away, Ed" he said, and for once he was the one steadying me as we walked out of the room and down the hallway to the lounge, where we both sat down to try to process what had just happened.

"It never gets easy," he told me. "I guess this is your first time. Unfortunately, I saw a lot of dead bodies in my day. Did I ever tell you about how my own father died?" He had told me, and I remembered. His father—my great-grandfather—had been a drunk who was murdered in a Chicago alley when my grandfather was only 18 years old, back in the mid-forties. Grandpa had run away to join his uncle's carnival and he had gone on to investigate not only that murder, but many others, as part of the Hunter and Hunter Detective Agency.

"I think so," I said quietly, and he was quiet, too.

"It never gets easy, but it gets easier. Frank Murphy was a good man. He was my roommate for the last year and a half and we got to know each other pretty well; at least I think so. His wife died years ago and he was on his own; he didn't have a grandson like you to come and visit him." I smiled. "I wonder what finally killed him?"

We sat there for a while, just shooting the breeze like that, and I began to feel better. We heard people coming and going in the hallway and, after what seemed like an hour, Amber came to see us. "If you want to sleep somewhere else tonight, Mr. Hunter, we can arrange that," she told my grandfather.

"No, that won't be necessary," he replied, and we got up and walked back to his room behind her. Amber must be about 21 years old, and she's average height and on the thin side, with wavy brown hair that reaches down past her shoulders. When we got to my grandfather's room, we saw that a doctor was talking to a policeman. They stepped aside to let us in, then looked at each other and left the room.

"I wonder what the cop is doing here?" said my grandfather. "People in nursing homes die all the time." That made me wonder. He settled down in the easy chair next to the bed and I sat on the edge of the mattress. Mr. Murphy's bed was empty; the body had already been taken away and the sheets had been stripped. His possessions remained, however; slippers tucked under the edge of the bed, a book on the nightstand and, I assumed, clothes in the dresser and the closet. My grandfa-

ther and I sat looking at Mr. Murphy's side of the room for a minute, then I turned to face him.

"Do you think we should take a look through his things?" I asked, and my grandfather smiled.

"I was just thinking the same thing." I got up off of the bed and closed the heavy door that opened onto the hallway, then I walked over to Mr. Murphy's side of the room. My grandfather was watching me with a look of anticipation in his eyes. I picked up the book from the nightstand. It was a book of local history called *Forgotten: The Unknown Side Streets of the Windy City*. I held it up and showed it to my grandfather, then read him the title. He couldn't see far enough to read it himself.

"Interesting," he said. "I'll bet I remember some of those streets." I walked over and handed him the book, which he began to page through. I went back around Mr. Murphy's bed and be-

The magician wasn't half-bad.

gan pulling out drawers of his dresser to look inside. In the top drawer were the usual sort of things you find in any man's top dresser drawer: underwear, socks, tee shirts, and odds and ends that you don't have anywhere else to store. I felt around underneath the articles of clothing and found a small box. Taking it out, I carried it over to where my grandfather was sitting and sat back down on the side of his bed to examine the box. It was about six inches long by four inches wide by three inches deep, a box made of reinforced, colored cardboard with a lid. I opened it and saw a small sheaf of papers and photographs, along with a key.

"What do you have there, Ed?" said my grandfather as he closed the book.

"It's a box of keepsakes I found in Mr. Murphy's top drawer," I replied. Maybe there's something interesting in here." Just then, the door swung open and my grandfather and I looked up, both of us feeling like we had been caught with our hands in the cookie jar. It was Amber. Fortunately, she didn't seem to realize what we were up to.

"I wanted to let you know why the police were here," she told us. "They aren't sure Mr. Murphy's death was due to natural causes." Her voice was shaking a little bit. "I'm not completely sure, but I think he might've been... murdered!" She didn't have enough nursing experience yet to hide her emotions, and she put her hand to her mouth. "I'm not sure I should have told you that, but somehow I thought you should know." My father looked at her calmly.

"I had a feeling about that when I saw the way he was lying in bed," he said. "Many years ago—before you were born—I used to be a private detective. I solved some very unusual cases in my day. My Uncle Am and I were partners, and we had an office downtown in the Loop." Amber was looking at my grandfather with a mix of surprise and awe.

"Uncle Am?" she said.

"Yes," he answered, "short for Ambrose. When he died, I gave it up and went to work for the *Tribune*. I had started out as a printer—my father was a printer, too—and it came naturally to me. It was also a steadier line of work than the detective business. I managed to stay there till I retired, and just in time, considering what's happened to the newspaper business."

"Ambrose?" she said. "And I'm Amber. Funny, that." She looked at me. "Your grandfather goes by Ed, doesn't he? And so do you? Ed and Am. Just like us!" I hadn't thought of it that way, but I realized she was right. Me, Ed Hunter, grandson of a detective, and I had a crush on a girl named Amber. Another duo going by Ed and Am. Maybe together, we could solve a murder.

"Amber," I said, "did you hear any more of what the policeman was saying?"

"Just that his death didn't look natural," she replied. "He said something about bloodshot eyes and that it looked like the covers had been hastily rearranged." A bell rang in the hallway. "I have to go," she said, "but we need to talk more about this!"

After Amber left the room, my grandfather and I began looking through the box I had found in Mr. Murphy's drawer. On top of the sheaf of papers was a folded letter. I unfolded it and read it aloud to my grandfather.

"Dear Frank," it began, "I can't believe I've found you again after all these years! Ever since Mike died, I've been wondering what happened to you. I still remember that night on the Ferris wheel and how you told me you were in love with me. I never should have let you go. I'm sorry!"

"This is kind of personal," I said.

"Keep going," my grandfather replied. "Maybe we'll learn something useful."

I scanned down the page and turned over the letter. Near the end, the writer—who signed her name as Molly—said that she was going to find a way to come to Chicago to see Mr. Murphy. "It may take some doing," she wrote, "and I'm not the girl I used to be, but I'll get there and then we can be together again." She signed it, "Love, from your long-lost flame."

"So a woman named Molly found Frank Murphy after a long time apart and was going to come here to reconnect with him," my grandfather mused. "I don't see how that could lead to murder. He never said anything to me about it, in any case. What else do you have there?"

"There are some photographs." I looked through the ten or so small pictures and stopped when I saw one, a black and white shot of a pretty young woman that looked like it had been taken in an old photo booth. On the back, written in black pen, it read, "Molly Czerwinski, 1954."

"This must be the same woman who wrote the letter!" I exclaimed.

"Stands to reason," said my grandfather. "And what about that key?"

I turned the key over in my hand. It was nondescript, not a skeleton key or anything special, just a key, tarnished with age, fitting a long-forgotten door. "I wonder why he hung onto that in a box with important souvenirs." All of a sudden, I thought to look at my watch. "It's almost time for your dinner!" I said to him, and he looked at me with understanding. I think he knew that I was itching to leave.

"Why don't you get going, Ed? I know it's early for you to eat, but you know how it is here." I stood up and leaned over to give him a quick hug, then said goodbye and walked out into the hallway, hoping to see Amber at the nurse's station, but she was not there. I passed through the sliding glass doors and out into the sunlight. Around the side of the building, I noticed that the carnival crew was still packing up their equipment, so I wandered over to watch.

The performers doubled as the work crew, so the ringmaster was folding up tables and the magician was doing the same to chairs. They looked up as I approached and the ringmaster said hello and asked if I wanted to get a taste of the exciting carnival life. I chuckled and said, "Sure! How can I help?" He admitted that his back was aching, and

I offered to help carry folding tables and put them in the small truck they used to travel from place to place.

The ringmaster introduced himself as Carl Bemiss and said he was from Milwaukee. "I've been with this outfit for twenty-five years now," he remarked, "and things sure have changed." He glanced up at the outside of the nursing home and said that he never expected he'd be hosting Carnival Day for a crowd of old folks. "Don't get me wrong, work is work," he was quick to add, but I smiled and nodded that I understood what he meant. "What's a young fellow like you doing here? Do you work here?" he asked me.

"No, my grandfather lives here. I'm Ed Hunter," I said, and held out my hand. He shook it and replied, "Nice to meet you, Ed. I saw you and your grandfather watching the show earlier. Did he enjoy himself?"

"He sure did," I told the ringmaster. "He used to work for a carnival himself, a long time ago. The Hobart outfit. Ever hear of it?"

He looked introspective for a moment, then said, "Hobart? I don't recall that one, but it could be before my time. Let me ask Flo. She's been around a lot longer than I have. She does the books and travels with us." He walked over to another trailer that was parked nearby and tapped on the door. An old woman opened it and they exchanged words. When he came back to where I was putting the last table in the truck, he said that Flo didn't recognize the name.

I brushed my hands off and he thanked me before going back to the business of making sure that every trace of the carnival had been removed from the parking lot before they left. I went to my car and drove home to my apartment on the near North side.

3

It was a couple of weeks before I made it back to the nursing home to visit my uncle. I quickly forgot about the carnival and didn't think much about Frank Murphy or whether he had died a natural death. I guess when you're young, you think about yourself and your life so much that there's not much room to think about anything else. The one thing that did creep into my thoughts on more than one occasion was Amber, the nurse. I still had hopes of making a date with her, so when I went to visit my grandfather I was happy to see her stationed behind the front desk.

"Hi, Ed!" she told me. "I've been wondering when we'd see you again!"

I smiled. "Anything new?" I asked. "Has the case of Mr. Murphy been solved?"

She frowned. "You shouldn't joke about that, Ed. From what I heard, the police decided not to investigate any further because they couldn't be sure there was anything unusual about the way he died. But there have been whispers."

"What sort of whispers?" I replied.

"Not the sort you'd like. Some people here are blaming your grandfather. I know it doesn't make any sense, but you can't tell some of these people what to think." I looked at her quizzically and said I'd have to talk to my grandfather. I walked down the hall to his room, and when I entered, he was alone. The other bed had remained unoccupied ever since Frank Murphy died.

For a change, my grandfather was awake. He was sitting in the chair next to his bed, reading *Forgotten: The Unknown Side Streets of the Windy City*, the book we found on Mr. Murphy's nightstand. "Hello, Ed!" he said, looking up at me. "I'm so glad you decided to pay me a visit! I've been looking through this book and I've found some interesting things."

I sat on the edge of the bed and waited for more.

"Frank turned down the corners on some of the pages, so I can tell what he was interested in. Look here, on page 39." He showed me the book. "It's about the neighborhood where my father was murdered! It has changed quite a bit since the forties, but back then it was pretty rough." He turned the pages and came to another one whose corner was turned down. "And here, it talks about the area around Grant Park, down by the lake. I remember spending quite a few nights there with your grandmother." He looked wistful.

"Grandpa," I began, "has there been any more talk about Mr. Murphy's death?"

He looked at me quizzically. "Death? What do you mean?" I could tell that he wasn't fully comprehending what I was saying, and I wanted to tread carefully so as not to upset him.

"You know, Mr. Murphy? Your roommate?"

"Of course I know him!" he replied. "He hasn't been around lately." He looked around me and over at the empty bed where the dead man had lain. "I need to return this book to him when he comes back."

It was then that I realized that my grandfather had forgotten about Frank Murphy's death. I wondered what else he had forgotten, and I knew that any investigation on my part into the death could not rely on my grandfather for any significant help. I stayed with him for about an hour that day and looked through the book about Chicago, noting the pages with the corners turned back but not seeing any pattern to them. When it was time to go, I said goodbye and gave him a hug before I walked down the hall to the nurse's station.

"Amber, do you have a minute?" I

He was sitting in the chair next to his bed, reading *Forgotten: The Unknown Side Streets of the Windy City*.

asked. "Sure, Ed! What's up?" she replied.

"I don't think my grandfather is upset about what anyone else here thinks about him and Frank Murphy's death. In fact, I don't think he even realizes Mr. Murphy is dead," I told her.

"I'm not surprised," she replied. "Short-term memory can be a problem for many of the people here, your grandfather included. I guess it's for the best sometimes. I have things in my life I wish I couldn't remember sometimes!"

I wondered, but didn't ask, what those things were. She looked down at her computer screen, then back up at me. "Ed, I don't know what happened to Mr. Murphy, and the police closed their file after barely looking into it at all. I don't think the death of an old man in a nursing home is worth their time. Especially not in Chicago."

"Do you think there was something funny about the way he died?" I asked.

"I'm not sure," she said, "but at the time it seemed that way. What really bothers me is the way some of the residents here look at your grandfather now, as if he could have had anything to do with Mr. Murphy's death."

"We weren't even inside the building when he died," I reminded her, and she nodded.

"That's what I mean. It makes no sense." She shook her head. "It's bad enough to have to come to terms with the possibility that one of our residents was murdered right in his bed and no one sees the need to investigate, but it's even worse to think that your grandfather has to deal with people thinking he was involved."

"What can we do about it?" I asked.

"I've been giving that some thought," she told me. "Maybe you and I, together, can try to figure out what happened to him? At least we could convince the other residents that it was nothing to do with your grandfather."

I looked at her for a moment longer than I needed to and agreed in a heartbeat.

4

We decided that the first step in the investigation was for me to talk to the other people who lived in the same hall as my grandfather. The only problem was that they either were asleep, out of their rooms for therapy, or not very talkative. One woman who didn't fall into any of those categories was Gert Rosen, who lived across the hall and two doors down. I knocked on her open door and she invited me in. She was a tiny woman, whose feet didn't touch the floor when she was sitting in the chair next to her bed, which is where I found her.

"Hiya, handsome!" she said, and smiled, showing me her dentures. "Come on in!" I could tell right away that she wanted to talk, though I had no way of knowing whether she'd have anything to say worth hearing.

"My name is Ed Hunter," I began, and she stopped me.

"I know who you are! I've seen you coming to visit your grandfather. What can I do for you?" she asked.

I told her that I was asking people about the carnival troupe that had been there a couple of weeks before.

"Sure I remember them!" said Gert. "That ringmaster was a fine-looking man." I got the feeling that Gert wasn't too particular. "I always liked going to the circus when I was young. I really liked the sideshows. I remember there was a woman with alligator skin, a man who was a human pincushion..." I stopped her.

"Do you remember the Hobart Carnival by any chance?" She looked at me slyly.

"No, can't say that I do. But I remember Ringling Brothers coming to town year after year." We chatted like that for a while and eventually I got around to the question I really wanted to ask:

"Did you see anything unusual the day the carnival troupe was here?"

"Unusual? What do you mean?" she replied.

"Like someone in the hall who shouldn't have been there, or anything like that?" "Hmm. Let me think." She tilted her head. "There was something... but I can't be sure." "Take your time," I said, encouraging her. She shifted around in her chair.

"I did see a woman I didn't recognize. She was coming down the hall when I came back in from seeing the show. I had to come back to my room before it was over, and I move pretty slowly, so I got a head start. I don't think she belonged here, and I don't think she realized I noticed her."

"What did she look like?" I asked, leaning forward.

"She wasn't young, but she wasn't old enough to live here. Oh, and her hair was dyed red. That much I do remember."

"Do you know what she was wearing?"

"I think she had on slacks and tennis shoes," she told me, "but that's about all I can tell you." Just then, a nurse came in and said it was time for physical therapy. I stood up and excused myself, thanking Gert for her help.

"Be sure to come back soon!" she told me as I left the room. I smiled and said I would.

The next room down the hall was empty, but the one across from that wasn't. I knocked on the door. I could see from the partially open door that there was an elderly man sitting in a chair inside the room, looking out the window with a vacant expression. The nameplate outside the door said his name was Sweeney. Gently, I pushed open the door and stepped in-

side, speaking loudly as I entered. "Mr. Sweeney?" I said, "Hello?" He did not turn his head. He must have been hard of hearing. I waved my arm back and forth in the air, and the motion must have caught his eye because his head swiveled like an owl's to face me.

"Get out of here!" he said in a surprisingly loud, strong voice.

"I'm Ed Hunter," I began, trying to explain who I was and why I was in his room. "I said get out!" he yelled. "I'm waiting for Yolanda. She'll be here any minute."

"Okay, okay" I replied, putting my hands out in front of me with the palms down, using a calming motion as I backed out of the room. Chicago sure has some weird people, I thought. I headed back to the front desk and told Amber about Mr. Sweeney and Gert. She laughed.

"Old Mr. Sweeney is harmless. He thinks all of the nurses are named Yolanda. I think she was a woman he knew a long time ago. He's obsessed with her. You won't get anything useful from him." I told her about my conversation with Gert. "A woman from the carnival was inside the building?" she said. "I don't remember that, but maybe she needed to use the bathroom. Let me check something." She swung around in her swivel chair and started typing keys on her keyboard. In moments, a web page for the Johnson Traveling Carnival popped up, and she turned the screen of her monitor slightly so I could see more easily. "This is the outfit that we hired to come for Carnival Day," she said. "They travel around to senior centers and anywhere else that will have them. It looks like they're based in Milwaukee."

"Is there a schedule?" I asked. She typed a few more keys on her computer keyboard and a web page with a schedule popped up on the screen. I leaned forward and stared at it, my arm brushing against hers. She did not move her arm.

It was October 19th, and the carnival had visited Chicago two weeks before, on October 5th. The weather outside had been in the 60s when my grandfather and I sat outside watching the show and, in unpredictable Chicago, it was even warmer today. From the schedule, it looked like the carnival was making a southern loop for the next couple of weeks, undoubtedly following the warmer weather. They were in Jefferson City, MO, this weekend at another nursing home, this one called A Place for Seniors. There was a phone number on the website, so I pulled out my cell phone and dialed the number. I got a message that was in the voice of the ringmaster, but I hung up before leaving a message.

"What are you looking for, Ed?"

"I'm not exactly sure," I said. "We don't know if Frank Murphy was murdered or not. We don't know why the woman from the carnival was inside the building. My grandfather doesn't remember anything, and some of the other people here seem to blame him for Mr. Murphy's death. I'm at a loss. I don't know whether we should be following this lead or not—or even if it is a lead."

She was looking at me, her eyes shining. "Ed, I'm proud of you. You love your grandfather and you're trying to help him. Whether Mr. Murphy was murdered or not isn't the point. You want to clear up the mystery and make your grandfather happy. And that's worth the trouble." I could have kissed her, but she was on the clock.

"Do you know what I think?" I said. I think I'm going to see the carnival again next weekend. Where will they be?" We both looked back at the computer screen to review the schedule. Next weekend, they were scheduled to be at an assisted living facility in South Bend. "Are you working next weekend?" I asked Amber.

"It just so happens, I have next Sunday off," she told me, and smiled impishly.

5.

The days dragged that week as I waited for Sunday to roll around. When it finally did, it was a chilly morning, and it had rained the day before, but the forecast for that afternoon looked warm and sunny. The forecast for South Bend was similar, so I guessed that Carnival Day would be happening outside, just as it had three weeks before when my grandfather and I attended. I pulled up outside the nursing home and Amber was standing outside, waiting for me. She looked terrific in jeans and a leather jacket, her hair pulled back in a ponytail. She looked younger than she ever did in her nurse's uniform.

She pulled open the passenger door and joined me. "Hi, Ed!" she said, and gave me a big smile. "Let's get going!"

The ride from Chicago to South Bend is a quick trip along Interstate 90, passing out of Illinois, past Gary, and then a straight shot after you've gotten around the southern shore of Lake Michigan. There wasn't much traffic on a Sunday morning and we were there in less than two hours. We chatted about our jobs and our families and it became clear to me that she was hoping to move on from the nursing home eventually and work in a hospital. I told her about my work at the insurance company in the Loop, playing up my skills as an investigator, though the truth was that I rarely left my desk.

Forest Glen Assisted Living was on a quiet street not far from the University of Notre Dame. I parked the car, and we walked in the front door and straight to the nurse's station. Amber took over; being a nurse in another long-term care facility, she was able to establish a rapport with the older nurse behind the desk in a matter of moments. "We're here to see the carnival," she said, adding that the show had visited her workplace in Chicago a few weeks before and, since we were in the neighborhood, she wanted to see them again to decide if they should be invited back. The nurse told Amber that the carnival was already setting up outside and we were welcome to go out into the courtyard to say hello. We walked back out the front door and made our way around the outside of the building until we found the courtyard where the carnival folks were setting up. I recognized Carl Bemiss right away and introduced myself.

"Ed Hunter? Sure, I remember you. A few weeks ago, right? In Chicago?" I said he had a good memory, and he replied that he didn't meet that many young people these days. "Your grandfather was a carney, didn't you say?" I allowed that he was right and said that we were in town visiting the university and heard that they were in the area, so we stopped by. He smiled.

Just then, the old woman I had glimpsed three weeks earlier approached Bemiss. "Flo," he said to her, "do you remember when we were in Chicago a few weeks back and I asked if you recalled an outfit by the name of Hobart?" She cocked her head at him and squinted. "Well, this young fellow here is the grandson of someone who worked for that concern. Ed Hunter's his name." Flo turned and looked me up and down. They both ignored Amber completely.

"Ed Hunter, you say?" Flo asked me. "You sure don't look like the Ed Hunter I knew. For one thing, he wasn't as tall." She looked at Amber for the first time. "But I can see you've got his eye for the gals!" She let out what could only be described as a cackle.

"You knew my grandfather?" I asked

in astonishment.

"I was a kid in Cincinnati when he came to visit my mother. I'm named after her—Florence Czerwinski. I'll never forget that visit, and she never forgot it either. It led to him solving the murder of a midget! Did you know that?"

My mouth was hanging open and so was Amber's. "Why don't you come back to my trailer and have a cup of coffee? We can compare notes," she said.

Her trailer was more like a camper, with a small office in front and what I assumed was a bedroom in back, though a curtain blocked it from view. Flo cleared papers off a couple of stools and told me and Amber to sit down, then fixed coffee for the three of us from an ancient pot on a hot plate. "Funny you should show up here," she said, rummaging through a pile of old ledgers and papers on the floor next to her desk. "I was just thinking about your grandfather and that poor, dead midget." She yanked a book out of the pile and I saw that its cover was turning brown. "Take a look at this," she told me, handing me the volume. I flipped it open gently and saw that it was a scrapbook.

"Let me see, Ed," said Amber, edging her stool closer to mine. As I flipped through the pages, I saw brown newspaper clippings of ads and ballyhoo for the Hobart Carnival. I looked at Flo.

"I thought you said you'd never heard of the Hobart outfit," I asked her.

"I forgot," she replied. "After Carl asked me that day in Chicago I got to thinking, where did I know that name from? And finally, one night, it hit me. My mother had told me about it. I started rummaging through old things and found this."

I turned a page, and there was a photo of my grandfather as a young man. Standing next to him was his Uncle Ambrose, a chubby man with a walrus mustache. They both were smiling as if

Flo turned and looked me up and down.

they hadn't a care in the world. "That's my grandfather and his Uncle Am," I showed Amber. "Ed and Am," I said. "Just like us!" She smiled at me and we kept looking through the book. Flo pointed out her grandmother in a photo and we saw more of her, but no more of the Hunters. I closed the book and handed it back to her. "Did you know my grandfather was in the audience that day in Chicago three weeks ago?"

"I wish I did," Flo replied. I would have gone up and given him a big hug and shared my memory of him coming to visit my mother all those years ago. Will you tell him I said hello? He probably won't remember me. I was just a little girl. But he might remember my mother."

I said I would, and she showed us out of the trailer. Amber and I hung around and watched the carnival's show again. I admired how fresh Carl Bemiss, the ringmaster, seemed to be with his audience, even though his spiel and patter were identical to what I'd heard three

weeks before and I was sure he could rattle it off in his sleep. When the show ended, we all clapped and Amber and I got up and thanked the ringmaster before saying goodbye. Flo was nowhere to be seen. Amber stopped by the front desk again to thank the nurse for letting us watch the show, and we headed out to my car.

"Now what?" she said to me as I started the engine. "We don't seem to have found out anything of use."

"That's where you're wrong," I told her, and showed her what I had hidden in my shirt. She was startled, and she stayed that way as I began to drive back to the Windy City.

6

We pulled into the parking lot of my grandfather's nursing home around seven o'clock that evening. We had stopped for a quick bite to eat at a place off the highway, but I had been intent on getting back to see my grandfather before visiting hours ended for the day at eight o'clock. I had told Amber what I planned to do, and she was excited and a little bit nervous. "Why don't you call me later?" she said and surprised me with a kiss on the cheek before she walked across the parking lot to get in her car.

I went into the nursing home. The nurse at the front desk didn't even look up from her computer screen when I passed on my way to my grandfather's room. I walked down the familiar hall and heard the strains of the *Jeopardy!* theme music coming from other rooms, but my grandfather's room was quiet. He was sitting in the chair next to the bed, reading, when I gave a quick knock and walked in. His new roommate, a man even older than my grandfather, was lying in his bed, snoring gently.

"Hello, Ed!" my grandfather said, and I responded in kind. "I didn't know you were coming by today!" He closed the book he was reading, and I noticed that it was the one we had found on Frank Murphy's night table after he had died.

"Grandpa," I began, "I need to talk to you about something. Can we go down to the lounge?" He gave me a puzzled look, reached over and grabbed his cane, and joined me as we walked slowly down the hall to the sitting area referred to as the lounge. There were a couple of other old folks there, sitting at tables with cups of coffee or just chatting quietly. We found a small table near a corner of the room and sat down.

"What's going on, Ed?" he asked me. "You have a serious look on your face." I smiled at him to try to ease the tension.

"I took an interesting trip today," I began. "Amber and I..." He smiled widely, and I stopped him: "No, no, nothing like that," I said. He shook his head in amusement. "We drove to

South Bend for the day to visit another nursing home."

"Another nursing home?" he said and asked "Why? Don't you see enough of this one?"

"It was the carnival," I told him. "You know the carnival that was here the day Mr. Murphy died?" He looked confused.

"Carnival?" He said. "Why would you do that?"

"I think you know why, Grandpa," I told him.

He looked at me for a few moments, then he smiled wistfully and said, "Did you see her?"

"Yes, I did. And she remembers you." I reached into the inside pocket of my jacket and took out the two photographs I had stolen from Flo Czerwinski's scrapbook when she was out of the room making coffee for me and Amber. I showed him the first one. "Do you remember when this was taken?" I asked. He took the photo of himself as a young man, standing next to his uncle, and looked at it.

"Such a long time ago," he said. Even Uncle Am looked young then. "This was taken when we were still working for old Ben Starlock. He's been gone a long time. Those were simpler times, Ed, even though they didn't seem that way then."

I prodded his memory a little bit. "What case were you working on then?" He thought for a minute and said, "I really don't know, Ed."

"I think I do," I told him, and held out the other photograph.

"Flo!" he said. "Where did you get this?"

"Amber and I visited her daughter in South Bend today, grandpa."

"Her daughter?" he said. And then I knew I was right. My grandfather didn't know Flo Czerwinski from her daughter. His confusion came and went, but this time it was clouding his ability to separate the past from the present.

"Yes, her daughter," I said. That's who came looking for you that day, while you and I were outside watching the carnival. When she came into your room, Frank Murphy was here alone. I think he may have already been dead by then. She must have seen him, realized he wasn't breathing, and quickly gone back out to her trailer without saying anything to anyone."

"Do you mean...?" he asked.

"I think someone else saw her come and go from your room that day. And I think that when it got out that Mr. Murphy had died and the police were here, that person got a little confused about what happened and the timing and thought you had killed him."

"Killed him?" said my grandfather.

"Yes," I said, "when the truth is that he just died. Nobody killed him and nothing unusual happened. Some people here have been blaming you for his death, and it was all a mistake."

"I'm not so sure about that, Ed," he said, and reached for the book we had found on Mr. Murphy's night table. "Take a look at this." He opened the book and took out a folded piece of stationery. On it was a handwritten note that read:

FRANK, YOU HAVE ALWAYS BEEN THE ONLY ONE FOR ME. MEET ME LATER TONIGHT IN THE LOUNGE AND I'LL BE FOREVER YOURS. LOVE, G.

My grandfather looked at the note, which was written in a shaky, pink script. "G?" he asked. "Who's G?" I looked at the doorway to his room and out into the hall.

"I think I know," I said. "Come with me." He grabbed his cane, and I helped him to his feet; he was a little shaky in the evening. Out into the hall we went and crossed over to the other side. Two doors down was Gert Rosen's room. The door was open, and she was sitting inside, watching television. I knocked,

and she welcomed us in heartily.

"Two men at once!" she said. "My lucky day." We stood by the doorway. "Mrs. Rosen," I asked, "Do you remember me?"

"Of course I do! You're his grandson," she said, pointing the rubber tip of her cane at my grandfather. "I can see the resemblance."

"Gert," began my grandfather, "were you and Frank Murphy having an affair?"

She began to laugh, a thin, reedy sound that started out as a rattle and ended as a high wheeze. "Me and Frank Murphy? You have to be kidding. He was twice my age!" She winked at me. "Now your grandson..." she said, and smiled in what might have been an attempt at a seductive look.

"Cut it out, Gertrude," said my grandfather. "I'm serious. We think Frank's death may have been suspicious, and we found this note in a book by his bedside." He held out the note for her to take. She looked at it and began to turn red.

"That's embarrassing, Ed. Put that away," she said. "You shouldn't go through a man's private things, even after he's dead." Right then I knew that she had written the note. "Frank and I were friends. That's all. You have no right to speak to me that way." She was getting stern and, despite her tiny frame, she had an air of authority that my grandfather and I both responded to.

"Mrs. Rosen, when I was here a few weeks ago, I asked you if you had seen anyone unusual in the hall when the carnival troupe was here. Do you remember that?" I said.

"I sure do. The redhead," she told me. I took a chance.

"She was attractive, wasn't she?" I said.

"Not in any way you'd want to know," she snapped. "She looked like a floozy."

"Do you think Frank thought so?" I asked her, and looked at my grandfather, who seemed to have some idea of what I was doing. He had been a detective long ago, and I think he was remembering the thrill of the hunt.

"Frank wouldn't give a woman like that the time of day," said Mrs. Rosen.

"You don't think so?" I queried, and added, "That's not what he told you then, was it."

Before she could stop herself, she blurted out, "I told him he'd better not have anything to do with her or any other woman." She looked surprised at what she had said and started to cover her mouth with her hand.

"When did you confront him?" I asked her.

"Right after I saw that woman in the hall. I knew where she was coming from. I know her type. I went straight to Frank's room, and he was lying there in bed, looking like the cat that ate the canary. I got so mad at him!"

"What did he say?" my grandfather asked.

"He denied everything," she replied. "But I knew better. I know what kind of man he is and what kind of woman she is. I grabbed that pillow and..."

And that's when we knew. Old Mrs. Rosen had been jealous and confused and she thought her boyfriend Frank Murphy had been two-timing her. "You didn't mean to hurt him, did you?" I asked her gently. She started to cry.

"I never hurt a soul in my life. But I was so mad when he wouldn't own up to his rascally ways, I couldn't see straight. I pushed that pillow down over his face and the next thing I knew he wasn't moving. I put the pillow back on your bed"—she looked at my grandfather—"and got out of there, fast. I got back to my room before anyone saw a thing and just sat down here as if nothing had happened. I wish nothing had happened! I miss Frank every day."

She just sat there, shaking her head, tears beginning to fill her eyes. I looked at my grandfather and he stood, leaning on his cane, suddenly looking every one of his 84 years. "Let's go, Ed," he said softly, and we walked slowly out of Gert Rosen's room and down the hall, back to his own room. His roommate was dozing. My grandfather sat back down in his own chair and I sat on the side of the bed.

"What now?" I asked. He looked at the floor.

"Ed, I was watching Mrs. Rosen while she spoke, and I'm not sure I believe her. I can't tell if she is imagining what happened or if she's really remembering something. In any case, I don't know if there's any point in calling the cops."

I looked at him, stunned. "But grandpa! What if it's true? What if she really did kill Mr. Murphy, even unintentionally? We have to tell someone."

"To what end?" he replied. "Do you think it would change anything? Would they charge her with murder? Probably not. At the most, she'd be guilty of manslaughter and end up in a psych ward somewhere, spending the rest of her days locked up. I don't know. What do you think?"

I thought about it some and decided there was one other person I wanted to talk to. I told my grandfather my plan and left for the evening. When I got home, I telephoned Amber, who was home and awake. I asked if I could meet her, and we agreed to meet in an hour at an all-night lunch counter in the Loop.

Over coffee, we hashed out everything that had happened, from my first arrival at the nursing home a few weeks before to see the carnival with my grandfather, to Frank Murphy's death, and our suspicions, to our trip to South Bend, all the way to Gert Rosen's confession.

"Ed," she told me, "I agree with your grandfather. The police know what they're doing and they came and went. We've gone on a wild goose chase and all we ended up with is an unhappy old woman. I don't think taking this any further would help anyone or bring any kind of justice. We don't know if she's telling the truth or not. It could all be a fantasy." She looked straight into my eyes. "Do you know the one good thing that has come out of all this?"

I had a feeling that I knew, but I wanted to hear her say it. She took my hand across the table. "You and I have gotten to know each other better. I used to watch you come and go from behind my desk at the nurse's station and wonder about you. Now I know. And I want to know more."

And she did know more, starting right then. The weather got colder in the weeks that followed, as it always does in Chicago, but I didn't really notice because I was falling in love. New Year's Eve came and went, and a new year dawned for both of us. At the nursing home, one day ran into the next as they always did until March arrived. With it came a pandemic, and Gert Rosen was one of the first to lose her life. Amber and I agreed that we had made the right decision about calling the police. Together, we hoped to weather the storm, and I hoped my grandfather would hold on just one more year.

"A can of french fry oil! And super size it!"

Cartoons by Bob Vojtko

"My late husband never liked people."

"This is a good job for me. I don't take criticism well."

"What's it going to take to get you into this *casket*?

Zip! was a 1960s cartoon/pin-up digest from Humorama that provided "stream-lined humor," often at the expense of a beautiful young woman. In Bob's version, the humor takes a stab at the macabre.

ACME
Summer No. 1

STARTLING MYSTERY STORIES

50c

UNUSUAL - EERIE - STRANGE

THE
LURKING
FEAR
by
H. P. LOVECRAFT

HOUSE OF
THE HATCHET
by
ROBERT BLOCH

Jules de Grandin
in
THE MANSION
OF UNHOLY
MAGIC
by
SEABURY QUINN

AUGUST DERLETH
EDWARD D. HOCH
EDGAR ALLAN POE

Startling Mystery Stories No. 1 Summer 1966. One of several digests edited by Robert A.W. Lowndes for Health Knowledge. It ran for 18 issues from Summer 1966 to March 1971. See Peter Enfantino's series overview in *The Digest Enthusiast* No. 10, pages 46–61, June 2019.

Startling Mystery Stories No. 1
Review by Richard Krauss

" . . . classic bazaar tales and old-time favorites of uncanny mystery that have long been unavailable, as well as new tales of strange and eerie mysteries beyond the scope of the mundane crime reports that you read in the daily papers."
–RAWL Introduction to *Startling Mystery Stories* No. 1 Summer 1966

Famous Detective Stories December 1955.

Introduction
by Robert A.W. Lowndes

RAWL's introductory text and editorial commentary is steeped in enthusiasm for the stories and authors he presents, and a sincere interest in understanding readers' preferences. He imbues his magazine with a quality you might not expect in a magazine of horror, weird terror tales, or strange and eerie mysteries—warmth.

Village of the Dead
by Edward D. Hoch

This story introduced occult detective Simon Ark to readers in the Dec. 1955 issue of *Famous Detective Stories*, also edited by RAWL. It was Edward D. Hoch's (pronounced "hoke")(1930–2008) first published story. Long before the Jonestown Massacre of 1978, Ark investigates a ficticious mass suicide of 73 people in the remote village of Gidaz. The reporter Simon Ark teams with records the story, but deems there are too many things left unexplained for newspaper publication.

House of the Hatchet by Robert
Bloch (*Weird Tales* Jan. 1941)

A quarrelous couple make a pitstop at a tourist trap along the way to their second honeymoon hotel. "The House

Weird Tales Jan. 1941. Cover by Harold S. De Lay.

Weird Tales June 1928. Cover by C.C. Senf.

of Terror," where Russian director Ivan Kluva purportedly murdered his wife, is now an attraction. His weapon of choice: an axe—this is a Bloch story after all—and I'll bet you can imagine how it ends.

The Off-Season
by Gerald W. Page

The startling mystery of a supernatural serial killer slowly unfolds at Jason Fidler's Seaside Hotel. Author Page brings anticipation to a satisfying, if not an entirely surprising conclusion, over his six-page story.

The Tell-Tale Heart by Edgar
Allan Poe (*The Pioneer* Jan. 1843)

I first read this story decades ago and subsequently saw and heard it dramatized numerous times over the years. I wasn't really excited to read it again due to what I thought was my familiarity with it—but it surprised me. The writing is excellent. Poe builds the case for his narrator's madness through contin-

ual denial. The pace is quick, and drives home its point in only three pages. No wonder it's still considered a classic—and as I learned, one worth revisiting.

The Lurking Fear by H.P. Lovecraft
(*Weird Tales* June 1928)

A reporter heads to the Catskill Mountains and soon finds himself embroiled in a series of mysterious events—widespread destruction in the wake of a massive thunderstorm, disappearances, and a strange presence inside a reputedly haunted house. As he delves deeper he discovers threads that hint at devolution and the hideous fate it portends for mankind if he is unable to vanquish this unseen threat.

The Awful Injustice by S.B.H. Hurst
(*Strange Tales* Sep. 1931)

An obssession with justice drove Judge Romain to the highest court in his state, powering his success as its Chief Justice. And yet he retained a vexing pang of guilt that compelled

Strange Tales Sept. 1931. Cover by H.W. Wesso.   *Weird Tales* July 1939. Cover by Virgil Finlay.

him to seek absolution from medicine. One doctor leads to another—Doctor Sykes—scorn of the medical society, ousted from their ranks on charges or rumours of unethical conduct. His methods are, of course, unorthodox, but his results belie his reputation. He brings Romain into a profound state of hypnosis and discovers a truth so revolting it can never be revealed.

Ferguson's Capsules
by August Derleth

Newspaperman Tex Harrigan reported 17 adventures of supernatural encounters, compiled by Derleth for Arkham House in 1975 in the limited edition volume *Harrigan's File*. The investigative reporter began his career in Spring 1951 in the pages of *10 Story Fantasy*.

"Ferguson's Capsules" concerns the invention of an ecentric genuis whose weight-loss capsules deliver as promised, but includes a rather shocking side-effect. At first, the good Dr. Ferguson demonstrates his discovery on dogs and cats, but eventually seeks to prove its worth on a human volunteer. An atmospheric jaunt that coaxes pseudo-science into the shadows of horror.

The Mansion of Unhoy Magic
by Seabury Quinn (*Weird Tales* Jun/Jul 1939)

The prolific Quinn's first story of Professor Jules de Grandin and his associate Dr. Trowbridge appeared in the pages of *Weird Tales* in 1925. The popular occult detective starred in over 90 stories and one novel, *The Devil's Bride*, that was serialized in *Weird Tales*.

In "Unholy Magic" de Grandin and Trowbridge are joined by a young cab driver who reluctantly agrees to drive them to their friend's lodge for a hunting trip. On the way, they are chased by a strange, tall man running impossibly fast so as to gain on their speeding automobile. But before the stranger can reach them, de Grandin fires his

One of several advertisements for other Health Knowledge magazines. This one for *Shriek*, that shows the cover of issue No. 2., from its four-issue run.

gun and the man disappears without a trace.

The rest of their journey is uneventful, but their driver is so shaken by the event she asks to stay the night rather than face the road home, alone in the dark. De Grandin agrees and as the three settle in, the driver shares the story of the ecentric Colonel Putnam, a man intent on the resurrection of his departed wife and daughter.

By morning, murder is in the air as de Grandin, Trowbridge, and the driver delve into Putnam and his deadly pursuits. An excellent adventure that readers subsequently voted as the issue's best story.

The Cauldron

Three pages intended for a letters column, but since this is the first issue, this edition of "The Cauldron" features author biographies.

Ads for other Health Knowledge publications are scattered throughout the issue. A bit heartbreaking, since all the back issues were priced between 50¢ and $1.00 each, postage paid. For three bucks, readers could buy the full run (three issues) of *Chase*—America's Most Exciting Crime Fiction Magazine.

Startling Mystery Stories was a fine companion digest to *Magazine of Horror*. The first issue is a solid representative of its 16-issue run. Although most of the magazine was reprints, they were carefully culled from their sources by one of the best editors of the pulp and digest magazine heyday.

References

Galatic Central
Wikipedia

"I was terrified when the alien creatures abducted me, but I felt good when they examined me and said I have no medical problems."

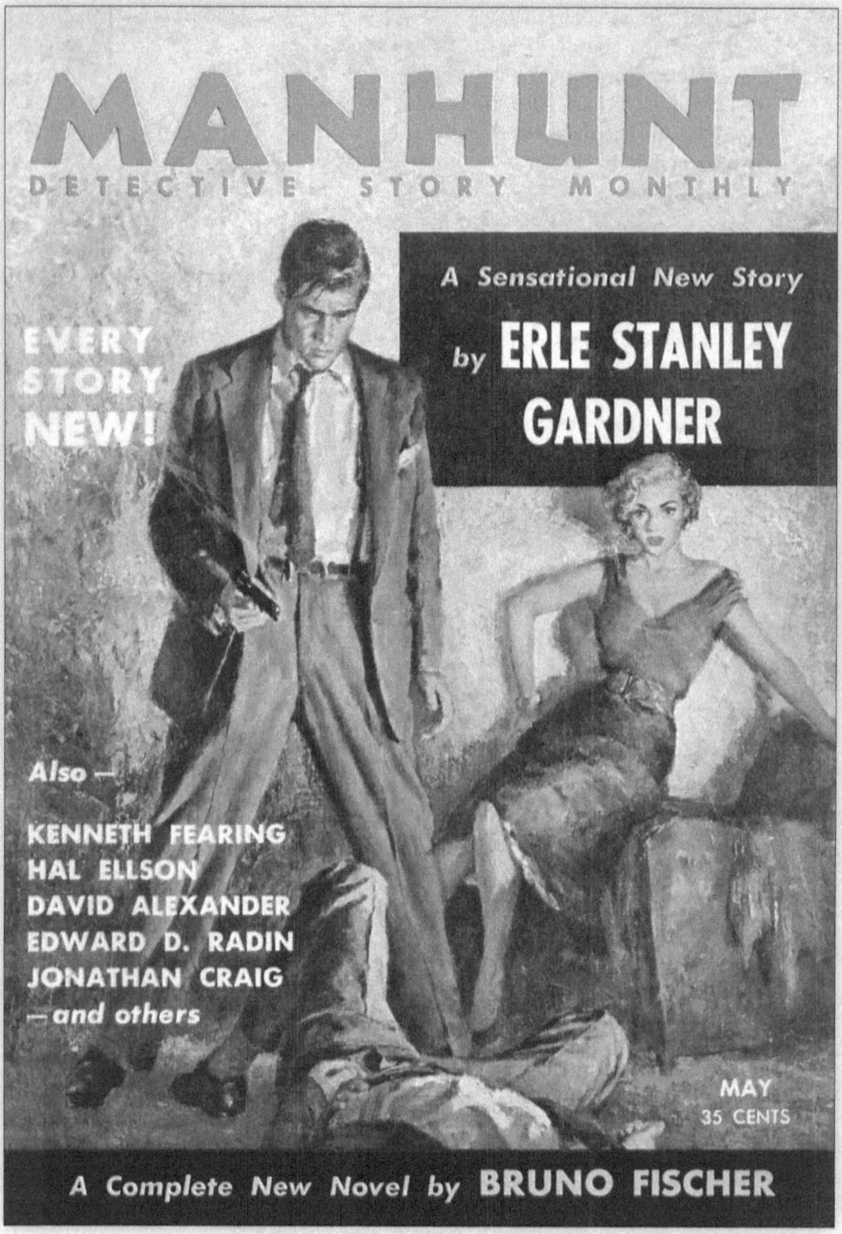

MANHUNT

DETECTIVE STORY MONTHLY

EVERY
STORY
NEW!

A Sensational New Story

by **ERLE STANLEY GARDNER**

Also —

KENNETH FEARING
HAL ELLSON
DAVID ALEXANDER
EDWARD D. RADIN
JONATHAN CRAIG
—and others

MAY
35 CENTS

A Complete New Novel by **BRUNO FISCHER**

MANHUNT
DETECTIVE STORY MONTHLY
1955 part two

Synopses by Peter Enfantino

"Oh, sweet Jesus, this is good, thought Crowley. She's the one. She's the one I've been waiting for all my life. I'm going to kill you with my fists, Katie."

–David Alexander "Mama's Boy" *Manhunt* May 1955

Vol. 3 No. 5 May 1955
160 pages 35 cents

Wrong Way Home by Hal Ellson (3000 words) ★½ illo: James Sentz

The very short saga of JDs Chiller, Knife, and Bomber and their gang-related violent actions. As with most Hal Ellson short stories, "Wrong Way Home" is filled with JD lingo and staccato sentencing and, as with most Ellson stories, the whole feels like a vignette within a novel about 1950s street life. Unfortunately, the eight pages here do not constitute a satisfying reading experience.

I'll Never Tell
by Bryce Walton (4000 words)
★★½ illo: Ray Houlihan

Anna's been stepping out on Glenn with Igor, the farmer down the road, but Glenn's stayed quiet for the most part. One day, when Anna brings Igor home for dinner, Glenn has had enough. A tough and violent little adultery story, with a satisfactory twist in its tail. The title refers to the mute narrator, a farm aide who witnesses and profits from the carnage.

Bryce Walton was one of those rare writers who managed to survive on a steady diet of short story sales, be they western, science fiction, or crime, and a few TV scripts. Walton was a regular contributor to *Ellery Queen*, *Alfred Hitchcock*, and *Mike Shayne*.

Mama's Boy
by David Alexander (6000 words)
★★★ illo: Tom O'Sullivan

Crowley is a muscle-bound sociopath who loves to ogle himself in the mirror while daydreaming about beating women. With the rent due, Crowley hits the Village with older marks in mind and an itching to do more damage than he's ever done before. At no time does this relentless peek inside the mind of a misogynistic psycho

I knew there'd be an initiation when I joined the gang. But I didn't know what it would be like . . .

Illustration by James Stenz for "Wrong Way Home" by Hal Ellson.

look away from its brutal violence but, rather, holds it up proudly in front of the reader. That's not a slam on David Alexander though, who perfectly captures Crowley's insanity through his thoughts:

> *Oh, sweet Jesus, this is good, thought Crowley. She's the one. She's the one I've been waiting for all my life. I'm going to kill you with my fists, Katie. I'm going to show you how a real man kills. He doesn't need a gun. I'm going to smash and break and keep on pounding until you're dead.*

Shake-Up by Kenneth Fearing
(4500 words) ★★★

Stenner and Frolich discover a pair of their fellow detectives are dealing in stolen goods and committing murder to hide their tracks. As Stenner and Frolich see it, the only way to make this situation right is to take the bad cops out.

Kenneth Fearing's second and final *Manhunt* story, "Shake-Up" is an intricately plotted (if a bit unbelievable with some of its coincidences) thriller complete with car chases and a bang-bang finale. Fearing was acclaimed for his poetry but is, perhaps, best known to crime aficionados as the author of *The Big Clock* (Harcourt, 1946), basis for the classic film of the same name starring Ray Milland (and later remade as *No Way Out* with Kevin Costner and Gene Hackman).

Tex by John Jakes (3000 words)
★★½ illo: Ray Houlihan

Dishonorably discharged from the Army, "Tex" is wandering, a powder keg ready to blow and today might be the day. Though he would go on to pumping out best sellers (*North and South*, The Kent Family Chronicles), writer John Jakes cut his writing teeth on the crime digests of the 1950s and 1960s, contributing two short stories to *Manhunt* and several more to the likes of *Terror Detective*, *Mike Shayne*, *The Saint*, and *Guilty*. "Tex" is suspenseful but feels incomplete, as though it was a small part of a bigger project.

I'll Get Even by Michael Zuroy (2000 words) ★½ illo: James Sentz

Sam is tiring of the bully next door but he can't find the nerve to deal with it. So he considers murder . . . over and over again.

We Are All Dead
by Bruno Fischer (11,500 words) ★★★ illo: Ray Houlihan

The payroll heist went off without a hitch until one of the guards ventilated Wally Gordon, leaving Wally on the edge of death. To avoid capture and the reveal of their identities, the rest of the crew had no choice but to finish the job. Oscar, Georgie, Tiny, Johnny, and Stella now each have a bigger piece of the pie. That is, until Wally's widow shows up, demanding her slice. Oscar manages to talk the girl into becoming his moll, so drama is avoided but then, after a dinner party, the entire crew gets deathly sick from food poisoning (in fact, Georgie succumbs from the foul chopped liver) and the thought occurs to Johnny that Wally's widow might not have gotten over his death just yet.

"We Are All Dead" is a fabulous caper "novel," but without most of the caper novel trappings. For one thing, the story begins in mid-robbery; we get no long descriptions of how the heist will go down or unnecessary character background. Fischer fills us in on what we need to know as the tale progresses. The finale is a nice (if overly exposi-

The Big Clock by Kenneth Fearing. UK edition, Bodley Head, 1947. Cover by P. Vinten.

tory) twist and double-twist that satisfactorily answers the question of who's knocking off the crew.

Protection
by Erle Stanley Gardner (4000 words) ★★½ illo: James Sentz

A life of crime and a prison stretch in the rear-view mirror, George Ollie reinvents himself as the owner of a successful diner. Engaged to his head waitress, Stella, life is looking pretty darn good. Or it looks that way until Larry, one of Ollie's former crew comes calling, putting pressure on George to cut him in on the profits from the diner. This con has some info on a job Ollie pulled years before, a bank robbery with fatalities, that the cops know nothing about. Turns out that maybe Stella has a history as well. A very good thriller with a nice change of pace climax; turns out that some of these hardboiled dames have more backbone than their men.

Hold Out by Jack Ritchie (1000 words) ★★ illo: Ric Estrada

Pete Harder's been kidnapped by two thugs out to blackmail Pete's boss. They want fifty large to give Pete back to the boss. But the scenario might not be as simple as it seems.

The Lady in Question
by Jonathan Craig (8000 words) ★★ illo: James Sentz

Third in the "Police Files" series, with Steve Manning and Walt Logan returning after a one-story hiatus. The detectives must investigate the death of singer Bonnie Nichols, a woman who had no shortage of beaus. "The Lady in Question" sees the series evolving (for this episode at least) into more of a *Dragnet*-type format. What will strike the reader funny is how many times, in this series, these cops are heading out for something to eat or drink. There's also some good "beat" dialogue from one of the chief suspects: "I cut her off cold after I met Bonnie. She flipped forty ways from the middle."

The Goldfish by Roy Carroll (3000 words) ★★★ illo: Tom O'Sullivan

Night club owner/bad guy Joey Manisetti has never forgiven Dolores for running out on him but when he discovers she's shacking up with his business manager, Maxie, Joey swears he'll treat her better. Well, what's Maxie to do?

El Rey by William Logan (1000 words) ★★ illo: Tom O'Sullivan

After climbing the treacherous El Rey, two lifelong friends discover they've forgotten to bring a marker to prove they've reached the top. "No problem," says one man, "I know the perfect marker!" A short-short with a very humorous twist.

Vol. 3 No. 6 June 1955
192 pages 35 cents
Cover by Robert Maguire

The Reluctant Client
by Brett Halliday (3500 words) ★★ illo: Dick Shelton

Mike Shayne gets a call from a terrified Mrs. Laura Jensen, who insists her jealous husband is going to kill her for the affairs he's conjured up in his head. Laura begs Mike to come to her beach house but, when Shayne arrives, the woman decides it was a bad idea and Shayne should leave. As the dick is leaving, he hears a gunshot and races back into the house, finding Laura Jensen with a bullet hole smack dab in the middle of her forehead. But was it her jealous hubby who ventilated her?

Mike Shayne is a guilty pleasure (like Shell Scott and Johnny Liddell) but I find the shorter cases much less satisfying. The action just starts kicking in and it's time to turn out the lights. Also, the usual PI tropes are evident: Shayne never thinks to call the cops before he heads for Laura's place even though he, himself, had urged her to do the same; and every gumshoe has to have his disbelieving cop and Shayne has his Sgt. Peter Painter, who automatically assumes Mike has offed the gorgeous dame lying on the rug.

Interrogation by Jack Ritchie (2500 words) ★★★ illo: James Sentz

Two detectives question a man for stealing lingerie from a clothes line but they suspect the guy's been up to nastier things with little girls. Jack Ritchie is one of those crime writers who can take a simple idea and turn it into a complex and substantive short story. Here. the two detectives let their Q&A devolve into something sinister and dangerous.

Manhunt Detective Story Monthly Vol. 3 No. 6 June 1955. Cover by Robert Maguire.

Body Snatcher by George Bagby (2000 words) ★★ illo: Dick Shelton

To keep up with the other women in the neighborhood, Yolanda has created a phony husband named Harry, who's on a stint in Korea. When the Korean War comes to an end, Yolanda finds she'll have to either live with egg on her face or find a Harry. A corpse in the river with a tattoo reading "Yolanda" tilts her decision.

Code 197 by Richard S. Prather (5500 words) ★★ illo: Tom O'Sullivan

Shell Scott finds himself dodging bullets and evading danger when one of his friends, writer Jim Brandon, is murdered just after finishing his scorching expose on communists in America. Evidently, the Commies figure Brandon told Scott what (and who) was in his manuscript and they attempt to tie up all loose ends. Some of the Shell Scott adventures can come off very dated and "Code 197" (which refers to the Penal Code definition of self defense) is one of those stories. There are still enough eccentricities to keep a reader's interest (the opening action sequence, set in a pet store, is really quite exciting) but the wrap-up is a letdown.

Decoy by Hal Ellson (1500 words)
★ illo: Ray Houlihan

Another of Hal Ellson's vignettes about street kids and the mischief they get up to, with the requisite staccato "beat" lingo: "I'm looking for Woody. He's a wino from way back. I got use for

him. He ain't around. I don't see him in the cellar. He ain't laying in the yard. I go to the alley where the bums sleep. He ain't to be seen."

The Careful Man
by Max Franklin (17,000 words)
★★★ illo: Tom O'Sullivan

Sam has a great scam going: he and his "sister" Mavis move from town to town setting up women. He scours the want ads for lonely women, determining if they have enough (but not too much, to avoid scrutiny) money to tide him over, marries, and then dispatches them soon after. With the help of Mavis, he makes thousands until he meets up with Helen, a shy, matronly farm girl who Sam quickly falls in love with. A good solid read, but the reader will see the payoff coming about halfway through the story.

The Makeshift Martini
by Jack Webb (5000 words)
★★ illo: James Sentz

Wells and Prouty, airport cops, have a dead blonde on their hands. Further, it turns out the woman was poisoned. But with an airport full of travelers, how does the pair whittle down the suspects? Other than the terminal background as a gimmick, the "Airport Detail" series is nothing more than just another 87th Precinct clone.

The Dead Grin by Frank Kane (1500 words) ★★½ illo: Lee

Johnny Liddell is asked by an insurance company to investigate a fatal shooting. Was it an accident or was it murder? No one can fool Johnny Liddell. Quite a bit shorter than the usual Liddell but this one's very enjoyable and has a nice twist in its final paragraphs.

Detail of the illustration by Ray Houlihan for "Decoy" by Hal Ellson.

Everybody's Watching Me
by Mickey Spillane
(For a synopsis see *Manhunt* Vol. 1
No. 1 in *TDE6*) illo: Ray Houlihan

The Vicious Young
by Pat Stadley (1000 words)
★★½ illo: James Sentz
A nasty short-short about a woman terrorized in a diner by a group of young thugs.

Vol. 3 No. 7 July 1955
160 pages 35 cents
Cover by Robert Maguire

See Him Die
by Evan Hunter (5000 words)
★★★ illo: James Sentz
A gang converges on a high rise apartment to watch the police battle a trapped killer in an apartment across the alley.

Illustration by James Sentz for "See Him Die" by Evan Hunter.

Solitary by Jack Ritchie (2500
words) ★★★★ illo: Tom O'Sullivan
An ex-con floats between reality and the fantasy he concocted while in solitary confinement.

The Baby-Sitter
by Jonathan Craig (6000 words)
★★ illo: Tom O'Sullivan
Fourth entry in Craig's "Police Files" series is more of the same. In this episode, Steve Manning and Walt Logan investigate the strangulation of Doris Linder, part-time babysitter, part-time teen-age trollop. Seems Doris babysits middle-aged men as well and one of them might have killed her to keep her quiet about her impending motherhood. Still nothing but cookie-cutter writing: the cops catch a murder, they interview suspects, they favor the most likely suspect, and the perpetrator turns out to be the guy the reader suspects all along. Either these are cops who have no life outside the badge or Craig chose not to dwell on that aspect of a continuing series. But by ignoring the background, these characters stay one-dimensional.

Scarecrow by David Alexander
(4000 words) ★★ illo: Dick Shelton
When Andy Tevis comes tearing into town, yelling that surly ol' Jeff Purdy done fell into the Winding River, Sheriff Estes and his deputy head up to interview Jeff's widow, Martha. After suffering abuse from her husband for twenty years, could Martha have pushed Jeff over the cliff into the Winding River? And what about that misshapen scarecrow up on the cliff? Could that have something to do with Jeff's "accident?"

The Watch by Wally Hunter (1000
words) ★★★ illo: Ray Houlihan
A creepy short-short a la *The Bad Seed*.

Manhunt Detective Story Monthly Vol. 3 No. 7 July 1955. Cover by Robert Maguire.

Juvenile Delinquent
by Richard Deming (20,500 words)
★½ illo: Ray Houlihan

When his "foster nephew" is arrested for murdering a fellow gang member, Manville Moon hits the street to find out what really happened. Moon discovers that the JD gangs are now backed by the mob and the gangsters are peeved that a private dick is sniffing around in their affairs. In the end, it's not the mob at all but, coincidentally, one of Moon's old flames who's been working a welfare scam for extra dough.

The worst of the five Manville Moon stories to appear in *Manhunt*, "Juvenile Delinquent" is a bloated and boring waste of space and time, redeemed only by a brief but exciting action scene in its midsection, where Moon must use his wits to get himself out of a basement filled with hopped-up JDs. The finale, with its contrived and unbelievable climax, is good for a few chuckles but nothing more.

The Big Score
by Sam Merwin, Jr. (7000 words)
★★★★ illo: Ray Houlihan

A quartet of over-achieving teen punks rips off and murders an old man in his own home, ignorant of the fact that he was mob-connected. A fabulously tense drama, with four well-delineated characters and compelling twists and turns. "The Big Score" resembles Merwin's first *Manhunt* story ("The Revolving Door" in February 1955) in that it involves the mob but contains much more unscripted dialogue and page-turning suspense.

You Can't Kill Her by C. B. Gilford
(4000 words) ★½ illo: James Sentz

The bottle means more to Van than his wife, Sarah, and whenever he gets liquored up, Sarah receives a nasty beating. Their handyman, Jassie, knows Sarah's about to boil over and use that shotgun on Van, so he handles things himself. Tedious backwoods drama.

The Death of Arney Vincent
by C. L. Sweeney, Jr. (2000 words)
★★½ illo: Art Gussman

Arney Vincent needs a new face after his latest bank heist so he goes to the Michelangelo of the plastic surgery industry and is very happy with the outcome. The doc has another idea how to make a quick ten Gs and Arney's listening. "The Death of Arney Vincent" is a very compact thriller, with a surprising (if a bit far-fetched) climax, that might actually benefit from its brevity.

Illustration by James Sentz for "Red Hands" by Bryce Walton.

Vol. 3 No. 8 August 1955
144 pages 35 cents

Red Hands by Bryce Walton
(4000 words) ★★ illo: James Sentz

The local hoods always made fun of "Red Hands," a brutish man-child who earned his nickname by nearly killing two men with his bare hands. Ed finds a way to profit on the half-wit but the plan backfires.

The Happy Marriage
by Richard Deming (4000 words)
★★★ illo: Tom O'Sullivan

When George finds a piano wire stretched across the top of his staircase, he becomes convinced his wife, Nora, and his best friend, Tom, are out to kill him. His suspicions are confirmed when he tapes the two making plans for an encore assassination attempt. But, rather than go to the police, George plans an elaborate scheme to rid himself of Tom but keep the wife in her place. Almost everything goes as planned. An amiable tale with a very satisfying twist in its final paragraph.

Make It Neat
by Frank Kane (5000 words) ★★

Judge Carter is murdered in his study and the gunman is spotted by the judge's wife as he makes an exit. After the woman IDs the killer down at the

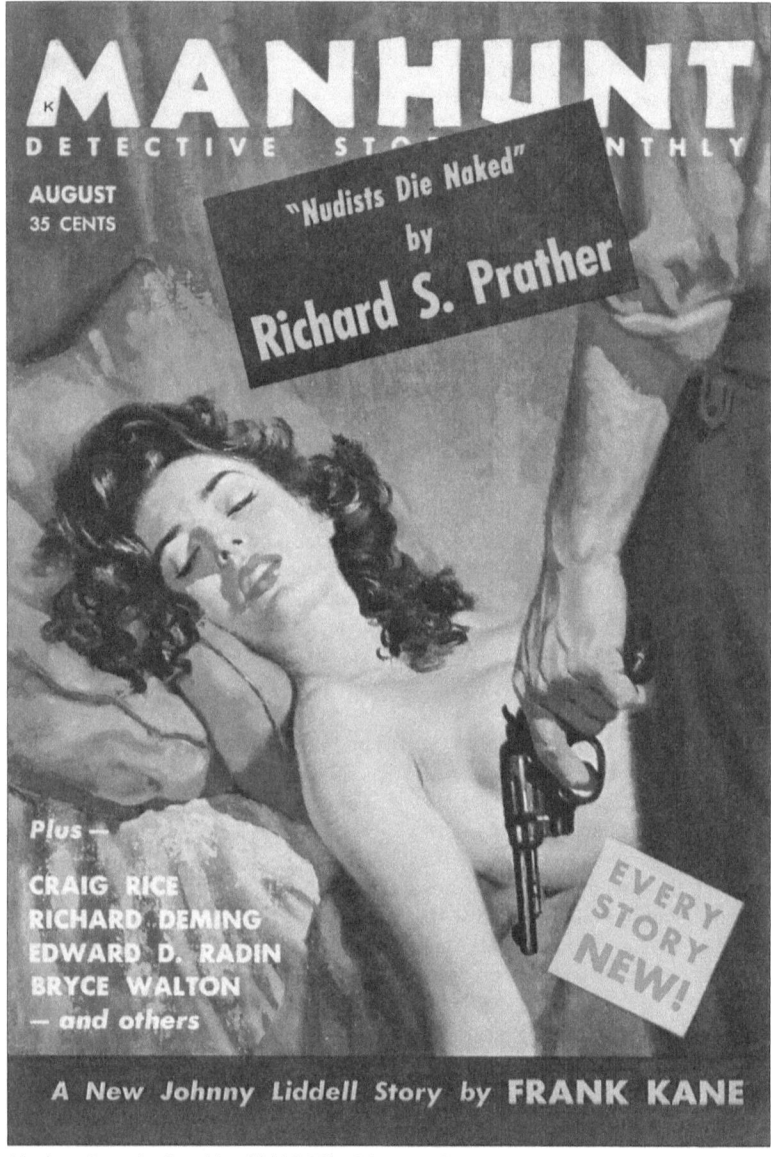

Manhunt Detective Story Monthly Vol. 3 No. 8 August 1955.

precinct, she herself is shot down on the building's steps. Weeks later, Johnny Liddell is called in by Citizen's Committee to look into why the police have been dragging their feet. No surprise, Liddell discovers the police department is headed by a rotten apple. Good set-up is marred by a hurried finale and unsatisfying answers.

Pass the Word by Jack Sword (3000 words) ★ illo: Ray Houlihan

Luke Caron has a worry-free strategy to smuggle 25 pounds of heroin in from Mexico and he's sure the mafia will want to hear his plan. He's right but the deal goes wrong. Subtitled "A Casebook Story," Jack Sword's gimmick is that the crime, and its aftermath, is told though a series of statements by participants and witnesses but the bits don't add up to a cohesive (or interesting) whole.

Shot in the Dark by Craig Rice
(9000 words) ★½ illo: Ray Houlihan

Manhunt's favorite lawyer/wannabe PI John J. Malone is parked with his love, Dolly Dove, when a shot rings out and a man stumbles through some bushes. Upon further investigation, Malone discovers a female corpse, ventilated five times. The body in question belongs to one Violet Castleberry, a very well-to-do matron with a yen for expensive jewelry. Who stands to gain from Violet's murder? Her best friend, Avin? Her step-daughter, Olive, next in line for the family fortune? Or is it the poultry man down the street? After an interminably long time, we get our answer in a silly expository near the rushed climax. "Shot in the Dark," like the worst PI fiction of the 1950s is cluttered with inane one-liners and situation comedy straight out of a B-film.

Nudists Die Naked
by Richard S. Prather (21,000)
★½ illo: Tom O'Sullivan

Shell Scott is approached by a woman who believes she's been targeted for murder. To his horror, Shell soon discovers the dame lives in a nudist camp and for the dick to go undercover, he'll have to take off more than just his gun. An interminably long and unfunny Scott episode packed with lame one-liners ("…never in my life had I seen so many naked women all at once. I didn't mind though: I'm broad-minded.") and a sense that Prather (who could do so much better) was cruising with

Strip for Murder by Richard S. Prather
Gold Medal 503, 1957.

this one. Later expanded into the Scott novel, *Strip For Murder* (Gold Medal, 1956)

Try It My Way by Jack Ritchie
(2000 words) ★★★ illo: James Sentz

A tense prison stand-off ends with a surprising climax.

Peter Enfantino is cofounder and coeditor of the *bare•bones* pop culture magazine. When not obsessing over the latest issue—or other Cimarron Street Books—he writes about various horror and war comic books on <barebonesezine.blogspot.com>, covering Warren Publishing (*Vampirella*, *Eerie*, and *Creepy*), Atlas/Marvel pre-code horror books (*Strange Tales*, *Stories to Hold You Spellbound*, *Suspense*, *Mystic*, *Uncanny Tales*, etc.), and DC's war comics (*G.I. Combat*, *Our Army at War*, *Our Fighting Forces*, *Star Spangled War Stories*, etc.).

VANGUARD
science fiction

K

JUNE
35c

FIRST ISSUE: KORNBLUTH · JONES · DEL REY · DE CAMP

SOS: PLANET UNKNOWN
By A. Bertram Chandler

EDITED BY JAMES BLISH

Vanguard Science Fiction Vol. 1 No. 1 June 1958. Cover by Ed Emshwiller.

At the Vanguard . . . But, Not for Long

Article by Vince Nowell, Sr.

It was as near perfect as a first issue could get, yet *Vanguard Science Fiction* probably fell to the competition during the time of declining lack of readership for "hard" science fiction.

Vanguard Science Fiction (June 1958)—saw but one issue: Volume 1, Number 1, with front cover artwork by Ed Emshwiller (EMSH). This was author James Blish's only attempt as an editor, working for publisher Larry Schecter.

Vanguard died after the first issue as part of the late 1950s–early '60s mayhem of science fiction magazine births/deaths and publishing abortions (such as *Beyond Infinity*, described in *TDE11*). Yet in my opinion it was one of the best constructed and well laid out SF magazines to ever hit the newsstands. (If, indeed it *did* hit the newsstands.) Plus, it carried numerous ads—the lifeblood transfusion necessary to keep a periodical publication in business.

First of all, James Blish as editor was a top choice. Look at the source-only bibliography at the end of this article. Anyone wanting to dig deeper into his accomplishments can do so at <wikipedia.org>. But there's more about Blish later in this article.

Vanguard kicked off with two interplanetary novelettes, one by A. Bertram Chandler ("SOS: Planet Unknown"), and the other by Cyril Kornbluth ("Reap the Dark Tide"). Chandler (b. 1912 in England. d. 1984 in Australia) was a merchant-marine officer who traveled worldwide until he decided to become a (prolific) writer of science fiction. He is a good representative, like Blish, of the carryover of authors from the pulp era.

Cyril M. Kornbluth (1923–1958)

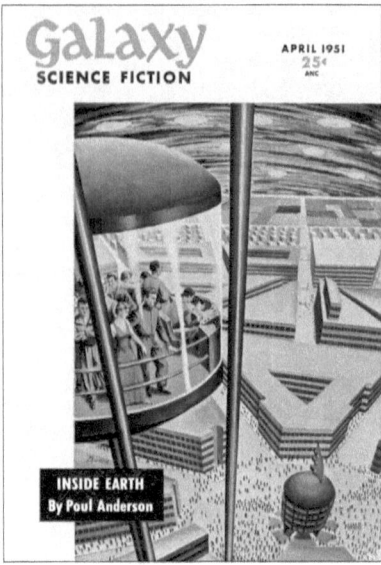

Galaxy April 1951 with Cyril M. Kornbluth's "The Marching Morons." Cover by John Bunch.

Dust jacket for *This Island Earth* by Raymond F. Jones, Shasta Publishers, 1952.

is well known to SF aficionados as a writer who used many pen-names, was a Futurian (one of the earliest SF-writer groups), and among other stories was famous for "The Marching Morons," first published in the April 1951 issue of *Galaxy Science Fiction*.

Kornbluth married Judith Merrill and they wrote together under the pen-name Cyril Judd, among others. Otherwise, his many other pseudonyms included: Cecil Corwin, S. D. Gottesman, Edward J. Bellin, Kenneth Falconer, Walter C. Davies, Simon Eisner, Jordan Park, Arthur Cooke, Paul Dennis Lavond, and Scott Mariner.

The fiction complement is rounded out with three short stories. The first is an interesting piece by James Gunn, entitled "When the Shoe Fits." In my view, James E. Gunn (who lived from July 1923 to very recently, having died in December 2020) didn't appear in *fiction* print enough, as he was a superb author. His anthologies and nonfiction works, such as the six-volume series *The Road to Science Fiction*, are good

examples of his capabilities. I treasure my copy of his edited work, *Alternate Worlds, The Illustrated History of Science Fiction* (A&W Visual Library/ Prentice-Hall, Englewood Cliffs, NJ, 1975). It is comprehensive, detailed, and beautifully illustrated. It is a collector's valuable resource.

The second short story is "The Strad Effect" by Raymond F. Jones. Drawing from the blurb that goes with this story, Jones (1915–1994) was a former radio engineer [*What's a radio, Daddy?*], who became a government meteorologist. He was well-known for his "pure" science fiction, i.e., loaded with factual backup. His most famous work may have been the 1952 novel *This Island Earth*, which was adapted into a not-so-great motion picture of the same name in 1955.

The last of the shorts—and it is very short—was "Farewell Party" by Rich-

Opposite: *Alternate Worlds, The Illustrated History of Science Fiction* by James Gunn, A&W Visual Library published by arrangement with Prentice-Hall, 1975.

ALTERNATE WORLDS

WORLDS

THE ILLUSTRATED HISTORY
OF SCIENCE FICTION

BY JAMES GUNN

WITH AN INTRODUCTION
BY ISAAC ASIMOV

RICHARD WILSON

The Girls from Planet 5

Dust jacket for *The Girls from Planet 5*
by Richard Wilson, Ballantine Books, 1955.
Artwork by Richard Powers.

Knapp in 1915, died in 1993). Del Rey was already well known for his enormous output of fiction, including the juvenile Winston Science Fiction series, and as the editor at Del Rey Books, the fantasy and science fiction imprint of Ballantine Books, along with his fourth wife Judy-Lynn del Rey (née Benjamin, 1943–1986). [Note: Judy-Lynn, born with dwarfism, was a fan and regular attendee at science fiction conventions who worked her way up the publishing ladder, starting with work at *Galaxy*.]

Del Rey earned his pay (if there was any to speak of) in his column, "The Tales They Tell," by reviewing John Christopher's *No Blade of Grass* (a view forward of a kind of pandemic, very well done, too), plus five other recently published SF novels. All in a day's work for Lester del Rey, I'd imagine.

On the last text page there is a notice about the withdrawal of the American News Co. from magazine distribution to newsstands. Blish (or someone) says

ard Wilson. Certainly an acceptable author, Wilson (1930–1987) wrote very little in the SF field. Perhaps his best-known book was *The Girls From Planet 5*, published by Ballantine Books in 1955. It is remembered as a "very different" kind of science fiction novel.

That leads us to the features in this sparkling issue. Excellent author, historical scholar L. Sprague de Camp (1907–2000) announced that he would be writing a column every issue (i.e., bimonthly, as promised in the contents-page indicia) on "odd by-paths in the history of knowledge, and occasionally [he would] review non-fiction books of interest to s-f readers." That sounds so interesting. It is a shame that only the introductory column ever got published.

Book reviews were the purview of author Lester del Rey (born Leonard

Lester del Rey

Illustration for Lester del Rey's column "The Tales They Tell," by Kelly Freas.

that *Vanguard* has a dependable distributor. *But* . . . it would be a good idea for readers to subscribe. Rates are $6 for 20 issues (a saving of $1.00). "But just to prove that we mean business," the article states, "we can give you a lifetime subscription . . . for $25.00."

So—here's the *first big question*: how many readers took advantage of that offer? Did they get their money refunded when there were no more issues? Did anyone sue? (Perhaps not. It wasn't such a litigious country sixty-three years ago.)

On the same (final) page is a listing of what was coming in the next issue. The lead novelette was by Lester del Rey ("Mine Host, Mine Adversary"), with another EMSH front cover to go with it. In addition, these were promised: "Mirror, Mirror" by Alan E. Nourse, a novelette about the invasion of Saturn [sic]; "To be Continued" by Damon Knight; and "Alone" by A. Bertram Chandler.

That brings us to the *second big question*: what happened to these manuscripts? Had they already been purchased by the publisher? Did they get returned to the writers? Or were they filed away in some dark and dreary basement, or have these works reappeared elsewhere under the original (or altered) titles? One tosses and turns

at night pondering such heavy conundrums.

The double-sided back cover ad was for Doubleday's Science Fiction Book Club—where you could get three (count 'em 3!!) hardcover books for a mere $1.00 if you joined and agreed to buy at least four more books (at reduced prices) during the coming year. Was it a great offer? You bet! But was the back-cover illustration of a girl wearing a small towel an accurate por-

Science Fiction Book Club's advertisement on the back cover of *Vanguard* No. 1.

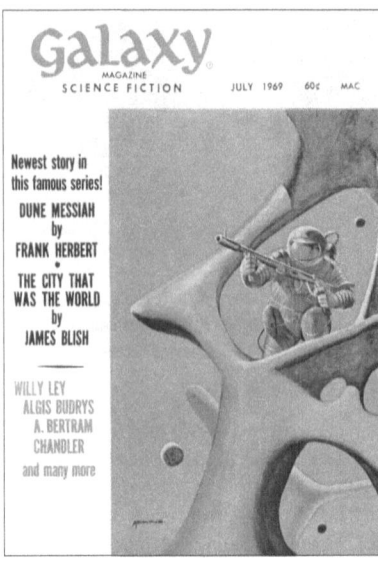

Galaxy July 1969 with James Blish's "The City That Was the World." Cover by Dan Adkins.

Galaxy Aug/Sep 1970 with James Blish's "The Day After Judgment" Cover by Jack Gaughan.

trayal for Isaac Asimov's *The Naked Sun?* Hell no! But it sure caught your eye, didn't it? So does the word *naked* anything!

There were ads for a record from Dr. Edward Teller (the so-called "father" of the H-bomb); Hi-Fi recording tape [*what's that??*]; the spoken words of art on records; astronomical telescopes; and a "fun game" based on psychology. But come to think of it, all these were offered by The Lawrence Company, which existed in a Box located in New York's Grand Central Station. So maybe the multitude of ads is deceiving.

So back to editor James Blish, whose first full-page editorial was entitled "In the Beginning." He presented the premise for *Vanguard SF*, and said any name association with the disastrous Navy program of the same name would have no effect on the magazine's high goals. Had his views become reality, *Vanguard Science Fiction* would have had a significant impact on the science-fiction publishing world. Alas,

it was not to be.

James Benjamin Blish (1921–1975), best known for his "Cities In Flight" novels, also wrote novelizations for *Star Trek*, among a prodigious output over many years beginning in 1935. He is credited with creating the term "gas giant" to refer to such large planetary bodies as Jupiter, Saturn, Uranus, and Neptune.

James Blish—Bibliography by Name of Publication Only.

The Planeteer (1935–36); *Super Science Stories* (1940) "Sunken Universe" (May 1942) rewritten as "Surface Tension" and published in 1952; *Stirring Science Stories* (1941); *Science Fiction Quarterly* (1941)—a "Doc" Lowndes magazine (see *TDE13*); *Cosmic Stories* (1941); another Lowndes mag *Future* (1941–1953); *Astonishing Stories* (1941); *Super Science* and *Fantastic Stories* (1944); Lowndes' *Science*Fiction* (1946) using the name Arthur Lloyd Merlyn (January 1946); *Astounding*

Science Fiction (1946–1957) the start of his cities-in-flight stories as well as "Get Out of My Sky" (Jan. and Feb. 1957, published later as a stand-alone novel; *Startling Stories* (1948); *Planet Stories* (1948–1951); *Thrilling Wonder Stories* (1948–1950); *Jungle Stories* (1948); *Fantastic Story Quarterly* (1950); the Palmer spin-off digest: *Imagination* (1951); *Two Complete Science-Adventure Books* (1951); and Ray Palmer's *Other Worlds Science Stories* (1952).

Blish wrote extensively for Horace Gold's *Galaxy Science Fiction* (1952–1970) including one of my all-time favorite stories by a SF author, "Surface Tension (1957). He also published stories in *Dynamic Science Fiction* (1953); *Worlds of If* (1953–1968); including "A Case of Conscience" (September 1953), expanded to a novel as *A Case of Conscience* (1958)—my second all-time favorite SF story. And he wrote for *Star Science Fiction Stories* (1953)—one of the first mass-market-paperback series that published periodically, such as a magazine would.

Blish also contributed stories to *The Magazine of Fantasy and Science Fiction* (1953-1980); *Fantastic Universe* (1955); *Infinity Science Fiction* (1955–1957); Lowndes' *Science Fiction Stories* (1956); Lester del Rey's *Science Fiction Adventures* (1957)—see *TDE7*; the digest-sized *Amazing Stories* (1960–1961); as well as *Impulse* (1966); *Analog* (1967–1968); and even *Penthouse* (1972).

And James Blish wrote for *Fantasy Book*, a very hard-to-find limited-run of issues by fan-turned-professional William L. Crawford. He produced a prodigious quantity of magazines and paperbacks, and started out with semi-pro fanzines before trying professional commercial publications. Crawford's Fantasy Publishing Company, Inc., or FPCI, was a science fiction and fantasy small press specialty publish-

ing company established in 1946. It was his fourth small press company. Crawford's first company was Fantasy Publications, which he started in 1935 in Everett, Pennsylvania, primarily to publish his semi-pro magazines *Marvel Tales* and *Unusual Stories*. He also published books.

Summing Up

Despite its many ads, one has to assume the 'zine didn't get the newsstand display it needed, nor enough subscriptions, or perhaps lacked the necessary publisher support to survive. The offer of cut-rate subscriptions to circumvent distribution problems wasn't a saving factor, either. Apparently lifetime rates, superior fiction by such big names as Lester del Rey, Alan E. Nourse, L. Sprague de Camp, A. Bertram Chandler, and the promise of more to come from such people as Damon Knight just didn't tickle the reading-urge at that time.

It was a more-than-decent first issue. It offered a lot of promise for the future. I was impressed; I kept my copy. But thankfully, I didn't send in $25 for a lifetime subscription.

Vince Nowell (Sr.), a sixth-generation native Californian, is a retired technical writer. As the editor of the Operating Manual for the J-2 rocket engine, he was on the project team for the Apollo 11 Moon Landing Program in 1969. His aerospace background encompasses missile instrumentation and test engineering. An avid reader since elementary school, Vince has been reading and collecting science fiction & fantasy since 1950. With a degree in history, a subject he taught in community colleges, he now enjoys researching the history of SF magazines and the backgrounds of authors.

"The Dark City Mystery Magazine is the product of a community of crime and mystery writers and fans who spend an inappropriate amount of time exploring the dark side of human nature as expressed by its criminal behavior."

–Steve Oliver <TheDarkCityMysteryMagazine.com>

The Dark City delivers a sharp package. It's simple cover design—with art that reflects the lead story—is clean and distinctive. The interior pages feature generous margins and a large, slightly decorative serif font that entices and speeds reading. There are no bonus features or editorials here—only stories. So, let's get started:

Phrenology
by Natalie Harris-Spencer

As her thirtieth birthday dawns, Millie suffers a milestone crisis. Her anxiety-wrought mental matter has twisted expectations of competing societal norms into a state of panic. She's thirty, unmarried, and childless. Even with over one thousand Instagram followers, her life feels meaningless. Her commitment to her current beau is based more on longevity than lust or love. A master of stymied emotions, she fantasizes about his romantic proposal on her thirtieth birthday one minute and "slamming his nasal bone up behind his eye sockets" the next.

The opening half of the story is all Millie. Sebastian, who arranged her birthday get-away to a Grade B hotel in picturesque Portmeirion, is painted in unflattering flourishes.

By the second half, it's Sebastian's turn to unload his angst. Turns out their duality is perfectly matched. They both fantasize about murder. And a milestone birthday is the perfect excuse for something special.

Funny, entertaining, and suddenly very somber, "Phrenology" gets this issue off to an outstanding start.

The Fourth Dubliner by D.C. Koh

Gerry O'Brien is young and fresh off the boat when he arrives in Westchester to make his fortune. His only relative, an uncle, helps set him up with a decent job. But from there, the lad is on his own. His night life soon migrates to McDade's Pub where he's drawn to the only Dubliners in sight—Iron Mike McGinty, a hard arse prone to heavy

The Dark City
Crime & Mystery Magazine Vol. 6 No. 1
Review by Richard Krauss

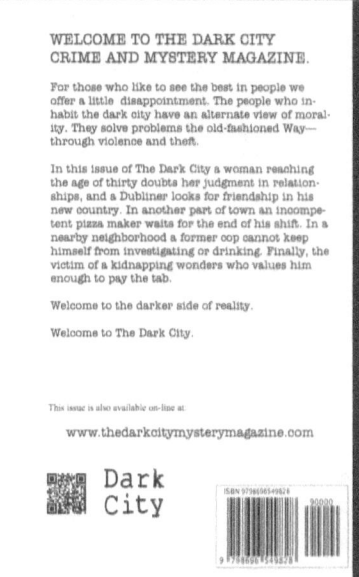

The Dark City Crime & Mystery Magazine Vol. 6 No. 1 front and back covers. Cover illustration for "Phrenology."

drinking and ill temper, and Sienna, the young barmaid whom all the boys desire, but none shall gain her confidence.

There's nary a fight allowed at Mc-Dade's, and that's all fine and good, until one night Iron Mike flashes a Smith & Wesson .38 caliber. From then on, it's every Dubiner for themselves.

Excellent characters, settings, and dialogue in this ethnic excursion. The ending is solid, but abrupt; and may take a moment to coalesce.

End of Shift
by Peter Emmett Naughton

"Jake wasn't terribly good at his job." That's a fact. Working nights for minimum wage assembling pizzas, with no plan for what's next evolves to drudgery in a hurry. Jake's head is not in the pizzas. His boss knows it and puts Jake next in line for the firing prod—just ahead of Steve and Mike. It's all menial, until the night a "tall figure dressed in

blue jeans and black sweatshirt, a long, gray coat over it, and a balaclava covering his face," walks in; the door left unlocked after closing. He's come for takeout of a different kind.

Another fast-paced, well-written crime story, entertaining from start to finish.

Front Window
by Michael Zimecki

Five years into retirement, ex police officer Stan Sikorski still lives by a code. No beer before Noon, none of the hard stuff before 3:00 pm. He peers out of his front room window when he's not watching TV. Across the street are million dollar homes, whereas his side is visibly working class.

On this particular day, a drama unfolds on the rich side. He speculates an obvious domestic dispute hides deeper drug-related crimes. The couple in question are separated and hauled off in handcuffs. When family services arrives a few minutes later, and a younger woman is helped out with her baby, Sikorski's musing morphs into the sex trade.

Great characterization colors a somber day in the life of a man with too much time on his hands and not enough of a life outside of his old job.

The One What Owns You
by Scott Edelman

Larry's first reaction to his kidnapping is a misplaced sense of pride. He, Larry, was a person of enough import to be kidnapped! But his sense of importance soon fades. As the reality of his helplessness washes over him, he begins to rethink his life. His life, if he's fortunate enough to survive this ordeal.

Summary

Wrapped in enticing design, this edition of *The Dark City* provides an outstanding collection of crime stories. Every one is fast-paced, peopled with solid characters, smooth prose, and varying levels of the seven deadly sins: pride, greed, wrath, envy, lust, gluttony, and sloth.

The Dark City Vol. 6 No. 1 October 2020
Editor/Publisher: Steve Oliver
Contributing Editors: Barbara Curtis, Darin Krogh
5.5" x 8.5" 122 pages
Print $6.99 Kindle $2.99
<TheDarkCityMysteryMagazine.com>

"My spaceship can travel to many different
planets. As long as it doesn't rain."

FROM THE PAGES OF THE PAST

ISBN 9780970169914 $9.95

ISBN 9780970169921 $16.95

ISBN 9780970169907 $14.95

NEW COLLECTIONS FOR THE PRESENT

BY NOTED AUTHOR C. M. EDDY, JR.

FOR MORE INFO AND TO PLACE AN ORDER GO TO

www.fenhampublishing.com

MICHAEL CHOMKO books

Your source for Adventure House, Steeger Books, Stark House Press & Other Fine Pulp-Related Books & Periodicals

REGULAR CATALOG ISSUED

mikechomko@gmail.com
https://sites.google.com/site/mikechomkobooks/

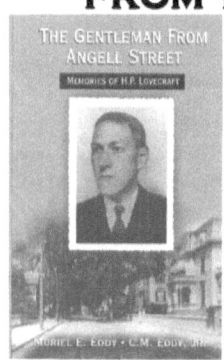

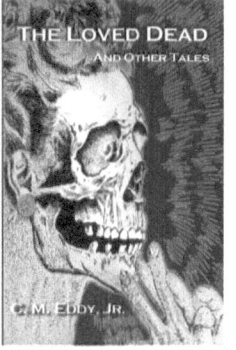

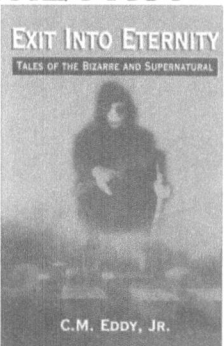

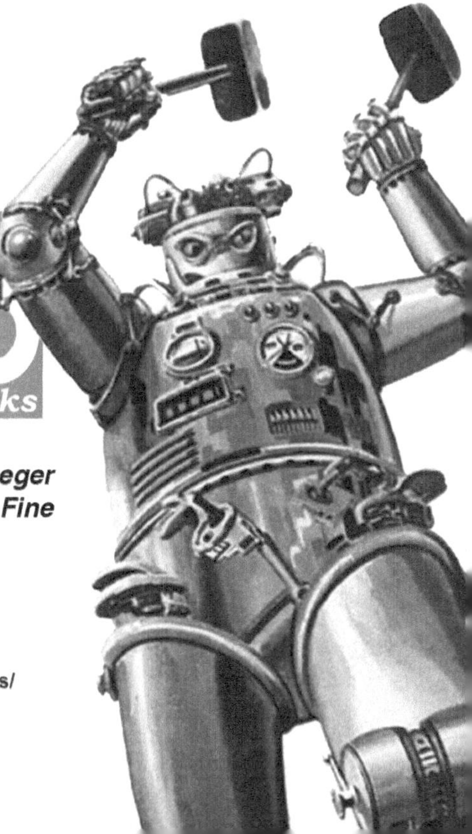

OCEAN DE VILLE

Fiction by Robert Snashall

"A towering monster, an eclipsing mechanized sky-scraper, on tread four stories high, with a revolving steel wheel of gigantic scoops of dragon's teeth, was tearing chunks out of the ocean floor."

It was the perfect potato chip—circular, rounded edged, baked golden crispy. The chip—tantalized, the wonder of all flavors, salt spice and fat. Bif tipped the chip like a cartridge between his right upper and lower incisors, cleanly biting off a pie slice into his mouth. No breaks, no splits, no crumbs, the procedure was done flawlessly, a skill honed over many seasons on the sand. It was a hobby. He made his own chips with his own seasonings of savory and unique spices. In a chip factory, seasoning is sprayed on. Pals called him "Sprayer," which dovetailed

nicely with body surfing, his numero uno pastime.

Bif crunched the slice, salt-caressing tongue nirvana. There was a practical angle. He held up the chip, centering it over a background of the ocean surf. Through the slice notch in the chip Bif gauged the wave sets. Were they coming in smoothly, regularly and out far enough but with some force of high tide pushing onshore? No. In front of him 25 yards out, tides rolled into each other with an upthrust of sand and shell. Still, the receding sun drenched

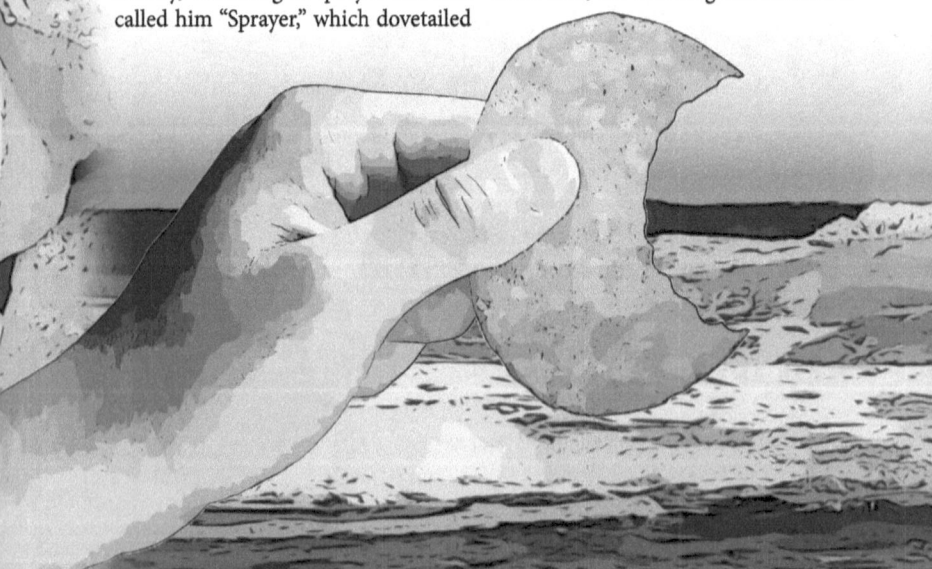

the swirl in gold. The cross currents carried their own chaotic regularity, nature's mantra of meditation with some kick to prevent nodding off. Bif was transfixed.

Then, at the tidal confluence, it shot up. A fin? No. A limb like an arm and hand, bobbing. Did the buoy break the spell? No, it intensified. It motivated Bif to move. This was worth checking out even if it meant removing his toasted buns from the warm embrace of the sand. The hand beckoned him. Could it be?

Bif pushed ahead against the slamming surf. Between waves and off to the side avoiding the vortex, he could just make it out. The arm was green. Triton be praised, it was her! Relief swept over him. He went into beach mode: deep throbbing copaceticism. "Be still my heart."

Taking his sweet time, Bif cleared the wave sets, only to find the arm had vanished. Now he was bobbing. Then he noticed the torpedo stream, heading on the slant to the horizon, toward a black hulk. "Thar she goes. To that humongo derrick or whatever. She's gonna have some fun with it, chase it away," he reckoned. "Works for me. I'm hungry."

No matter. The idea was not just to walk onshore, but to catch a wave, the last wave, to ride in, body surfing. This had to be done right, especially since she wasn't going to be there to help. It could take time. Bif side-stroked south further away from the tidal clash. Then, he positioned so that the water was waist high, letting his legs drift down so that his feet anchored in the sand. The waves were coming in sets of three swelling to what looked like four feet. Now it was a matter of getting up to a wave and pushing off toward shore just before the wave broke. He thought he had one, but no it slipped past him, his timing off by a split second.

This would be tricky. He surfaced, stroked out, repositioned. He dove under the first two waves. Now came the third, the largest. Bif braved looking up. What he saw was the Wave du Jour, now just beginning to curl, challenging. "What are you going to do, mortal?" The decision had to be made fast. "Go!" He pushed off.

BAM! Bif was thrown up, air borne, then plunged. A head over heels spin could mean a broken neck. He aligned his body to maintain form. He tucked his head between arms with fingers tight pointed straight ahead as the thrust propelled him through the countervailing currents left and right. Rallying strength, he steeled into a nautical nosecone.

Catapulted toward the shore in an unrelenting tidal sweep, there was no

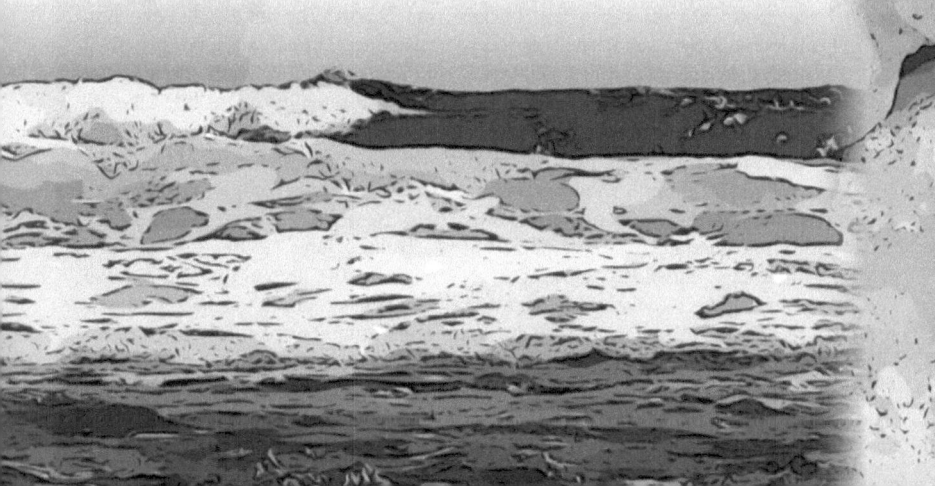

let up to catch breath. Eyes wide shut his body sizzled. Was it sea fever? No, the shoving water was foaming, electrified. Bif shot on shore hitting hard, sand ground into chest. To break the momentum, he careened to his side letting the tide flip him over, over the dry sand, over the dunes, up to parked fenders, dripping salt.

Slowly rising on all fours, he moved his limbs. No breakage! And his chest wasn't heaving. He wasn't out of breath at all. His skin sporting a patina, he was invigorated. "Must be in really great shape," he beamed, "and they say chips aren't a health food." As he sprung onto dry land, he noticed some stiffness in his hands. He paused to flex his fingers. They cleaved together, a tad greenish. "Cold seawater, nature's own ice pack."

He shivered. But it wasn't just the thought of 'cold,' for he did not shake alone. The sea shook, the shore shook, pounded by an unnatural fracturing tremor. From deep down, the earth rumbled. Bif craned his head daring a look in the direction of the sun. He did not need to shade his eyes. "That derrick metamorphed!"

A towering monster, an eclipsing mechanized skyscraper, on tread four stories high, with a revolving steel wheel of gigantic scoops of dragon's teeth, was tearing chunks out of the ocean floor. The rapacious beast blew out an arcing flume of sea flesh. Razor teeth of the cavernous bucket maws slobbered sand, shell and seaweed, green, gangly, ripped, helpless. It couldn't be her, could it?

He scanned the beach. There it was—the big pulsating pile, the monster's kickoff dump of sand, ocean alluvium swarming with organisms once thriving, once alive. Geez . . . there was something embedded, glowing . . . a blue light . . . yikes, that once was green?! . . . faintly pulsating . . . fading . . . fading . . .

"NOOOO!" A searing stab gutted him. "Oh Gawd please!" His heart tanked. She turned blue if injured. "Not HER!" Employing muscles unaccustomed to running, he dashed onto the pile. He clawed madly like a rabid badger to reach her. "No, no, please no!" He pleaded to the universe, his life ebbing away. She was his life. Flirtatious, mischievous, it was like her to taunt the beast. Over the primordial millennia, the oceans had bore many beasts. But this one was different—a man-made mass marine murder machine that would ensnare, extinguish her.

"It—it can't be!" The light died. Bif's head sunk, both arms stretched to pull her form out. All he got was a handful of wet, viscous seaweed and algae. He could only look at it, or try through the tears. But wait. Focus. Wait. It was teeming. Yes . . . critters. Hundreds and hundreds of minute critters, with translucent bodies and eyes. Blue eyes. It wasn't her! It was a swarm of slightly glowing sea lice! Bif laughed, caressing the little buggers so itchy if they got under your swimsuit.

Bif quivered, indulging in mojo-rocking paroxysms of relief. "Sea lice, my buddies."

He cupped them in his hands and, in a pang of anxiety, glanced at the sea. It was quiet. The monster sat, still. It had stopped . . . for now.

To aid recovery, Bif sought shafts of sun. "Ahhh." The sun dappled over him raising devotional goose bumps. Then it occurred to him. Wasn't there something he actually had to do? Like, be somewhere? He had to think, an ordeal at the best of times, now added to the stressors of hulk compounded by hunger. "Be where?"

Hulk, hunger. It hit him. He grimaced. "The dog-and-pony luncheon featuring proposals pitched by developers competing to clinch the city contract." Bif only had himself to blame for getting involved in local politics. He awoke one morning as an elected beach community rep, standing in for all the sand fleas and crabs.

"To have to put on a collared shirt and suffer suits," Bif wailed. Bif went into default, pivoting in his head to happy talk. "Oh joy," it came to him "the luncheon, you silly," Bif self-chastised, "is at Primo's Ice Cream Parlor & Beach Burger Bistro." As beach rep he had actually had a hand in booking the place. Good grief! He had planned for this! He cracked a smile: Visions of banana splits danced in his head.

Bif pulled up the umbrella, threw the towel around his neck, grabbed the book—an adventure tale of derring-do, naturally—and the bag of chips. Along with the she surf, that's all a guy needed to be happy—towel, book and chips with a little sun protection to be socially responsible. He could even see his beach shack from where he sat, front door always open to welcome the sun. What was not to like?

"Well, if it ain't Mr. Bif," the taunting growl broke the solitude, "having another play day lollygagging in the widdle waves are we?" It was Toik McGoik, former big wave surfing dude who boasted taking the Waimea trophy in '63. No one ever saw the trophy. If there was one, it was kyped out of a pawnshop. "How's the, heh heh, what do you call it, oh yeah, body surfing going down." That was the thing about Toik, to him anything any less than surfing with a board didn't deserve to be anointed as "surfing."

"And with that body!" Toik was getting personal. "One wipeout in the bunny waves, hey hey, and it would be all over for Biffy in a jiffy"—and that from someone who couldn't bend over through the flab to retrieve a fallen chip. He had sold out ages ago, trading in his jammies for a third hand polyes-

ter jacket with flaring stains and pointy booties. He provided vita-puffed atrophying muscle for Beachfront Freddie and the Development, an employment for which Toik was gratingly grateful.

"Here's a message from Mr. Fred." Toik did double duty as the Kahuna's messenger boy, popping Babble Bubblegum he wadded within blubbery jowls for emphasis. "You and your playmates are going to have to" >POP< "steer clear of frollicking on the beach tomorrow, yous got other things to do."

This was serious. "Why?"

"Oh Mr. Bif, how many times do I have to tell ya? You don't ask questions! Ah, but I'll give you this one, gratis—you look so, so hungry. You see that big beauty over there? Tomorrow's demo day doncha know, and" >POP< "Mr. Fred will be at the controls! You're gonna hear the spiel. He doesn't want garbage on the beach. He's showing yous city hall guys his advanced sand dredging with all the" >POP< "bells and whistles. He can plow the sea to kingdom come!"

So that was it. Freddie was the man behind the monster. Engorging all living things in its way. And Her. Bif burned, quietly, white hot, "Up his crotch."

It was Toik's turn to ask questions. What'd you say?"

"Watch, my watch, I'll be late."

"Make sure you're not. It's hard to body surf with a broken board."

Bif ambled faster into the shack. He found his collared Orlando CrocWorld polo shirt crumpled up wrinkle free in the bottom of the hamper. It snugged clingy. This was going to be dreadful. A luncheon one day and demo the next, a tuxedo twofer. "Oh, the sacrifices!" Bif invoked the gods. "Spare me, lost beach time!" A ray flooded the room. Bif squared shoulders, "Let's make the most of it. I'm going in." From the recesses of the spice cupboard above the stove, he grasped his emergency stash of chips bagged just for this type of occasion.

Bif pulled into Primo's early so he could see the set up before the developers arrived to cramp his banana. But not early enough. As Bif purposely moseyed up to the entrance, WHAM! He got shoulder checked. Spinning around, he came nose-to-nose with Aspaccia Calliope, sharply schnozzed, in tailored sharkskin with a hint of lace.

"Well, if it ain't beach baby Sprayer," Aspaccia smirked.

"High and dry," Bif greeted his acquaintance from designer pina colada days while checking for nosebleed.

"Still alone building sand castles," Aspaccia snarked.

"Not quite."

Switching to smarmy, she polled him. "You cronies in Freddie's pocket, Bifo?"

Bif had to hand it to Aspaccia. Though arrested at the hoary yuppie stage, indulging in too-tasteful beach gentrification, she had the cahones as a developer to stand up to Freddie and The Development. She deserved a spoonful of sugar-coated lip.

"Looking forward to your proposal, Ms. Calliope." Bif's grin split his face.

"Really? Do tell."

OK. Time to show some cards. "I don't like messing the ocean," he splained, "besides, it stirs up a ruckus."

"I'm sure. Your life of naps is . . . precious."

Primo set the parlor stage that usually featured boss beach bands covering rock hits on weekends. A table, pitchers of water, linen napkins and real silverware, with identifying maker marks scraped off, awaited the contending developers onstage. The developers perched over city pols including community reps that crowded around a few tables with the general public squeezed in the back booths. Parched, Bif noticed his table had no water.

But it was Ocean de Ville's greatest show, an over-the-top battle royal, Calliope versus The Development. Speakers in the parking area were set up for the overflow public, which could sit back in their cars drive-in style, following the blow-by-blow. This was a Primo production. He would operate a retro projector screening a few slides. The linen and silver accompanied Primo's signature cuisine—burgers, chips and sundaes. It was Primo's classy touch, politically savvy, very beachy keen.

Aspaccia Calliope led off. Behind her on the screen was a panoramic drone shot of "Ocean de Ville—Communities by Calliope" stretching across the land spit from the bay to the sea. Neat, concentric residential gated neighborhoods, a sprinkling of swimming pools surrounded spokes of boutiques with anchor organic grocery marts 'n' tony salvage hardware stores nestled neatly among salons galore.

This was followed by a street level cutaway shot featuring commercial and office space limited to three stories. "The idea is to keep the community low to the ground. This preserves the open sky, protects in hurricanes, and places less stress on the land needing but modest annual beach replenishment." She hugged herself.

"We envision renovating and extending the boardwalk to the city limits, lining the promenade with pastel cabanas accessorized for devices. Classic beach facades would be kept to retain character while modernizing the interiors to accent," she finished in a flourish, "*Euro Ambience.*"

Her mouth blazed Cheshire superwhites evened courtesy of avant-dentistry. But she rated only silence. A professed cynic, she really needed her feet kissed. Mortified, Aspaccia froze into a grimace.

Next up: Beachfront Freddie, throwing his considerable weight and hair oil around, scratching his balls. While behind him the screen remained dark, he didn't miss a beat. He came out alternating swinging and scratching. "So, what're we supposed to do then with our beautiful sky-view grand condo communities of families enjoying unparalleled access to the beach? Tear 'em down? No way! Such waste won't fly! We need to build on what we got. Make Ocean de Ville greater again!"

Freddie was going for entrenched self-interest, especially his own since, Bif knew, for every skyscraper Freddie leveraged, The Development had its hand in the til in deVille.

Then, the clincher: "We have to save money. This is going to take more beach replenishment. We have to save money. Our incremental sand nourishment to build up the beach every season is a budget breaker. We have to save money. Let's invest now in replenishing the beach for years upfront and pay off the expenditure with inflated dollars later."

Up on the screen, consuming the entire frame, was the mechanical monster. "Urk!" Bif squeaked like a tread chink.

"We have the means that can do the big job with continual scooping efficiency, and," Freddie pounced, "save money! Our dredge cut its teeth in surface coal mining as a bucket-wheel excavator leveling terrain." Father Freddie chuffed. "We rebirthed it to be the marine-ready, Gem of Neptune! We can mine the ocean for sand out to where the cruise ships float and pile it onshore in a single operation, finishing fast with reserves for stockpiling." Freddie changed the tempo, dropping an octave. "As an added bonus, hey hey, the Gem can move onshore for fast—clearance—projects."

"Girrurkkk . . ." Bif swallowed refluxed acid at the nightmare of this juggernaut jackboot, not to mention it would give amphibians a bad rap.

"Ooooowoowooo!" The city boys emitted squeals of joy. They were bought, no questions asked, no sweat. Freddie wrapped it. "We're ready to show 'er tomorrow. We would save money! Who's for *saving money*!"

At the thunderous applause line, city hall jumped up as one. Save Bif. He figured it came down to horizontal concrete versus vertical concrete. Either way, hedging its bets, money would win. It was a done deal. Ocean de Ville would skyrocket with skyscraper condo towers on foundations of sand dredged up by Freddie.

Freddie bowing, did a flapping cock-of-the-walk disco move, scratching the cock, throwing out a big smooch to a seething Aspaccia.

"Yaahaa!" Aspaccia bellowed at Freddie upsetting Bif's collapse into comfort food reverie of a bodacious banana split—slathered in anchovy paste?

"So Mr. Bigshot, it's your way again," she frothed, "Beachfront behemoths!"

"Without a percentage to you, eh, Calliope." Freddie loved business chats. "And I will be operating The Gem actually doing the heavy lifting while you, mizzy, buffed up by your podunk MBA, run off at the mouth for the chi chi set." He preened, scoring for Team Development. "By the way, you may want to take advantage of a makeover from one of those hoity salons you push should you ever manage to pull down a development and get yours."

"*Mine*?" Aspaccia exploded in a display of plumage for all to hear. "I'll get mine when you *get yours*, sooner than you think Bigstuff!"

She huffed and puffed until Primo intervened. He smoothed the ruffled feathers directing everyone's attention to the burgers and chips about to be served. Freddie fancied himself to be a man of the streets, a survivor, who distanced himself from trouble he stirred up. He claimed his seat, arranged by Primo, next to Bif outside of Aspaccia's reach at a table of the community reps. Toik, blowing Babble bubbles, had Freddie's back for extra insurance.

Bif dove into the French vanilla scoop with caramel dipped crushed peanuts riding the groove of a split banana. He had prevailed on Primo to come through with this emergency first aid for overexposure to business bullshit. Freddie, scratching his crotch, locked on to the gaff.

"So, you are Biffy, the body surfer sprayer." Toik had done admirable staff work filling Freddie in on the locals. Freddie gripped Bif's rigid hand in an alpha power vice. "You're taking your sweetie before they serve you the kiddie plate?"

"Dessert first!" Bif held his ground, his lip quivering, more from the obstructive peanut chunk wedged between his upper incisors. "Making sure I get the good stuff."

"Yeah, I'm sure you will. Ugh arghhh." Freddie was scratchin' in overdrive.

"You'll spare my shack then?"

"Ha, that beachfront location is ideal for a dune dump!"

Bif blanched. "A dump of dredged sand from the shelf, yanking sea life pristine from the ocean?"

"Yeah, well, when setting up a photo shoot of the rig today, I dipped into your pristine ocean for the wide-angle. The sea snatched me with filth. Now I got this itch." No doubt about it. The table was rocking up and down, Freddie was scratching to beat the devil.

Freddie draped a lugging arm around Bif. "So we scoop up a few broken up barnacles, shells, seaweed. We'll clean it up, see. Recycle real tidy like,

dispose sludge . . ."

The room darkened.

" . . . bodies."

It was pitch black. There was a rustling about, a clattering of plates on the tables. The drama was heightened by a scintillating sizzling. Mouths watered, stomachs groaned. This was pure Primo. For added effect, Primo had the lights go out for the entrance of the main course. As the lights came up, the luncheoners were greeted with Primo's finest: burgers and chips.

Inevitably, there were critics.

Aspaccia gingerly forked the top bun off methodically checking for gristle and fat. She swept her platter aside with a resounding "harrumph!" With dissected burger splayed all over the linen, she clenched fists, pursed lips, glowered.

"This better be steak," scoffed Freddie, "I don't do less." Yet under the bane of torrential itching impairing all critical faculties—"GAACK!"—the captain of the Gem of Neptune plowed into his platter full steam ahead, hoovering burger and a most generous portion of chips. "Yum yum, Primo's a chum."

Freddie was making a feast of it. He snarfed Aspaccia's cast off burger, throwing bits to Toik, who, wagging tail, abandoned his post in a frustrating attempt to roll the spare tire and snag the scraps.

Primo chose that moment to turn the lights off and on, off and on, to announce the next course, sundaes.

Freddie wolfed an oozing burger bit dripping molten cheese. "Yummmm!" Freddie hummed. "I'm taking a bite outta Aspaccia's bummmm!"

"YYYEEEK"—a piercing shriek shredded the skin off diners' eardrums. Strobe-silhouetted, Banshee Calliope cycloned around the table swirling behind Freddie. As Freddie's maw opened wide to catch the last bite o' burger, manicured tentacles of rage lunged for his throat.

"Arrgbooglawfff," he gurgled. Community reps strained forward to hear his every vital word and tried to think of something clever, career-enhancing to say.

The lights came on. Freddie contorted. "Oooo ahhh oooo ahhh–" His arms flailed, launching Aspaccia as she roared, "ARRUUUGALAAA!"

Freddie clawed for that last scratch of itch in inaccessible places. "YIM-mmfffff . . ."

He stiffened. Bif caught it—Freddie's black eyes turned blue.

Hyperventilating, Aspaccia crept down from the ceiling and fled through the swinging saloon parlor doors.

WHAP! Freddie's head lurched forward, smack into the platter.

Beachfront Freddie was dead.

Police Detective Sergeant Lacumbray Swade dipped her professional finger into a melting sundae, tonguing the fudge trickling down to palm. "Primo whips up the best, bar none," Swade staked it out, "and you can take that to the bank." It was the beginning of the off-season, but, as Detective Swade said, "There's no off-season for murder."

This looked like an open and shut case. Plenty of witnesses. Motive, opportunity. And means—those fingertip bruises on Freddie's neck testified to the choke. The innocent don't run. Yet, Slade's brow furrowed, the telltale sign of dyspepsia. Was the game a-foot?

As this was the hottest item to hit the beach since two harbor seals were caught on phone video humping a whale in a piece dubbed "A Shaggy Seal Story," the local press leapt to the chance before the national stringers could steal the action. Primo's was covered before the crime scene tape went up.

Punching out of outlet sales features, Jayceel Warbox of Boomer Beach WLCE-TV came armed with mic thrust up and out like a bayonet set to receive cavalry.

"Detective, detective, isn't it clear what happened here?" Though two feet away with camera "rolling," Jayceel was yelling as if she were the lead dog of a press pack hounding at the scent.

Slade, in stride, shoved the mic from her tonsils. Slade was thorough. "There will be a full investigation."

"Wasn't the victim an awarded developer?"

Slade knew the beachfront bwana had bit it. Slade wasn't spilling. "We need to confirm identity, notify next of kin." Toik McGoik, compressing quaking midriff, curled up in a corner with a gallon of rotgut red, >POPPED<, and bawled like a baby.

"Well, it was done publicly, you know who the suspect is, right?"

"There's a person of interest."

"And how it was done."

"No comment now."

"If not now, when?"

"After the medical examiner."

An all-points bulletin was put out for the obvious suspect, Aspaccia Calliope. She didn't get far, but far enough. The patrols under Sergeant Daff O'Toole had the place pegged. Aspaccia Calliope was holing up in the mauve light district loft chapel of her tantric yoga yogi.

Slade arrived pronto after getting the call. "What's the sitch, Sarge?"

"She's up in the second floor."

Slade took the bullhorn. "Aspaccia, this is Police Detective Sergeant Slade. We need to talk."

"I'm getting *mine!*" Aspaccia screamed, prompting a guttural riposte from inside the roost. "Ooooyeahhh . . . "

That got Slade's attention. "Is she holding a hostage, O'Toole?"

"That's the thing. We don't know

which one's the hostage."

"Ah-ahh-ahhh-OMMMM!"

Slade sized it up. "Bhagwan boffing."

Slade's phone rang the William Tell Overture Finale, a.k.a. "The Lone Ranger Theme." "The medical examiner has a preliminary finding," Slade relayed. "Stand down. There's a new angle. Let's go, check it out, Sarge."

Bif's phone rang the chorus of Donovan's "Atlantis." "Hey Bif, Primo here, how's it hanging?"

"Doing sand angels. It took my arms, powered like paddles from a Polynesian war canoe, just three arcs and I was down through dry sand to wet."

"So you feeling okay, Sprayer?" Primo sounded fragile.

"Never better Primo." Bif reassured. "Pouring on more lotion though, to stay hydrated. What's up?"

"A finding from the medical examiner. Got the word from my livewire source in the morgue." Primo panted. "Poisoning! It looks like Freddie keeled from something he ate. If it's from the kitchen, I'm scrod. I'm checking on the other diners. The cops are making the rounds. Expect a knock on your door."

"How's it going so far?"

"So far, so good. Phew, glad you're all right, Bif!"

Dear, sweet Primo what a dessert of a guy. Bif'd miss Primo, especially the banana splits. "Something tells me you're in the clear, Primo."

Bif stretched out on the beach. Soaking up the rays, he charged his batteries. Then, juiced, he sat up, scanned the coast. In the water, the Gem of Neptune sat, waiting. Bif reflected, "If you make it, they will come. A new Freddie will be spawned to take over the steel leviathan, it's just a matter of time. That's the future—until Nature knocks out the shore—the Big KO."

But why ruin a good day with dredged dread when there were welcoming waves? It was time to cut bait. Decked out in a new swimsuit, Bif reached for a chip, bit off a notch, gauged the waves. They looked perfect. "Seize the surf!"

He dove in, hugged with a laugh and a song. Catching the lateral flow, his legs jetting in muscular frog kicks, his fingers finely joined, he was carried further to the south. Within a few surfacings, he was even with the lower city limits of Ocean de Ville. At this rate, in a few more waves he would be outta state, moving toward the sun.

She was with him, by his side, teasingly dangling ambrosia chips. Green locks flowing, sun crystals sparkling, her streamline body gliding sinuous in the current. Loving his surfing body, she bestowed special torque, an extraspecie melding. She was his green nymph mate. Nerena. In her strength, he found breath. She guided him with her enchanting joy. They were on their way. On their way to where the waves lap up in the land of the palm trees at the House of the Six-Toed Cats. Home. One with the sea was Bif, stoked on chips with a dash of sea salt.

Detective Sergeant Slade had to nod in appreciation. She and Sergeant O'Toole had searched the shack of the beach dude called "Sprayer". Entry was no problem; the front door was wide open. They walked right in with the sun. There was no hiding the chip paraphernalia. "Quite a spice rack," Slade mused. "Get a load of this–" Tucked up in the open cupboard, was a jar of the finest transparent blue grounds. "Blue, now there's a twist, not the usual color of food." Slade was thorough. She collected a sample.

The lab guys burst a few brain cells on the sample. The medical examiner, nailing cause of death, owed them. Aspaccia was off the hook. "Freddie was a beefy operator," Slade said on background to the press, "Ms. Calliope would have had her hands more than full going for a death squeeze. Such pampered phalanges."

Slade's story made Jayceel Warbox of WLCE drool.

"We got our tips from the chips." Slade relished the reveal rollout by the beach. "The crab bay chip seasoning was spiced with protein toxin harpoons of translucent jellyfish larvae with blue eyes also known as 'sea lice.' The toxin can be discharged with physical or chemical pressure even after it has been crushed and dried out. Well," Slade enthralled Jayceel, "mastication is physical and human salt is chemical. In a concentrated form, the toxin was lethal when ingested, causing an explosive allergic anaphylactic shock. It's a case of interior seabather eruption, the Big Bitch of an Itch."

"When the lights were out," Slade summed up, "Freddie was slipped some chips on the sly that didn't agree with him. That didn't improve Freddie's health. He was already scratching a surface attack that looked like raw hamburger from a little dip he took in the 'pond.' It's as if the ocean had spread a netting of nettles neatly over his groin. So, it was an inside 'n' outside job. A low blow. A lousy way to go."

Jayceel pressed on, "You have a person of interest?"

Slade thought of the shack and the beach there. Halfway to water's edge, burrowing below windblown sand, there was the book, *Twenty Thousand Leagues Under the Sea*, opened face down, between two chapters. She didn't bag it as evidence.

"New person of interest?" Police Detective Sergeant Lacumbray Slade shrugged. Her brow rested unfurrowed. She looked out to sea. Calm. Her hands folded.

"No."

She watched a wave gently receding out, angling away. She smiled.

"No. They're gone."

Robert Snashall is a DC outsider used to straddling the fault line. When not wrapped in Rose City weeklies, you'll most likely find him at Vista and Spring inhaling a Caesar.

20 Million Miles to Earth
Overview/synopsis by Richard Krauss

All references to Ymir were removed, as Harryhausen thought the public would confuse it with the Arabic title "Emir."

Of course, the Ymir (the creature never named onscreen), is the star and main attraction of *20 Million Miles to Earth*. And Raymond Frederick Harryhausen (1920–2013) is the famous animator/special effects man who brought it to life. Although the picture was Harryhausen's fourth solo effort, to me it draws a lot from the original *King Kong* (1933), by pioneer stop-motion animator Willis O'Brien. O'Brien was a mentor and teacher to Harryhausen, who worked beside the master on *Mighty Joe Young* (1949).

For me, *King Kong* and this film both provide a vivid cast with meaty roles that support the idea of a "monster movie" with a plot that attempts to rise above its strictly monstrous expectations. And like the great ape, Harryhausen does everything he can to give his creature some depth and evoke viewers' sympathies, although it is less successful on a cold-blooded reptilian than a warm-blooded ape.

The film was produced by Charles H. Schneer (1920–2009), who worked for Columbia Pictures as a scriptwriter and associate producer under Sam Katzman. He met Harryhausen through a mutual friend from their Army days. Their original collaboration was *It Came From Beneath the Sea* (1955), Harryhausen's second solo feature. From there, the partnership solidified and Schneer would produce

every other film Harryhausen made, except *One Million B.C.* (1967).

Harryhausen wanted to shoot the film in color, but the budget wouldn't allow it. In 2007, 50 years later, he worked with Legend Films on a colorized version that was released on DVD.

20 Million was directed by Nathan Juran (1907–2002), who won the Oscar for Best Art Direction in 1942 for *How Green Was My Valley*. His directing debut occurred when Joseph Pevney dropped out of *The Black Castle* (1952) shortly before filming began. Universal liked the results and signed him to a one-year contract. His first SF film for them was *The Deadly Mantis* (1957). With the success of *20 Million*, for Schneer, Juan earned a reputation as a fantasy and science fiction specialist. His other films in these genres included *The 7th Voyage of Sinbad* (1957, also with Schneer and Harryhausen), *Attack of the 50 Foot Woman* (1957), and *Jack the Giant Killer* (1962), which he also wrote. In 1959, he turned his attention to television, directing episodes for all four of Irwin Allen's series *Voyage to the Bottom of the Sea*, *Lost in Space*, *The Time Tunnel*, and *Land of the Giants*.

According to Wikipedia, Juran directed *20 Million*'s footage shot in America, whereas Schneer and Harryhausen handled the scenes shot in Rome.

Ad for *Amazing Stories Science Fiction Novel* from *Amazing Stories* August 1957.

The screenplay by Bob Williams and Christopher Knopf was based on an original story by Charlott Knight (1894–1977). Harryhausen isn't listed as a writing credit, but the film was based on his concept, which he called *The Giant Ymir*. In fact, that was the working title, before it became *20 Million*. It was also called *The Beast from Space* at one time. Many of the film's most iconic scenes were set in Rome, because Harryhausen wanted to vacation there.

Charlott Knight was an actress and writer, perhaps best known for the story on which the *20 Million* was based. Most of her writing credits were articles she wrote for *Collier's* in the 1950s, although she had written a few for *Thrilling Love* in the mid-1940s as well. Her acting credits are nearly all for TV series that include *Lights Out* (Miss Watkins in "The Silent Supper," 1951), *The Whistler* (Maid in "Stranger in the House," 1955), and *The Big Valley* (Mrs. Goody in "Boy Into Man,"

Amazing Stories Science Fiction Novel 1957.
Cover by Luigi Garonzi.

1967). She also had uncredited parts in *Valley of the Dolls* (1967) and *The Ten Commandments* (1956). She's credited as "Charlotte" in all of her articles and several of her roles.

20 Million was released in 1957. Henry Slesar was hired by Ziff-Davis Publishing to write the novelization for the only issue of *Amazing Stories Science Fiction Novel*, also in 1957. It's likely Slesar wrote his novel from the script, as the two mediums are markedly similar, and share quite a bit of their dialog. What follows is a detailed synopsis of the novelization, with major and some minor differences noted.

Chaos of Gerra

Before its opening credits, the movie features a short prologue highlighting mankind's scientific advances, "before most of us are even aware of them." Including interstellar space flight to "a point more than *20 Million Miles to Earth*."

After the credits, the novel joins the movie to open on the fishing village of Gerra on the island of Sicily. Seasoned fishermen Verrico and Mondello are aboard their longboat on the Mediterranean Sea, handling their big nets to harvest tuna. Onboard is eleven-year-old Pepe, who idolizes "Taixas" for its cowboys.

Suddenly, the trio and the surrounding fisherman all turn their attention skyward at the sound of an approaching roar. The puffy white clouds overhead spit forth a silvery object in a steep dive toward the water. A vast cloud of steam obscures the object momentarily as the strange craft tries to level itself and skips across the water only to career into the depths.

The impact creates a small tidal wave, as the fishermen scramble to distance their boats from the oncoming threat. One craft is scuttled, its occupants thrown into the sea. Another boat rushes to rescue the men, as Verrico and company watch. While the others continue to row toward shore, our intrepid trio decide there must be men aboard the craft and row toward it. (The impact wave and the scuttled boat are not part of the film.)

As our heroes approach the craft, they observe a gapping hole in its side, just above the waterline. Vericco and Mondello board the craft, while Pepe holds their longboat steady as best he can.

Inside, their eyes wash over an amazing array of scientific equipment. "Clamped to the far wall, they could see metal cylinders of varied sizes. One of the clamps was empty." (A detail not shown in the film.)

Verrico opens a bulkhead door as steam pours from within the chamber it secures. Walking through the futuristic interior of the slanting ship, both men hang onto railings and whatever else provides a handhold as they make their way downward. The next chamber they find is overwhelmed with dials, controls, gauges, instruments, wires, and tubing. There they find a man laid back in a massive chair. On film, Mondello places his ear to the man's chest. "This man—he still lives!"

Together, they drag the unconscious pilot back toward the open bulkhead hatch. (On film, the man is partially conscious and Mondello is able help him limp to the longboat.) Meanwhile, Verrico spots another man and carries him bodily to the safety of the boat.

The spaceship lurches from time to time during the rescue, and after the second man is aboard the boat, it begins to sink. Verrico leaps from the spacecraft, but his foot misses the boat, plunging him into the water, where he swims to the boat and climbs aboard with help from his comrades. (On film, he heads back into the spacecraft to continue the rescue, telling Mondello and Pepe to "Row, row." He doesn't get very far when it becomes obvious the spacecraft is about to sink. He dives into the water and swims to the longboat, now some thirty feet out.)

Mourning the loss of whoever else was aboard, Vericco crosses himself as the spacecraft sinks below the surface. The novel acknowledges the danger of the suction the sinking craft creates, but on film the massive hulk makes only a tiny ripple of foam as it slides out of sight.

The Best-Laid Plans

The majority of this chapter is background information about the spacecraft's mission, that does not appear in the film. Project XY began as a civilian dream "born in the great white shells of astronomical laboratories," then nurtered by industry and government.

By the time General A.D. McIntosh learns of the project from Dr. Judson Uhl, the secret plans are complete. Bypassing the step-by-step approach of launching satellites or a trip to the

moon, the XY-21 spacecraft is destined for Venus. Spectroscopic equipment has revealed "the presence of a group of valuable minerals—essential minerals to the full development of atomic power."

Now that construction of the craft is ready to begin, the President's personal recommendation to lead the project is General McIntosh. The General leaves construction of the vessel in the capable "hands of several hundred scientists and engineers," but handles the political firestorm that surfaces once a Congressional committee learns of the top-secret project. His fundamental opposition is Senator Banyon who nearly succeeds in scuttling the project until the President orchestrates a few high-level maneuvers and the oversight investigation ends.

Next comes the culling of some eight hundred "of the Air Force's best men" to find the seventeen required to make the journey. Unfortunately, only six men meet the exceedingly high standards of physical excellence, psychological acumen, "and that indeterminate quality of spirit that was needed for such an endeavor."

In the end, a committee of three— General McIntosh, Dr. Sharman (chief medical officer), and Dr. Uhl are tasked to find the remaining crew. It is at this phase, Sharman reveals his desire to join the voyage. He excels in all criteria lest one—he failed the gyroscope tests. Nevertheless, the General agrees he'd make an excellent addition to the crew.

How the remaining ten crewmembers were selected is a mystery; the novel now joins the movie's script, shifting forward in time to ground control where we find McIntosh and Uhl tracking the incoming spaceship. It's mission to Venus was successful, but its landing is off course.

A radar blip from Iceland shows the ship at two hundreds miles up, descending at thirty-five hundred feet per minute. Then a sighting in Marseilles, descent steady, on a trajectory for the Mediterranean.

The final report comes via telephone, confirmation the ship has come down a few kilometers off the coast of Sicily. McIntosh barks orders to Major Stacey, "We'll need the cooperation and courtesy of the Italian Government, so get the State Department on the phone."

Uhl advises, "Tell them to roll up their red tape and put it in a drawer and lock it up until this thing is over."

With that, the General and Dr. Uhl leave for Sicily!

The Monster Emerges

Meanwhile on the beach in Gerra, the fishermen are gathered around Verrico and Mondello who transfer the injured spacemen from their longboat to a pair of stretchers. The Commissario of Police arrives and directs the men to take the injured to the nearby Commune di Gerra. Then he orders Mondello to fetch the doctor, and while they wait, begins questioning Verrico about the spacecraft.

The fisherman explains he only saw one other, who was surely dead, but the craft was large enough to hold more, who most certainly perished when it sank.

While the men talk, Pepe slips away, attracted to a dark bit of cloth, perhaps a garment, floating close to shore. He soon discovers it's an air force jacket, complete with insignia. He's delighted with the find and scours the tideline for more treasures.

At first, he spies only splinters of wood, but then a glint of sunlight catches his eye and he finds a metal cylinder, stamped with the letters "USAF." He struggles with the clamps that secure its cap.

By now, Mondello has returned, the doctore is far away delivering a bambino. The Commissario is stiffled for a moment but then remembers an old doctore from Roma, who lives in a house on wheels, traveling with his American granddaughter. The doctore is familiar to Verrico, Pepe sells the man shellfish and anything else he'll buy.

Verrico calls out for Pepe, who looks about wildly for a place to hide his newfound treasures, and has to settle for a clump of sand.

When he joins Verrico, he identifies the doctore as Dr. Leonardo. He is camped on the Via Messina, "only a small kilometer beyond the residence of Signore Greppi." Mondello knows the spot and is quickly dispatched.

Young Pepe is immediately forgotten, and he is able to return to his treasures. He removes the clamp from the cylinder and shakes the gelatinous glob it contains onto the sand. "It was about fifteen inches long, bulky, and sand was clinging to its slick, wet-looking surface."

Pepe gingerly explores the strange glob, decides it's inanimate, and washes the sand off. It's smooth and semi-transparent. "There was something inside, something vague and shadowy, but nothing that Pepe's young eyes could identify." Suddenly elated, he wraps the thing in the flight jacket—he'll sell it to Dr. Leonardo!

Marisa Leonardo, the doctore's granddaughter, had furnished the old man's trailer so that at least he could live in relative comfort in the rather cramped space, before she left for the medical universities of the great United States. He was happy for her selections, but his zoological equipment was his primary concern. She knew him well and accepted his eccentricities with a warm heart.

Her parents had been killed when she was just eight during the great war. Dr. Leonardo cared for her despite his poverty, and eventually scraped together enough to send her to America, where relatives sheltered her and her academic skills earned her a scholarship for medical school.

As Marisa straightens the old man's bed, a knock upon the trailer's door draws the doctore from his study. It is Mondello, who comes with an urgent need for a doctor. Unfortunately, Dr. Leonardo is a zoologist, not a medical doctor. Grasping the desperation in Mondello's voice, Marisa, although not yet a full doctor, agrees to do what she can to help. The two leave for the Commune di Gerra immediately.

On his way to Leonardo's trailer, Pepe imagines he is defending a ranch from a black moustached cattle rustler. "Just as the villain raised his gun, the hero's right hand darted to his gunbelt swifter than lightning. Crack! The rustler clutched his midriff and fell to the ground." His play-acting ends as he arrives at the trailer and sees a pretty young signorina hurrying out with a black bag, running after Mondello.

Dr. Leonardo greets the boy and inquires about the purpose of his visit. No doubt to sell something at an exorbitant rate. Pepe ignores the friendly jibe, as he knows he has something truly special today. He requests the sum of two hundred lira and demands payment upfront before handing over the prize.

The good-natured Leonardo feigns doubt, but eventually agrees to pay the ransom. Pepe heads for the trailer's door after placing the gelatinous mass on Leonardo's work bench.

The Doctor studies the strange object and determines there is something inside. He begins to ask a question and then realizes Pepe has already gone.

The Doctor shouts from the doorway, "Where did you find this thing?"

"In the water, Doctor! In the sea."

The thing inside the blob quivers once, twice, and then is still.

The Commune di Gerra is home to the Mayor, the Commissario, and a hospital for the sick. The hospital floor is one large barren space, with three cots, and two patients—the two Americans from the spacecraft. The younger patient, his head wrapped in bandages, lay breathing normally. The older man was less fortunate. An oxygen mask covered his mouth.

Marisa Leonardo listened to the older man's labored breath as he lay motionless. "Not even her worst dreams had featured such a mangled, tortured face as this." She wondered what had caused such a nightmare.

She turns when the younger man lets out a grunt as he rises from his cot. His eyes remain closed, yet his head rises from his pillow. When she touches his wrist to check his pulse, he opens his eyes.

Anticipating his question, Marisa explains he's in Sicily, in the village of Gerra. The man asks about the others. She replies gently that his aircraft is at the bottom of the sea. Except, of course, the man beside him, who is in critical condition.

Despite her protests, the young pilot rises from his bed and bends over his companion's cot. "Doctor!" he shouts. "Dr. Sharman!"

Marisa continues to attempt to guide the young man back to his bed, but he rudely resists. When he dismisses her as "nurse" she explains she's not a nurse, she's a doctor—or rather "nearly a doctor." This label plagues the poor woman repeatedly throughout the novel and the movie in a labored bit of "whimsey."

The young man persists with Dr. Sharman, removing his oxygen mask, and eventually rousing him. Once the Doctor realizes they are back on Earth and the others have perished, he asks about the specimen. The younger isn't certain, but speculates it went down with the spaceship.

Dr. Sharman rummages beneath his blanket and passes his notebook to the younger man. "Make them . . . make them find it . . . my notes . . ." he utters.

His companion asks how long can it live? How long can it survive in the cylinder? But there is no response. The younger man replaces the oxygen mask, and returns to his cot.

Marissa produces a hypodermic needle from her bag. "What were you talking about?" she asks. "What specimen? I don't understand any of this."

Her patient replies, "You don't. And you won't"

Such a patient, she laments aloud. An all together joy. Yet she wishes him pleasant dreams—if he's capable of them—as she administers a sedative.

When she checks Dr. Sharman's pulse, she declares, "He—he's dead."

"I know," replies the younger man.

She asks him again to explain things, but he refuses to answer, claiming he can't.

"Can't?" she asks. "Or won't?"

"Both . . ." he says as he drifts off to sleep.

Despite his rude and secretive behavior, Marisa reflects on his handsome features as they relax. She tucks a blanket around him and brushes his hair from his forehead.

As evening settles on Gerra, a romantic moon shines down on Marisa as she treks back to her grandfather's trailer, and she can't help but smile.

As she walks, that same moon shines its beams through the trailer's window, illuminating the gelatinous blob on the doctor's work bench. The strange shape inside is more defined. It moves, struggling to free itself.

Slowly, a crack forms in the surface of the glob, and grows wider. Then, a tiny fist with three talon-like fingers emerges.

Despite her long day, Marissa does not feel tired. Rather than exhaustion, she feel energized, as she puzzles over the strange conversation she overheard between the Air Force men. Home at last, she puts down her surgical bag and shrugs off her jacket.

Then she hears a peculiar, sibilant noise that startles her.

When she sees the thing on the workbench, she pales, riveted in speechless awe. The thing is fifteen inches high; the moonlight revealing its grotesque reptilian shape. It hisses at her as if she had frightened it!

WIthout thinking, her hand shoots out and flicks on the overhead lights. The creature jumps at the sudden burst of brilliance.

Marissa calls for her grandfather, and he responds quickly to the urgency in her cry, clutching his dressing gown around his chest.

When he spies the creature, no explanation is required. For a moment, he simply stares at the thing in shock. Then his training and instinct return. He finds his gloves under the workbench, dons them, and gently reaches for the creature. Although it hunches its shoulders and raises its claws, it does not resist the old man's touch, as his fingers close around its scaly body.

The torso of the creature resembles that of a human being. The head is beyond classification. Its tail, that of a reptile; its legs with surprising articulation.

As he notes the remnants of the gelatinous mass on the work bench, he sumises it was some sort of egg.

"Pepe said it came from the sea," he says to Marisa, then directs her to open the empty cage in the truck.

He follows her outside, while holding the creature in his gloved hands. She opens a five-foot-tall cage on the truck bed, and places a blanket across its floor, at his direction.

Placing the creature gently inside, Leonardo closes the cage and securely latches its door. "Dr. Leonardo shivered in spite of himself."

"So ugly," Marisa says quietly. "And so very frightened." Her voice compassionate despite the alien nature of the beast.

They linger a moment and then return to the trailer, confused, fearful, and tired.

The novel follows the script closely in this chapter. Only a few details were changed. On film, Pepe shakes the gelatinous egg out onto the flight jacket rather than onto the sand, so there's no need to wash it off in the tide later.

The youngster practically follows Mondello to the trailer and viewers catch a good look at the cage in the back of the truck early on as Pepe lingers there until Mondello and Marisa set off, leaving Dr. Leonardo alone.

Illustration from page 19.

On film, Dr. Sharman is not wearing an oxygen mask.

Although Marisa ponders the specimen discussed by her patients, she never seems to connect it with the creature on the work bench.

The Things That Went Before

If moviegoers ever wondered about the flight to Venus and what transpired there, Slesar provides the details in this chapter—none of which appear on-screen.

The spaceship's pilot, Robert "Bob" Calder, recalls the chain of events that led him to his hospital bed.

The promise of flight had always intrigued Calder. "From box kites to model airplanes, from home-made gliders to circus stunting in the Flying School of Kansas, from the P-40's of World War II to the Thunderjets of Korea, Calder had known the sky firsthand."

When he heard about the opportunity to fly into outer space, he immediately applied. His first interview was conducted by Dr. Judson Uhl, who soberly contrasted the hardships of everyday routines like eating, drinking, and personal hygiene in a weightless environment with potential exposure to cosmic radiation that may cause sterility.

Despite the threats, Calder persists. He wants the most critical job, that of pilot and commander of the expedition. His next interview with a sour-faced Colonel goes poorly. The Colonel reduces Calder to a stereotype and treats him as such—a privileged flyboy, who hasn't really earned his rise through the ranks—Captain at twenty-one, Major at twenty-four. He believes Cauder's motivation is glory and fame, not grasping the odds of surviving such a dangerous mission.

It's difficult for Calder to control his temper under the Colonel's grilling and the interview ends in a shared disgust for each other.

Still, Calder moves onto the final interview with General McIntosh, who admonishes him for his hot temper. But the General's tone softens as they discuss the wonder of flight and the importance of the mission. Dr. Uhl and Dr. Sharman have given Calder the green light. The final decision now lies with McIntosh.

"The General walked towards him, and put his hand on Calder's shoulder.

"'Fly it for me,' he said softly. 'Fly it for me, Major.'"

Two months later, the starship XY-21 rockets into the sky, with now Colonel Calder guiding its trajectory. Aboard are sixteen crewmen.

Adjusting to the weightless environment is difficult for all, but impacts crewman Jensen the hardest. At first, the quiet mathematician is mildly amused by floating coffee and free-fall sensations, but as the days progress his giddy state becomes uncontrollable. It takes three crewmen to restrain him while Dr. Sharman prepares a sedative.

When he wakes, Jensen's calm demeanor has returned, but he never speaks again. He dies a silent death on Venus.

His is not the only personal mishap on the flight. Bailey is stricken by a strange fever. Key Kyoto goes berserk as the ship's destination nears. Mason and Cardell, who had been friends, suddenly become backbiting, bitter enemies.

Fortunately, the day of the landing, as the planet Venus hovers in the viewscope, a glow of harmony spreads throughout the crew and unites them in their excitement about the adventure ahead.

"For a moment, it almost seemed as if the yellow clouds of Venus had parted, like the Red Sea to Moses, to permit their entry on the silent, sandy world."

Colonel Calder turns the hatch's wheel and leads his crewmen out onto the spongy, sandy terrain. Visibility is poor, thanks to the yellow-reddish mist all around. Instead of exploration, the crew spends their first hours erecting a lighting system around the ship, so they'll be able to find it in the strange Venusian atmosphere.

By the second day, the crew widens the perimeter around the ship to fifty yards. Four men guard the ship while the others gather minerals and explore nearby. Suddenly, the power lines erupt in a shower of sparks and a strangled, terrorized shriek rings out.

As Shuster and Bailey rush to investigate, they find a strange reptilian creature, eight feet tall with a prehensile tail. Dead—apparently electrocuted by the relatively low voltage of their power lines.

Dr. Sharman examines the alien creature, but his attention is quickly diverted when Bailey falls into a dead faint. Inside the ship, Bailey's breath is labored, his voice choked, and his sputum and blood reveal an odd tinge. His system is overrun with some sort of poison.

Suspecting the rations, Calder makes a quick check of their food supply, but finds no trace of contamination.

A mere twelve hours after his initial collapse, Bailey is dead. The crew buries him in the spongy sands of Venus, with Calder presiding over the hastily assembled service.

Then the poison spreads.

"Almost within an hour of each other, the crew felt the sudden surge of dizziness and nausea; the strange combination of exhilaration and depression; the clutching pain at their hearts and lungs." The most severe cases looked after by those with milder symptoms.

In a matter of a few hours, eight of the crew are dead. After burial, Calder tells his crew they're cutting the voyage short and leaving for Earth immediately. They have not completed all of their mission, but they have gathered minerals, botanical, and geologic specimens—and the egg of a Venusian creature like the one that died on their power lines.

Shuster wonders aloud if God knows where Venus is.

"'Sure he does,' Calder answers. 'He'll know they're there. And they'll get special attention. Take my word for it.'"

Soon the spacecraft's rockets fire and the XY-21 heads home to Earth. A few weeks into its journey, a meteor strike cripples the craft. It crashes into the sea, most of its crew and cargo lost beneath the waves.

The Empty Cage

As day breaks, Dr. Leonardo checks on the creature. Once he sees it, he calls out to his granddaughter who comes running to his side. The creature has doubled in size, now standing three feet tall.

The zoologist immediately dons his hat and coat. They will leave for the Museo Zoologico in Roma as soon as he learns where Pepe found the strange egg. He leaves Marisa with the creature and heads for the beach.

Near the prow of an overturned fishing boat, Pepe play-acts a heroic cowboy fending off an Indian attack, his six-shooting blazing. The boy has built a sand castle fortress in the novel, while on film his cover is simply a wooden box and a wicker basket.

The boy spots Dr. Leonardo's approach and ducks out of sight. On film, this behavior is not explained, but in print we learn the boy fears the good doctor has come to reclaim his two hundred lira and take the brand new cowboy hat atop Pepe's head.

Leonardo finds Verrico and Mondello and asks them for the boy's

whereabouts. Mondello points to the box and basket, explaining he was there a moment ago. Verrico will tell the boy he's wanted and will send him to see the doctor tomorrow.

Leonardo explains he and Marisa are leaving for Roma. He turns and heads back to his granddaughter, as Pepe watches from his hiding place.

Just then, a massive sea plane lands in the harbor, its twin engines guiding it along the water, toward the beach. Its passengers, General McIntosh and Dr. Uhl are transported to shore by a skiff sent to fetch them.

On land, a dust-caked jeep arrives and the Americans are greeted by the Comissario of Police. Pepe watches it all in silence.

After introductions, the Comissario takes them to see Colonel Calder, who is waiting outside the hospital. The General and doctor express their congratulations to Calder on the mission and their condolences for the crew who perished. The Comissario agrees to loan them his office, where they retire to speak in confidence.

On their way to Roma, Leonardo and Marisa drive the truck and trailer cautiously along a narrow road. A wind rises from the south, catching a loose edge of the tarpaulin, flapping it against the cage in the back of the truck. In print, Slesar drops a bomb before the next scene change: "The cage was empty." On film, we simply see a shot of the truck and trailer on the road. It looks like it was shot "day for night," under a shadowy canopy of trees. We see a road sign that reads "85km a Messina," with no wind, no empty cage.

Back in Gerra, a black Alfa Romeo arrives at the police station, official flags fluttering from its front fenders. In print, its arrival attracts the attention of some villagers. On film, its sole passenger enters the station without fanfare or observation. As in the previous scene, it seems to be evening.

The man is Signore Contino of the Italian Department of State. After introductions, the Americans request the observation of complete secrecy. Once agreed, McIntosh reveals their successful mission to Venus. It takes some convincing, but once assurances are made McIntosh explains: The air on Venus is poisonous. The special breathing apparatus they developed was only partially successful. Several of the crewmen died on the planet, along with Dr. Sharman, who survived only a few hours after his return to Earth.

They brought back a sealed metal container with an unborn specimen of Venusian life. Now it must be found, so they can discover what physiological process enables life to survive on Venus.

"Not until that secret is learned can another expedition expect to return." And return they must, for Venus hosts "rare and precious minerals that would be of vast benefit to the security and the progress of our civilization."

Signore Contino agrees to provide divers to search the submerged spacecraft in the morning.

In print, we return to the wharf. Pepe watches in rapt attention as divers, outfitted with masks, air tanks and flippers, climb into boats. The General and his associates join the fishermen on the wharf.

Pepe listens in as the General asks Verrico and Mondello about the missing metallic cylinder. It must be found, and the General is willing to pay a reward of a half million lira to anyone who discovers it.

At this, the boy rushes forward. The savvy little hustler wants assurances he can keep his cowboy hat and that the reward will be enough to buy a horse.

Calder stoops to eye level with the boy to calm him and convince him to help.

Pepe leads them to a rocky cave where the discarded cylinder lay. He immediately asks them for his horses, but the cylinder is empty—useless to the Americans.

Calder is slightly more abrasive with the boy in print than onscreen, but the men quickly learn that it's Dr. Leonardo who has the cylinder's specimen. From Verrico they learn Leonardo is on the road to Messina.

Calder takes off with Dr. Uhl and the others to find Leonardo, while the General stays to pay the reward to Pepe. On screen, the General miraculously opens his wallet and withdraws all half a million!

By now the doctor and his granddaughter are well into their journey. In print, Marisa's thoughts drift back to her parents, their deaths during the great war, her life in America, and the rude American pilot she treated in the hospital.

Her reverie is broken by the flapping of the tarpaulin. She asks her grandfather to stop the truck; the canvas has come loose.

In the movie, the director cuts to a quick shot of two jeeps barreling down the rural road in pursuit of the truck and trailer.

Leonardo and Marisa meet at the rear of their truck to resecure the canvas. Leonardo hurls a strap over the back of the truck bed to the opposite side, where Marisa rushes to secure it. As she does so, a three-taloned claw wraps itself around her wrist. She screams and jerks her hand away in horror.

The heavy canvas tarpaulin is ripped apart before the pair's eyes as they back away from the truck with Marisa still screaming. Now the creature is revealed again. It's become the size of a man. It tears at the bars of the cage, breaking and twisting them until a gaping hole allows it to pass through.

The creature leaps to the ground as the humans retreat farther back alongside the trailer. Despite their fright, it appears the creature is not interested in them. It brushes by and disappears into the woods.

Leonardo verifies Marisa is uninjured from the creature's grasp. She is not. But the creature's hand was strangely hot. Suddenly, they hear sirens, Calder and the authorities have arrived.

Marisa recognizes Calder, but he barely acknowledges her presence, saying only, "Hello! It's you—almost a doctor." He directs himself to Leonardo, who explains what happened.

Dr. Url wonders about the creature's rate of growth. Calder can't confirm one way or another, the only data available would be in Dr. Sharman's notebook.

Calder refuses to explain more about the creature to Leonardo and refuses to allow him to join them. Calder and company will track the creature, Leonardo and Marisa will continue on to Roma.

"It looks like my patient's recovered," she says. Then adds in the novel: "But his manners are no better."

Horror Takes Shape

Slesar adds some useful background that doesn't appear in the movie. The creature is hungry, yearning for an unknown source of food it's never tasted. "A food that millennia of inbreeding on a world far away made necessary for its survival." How it grew to the size of a man without eating is another Venusian wonder.

We join the creature in the Italian countryside as it surveys a farm, scaring a herd of horses and then a flock of sheep, before it lingers over a lamb, that appears more curious than fright-

Illustration from page 27.

ened. In print, the creature moves on toward structures of the two-legged beings, driven by its hunger. On film, it's the barking of a dog that attracts its attention.

Here, Slesar adds a scene with a farmer, Vittorio, and his mongrel dog, Carlo. Vittorio is tired from a day of working his fields. He loves his old stray, but is angered by the dog's incessant barking. He peers out a window. "For a moment, he thought he saw a shadow cross the path of moonlight in the barnyard, a shadow bigger than a marauding fox."

Inside the barn, the creature's presence panics the horses. They break free from their restraints and stream out of the structure. Followed, on film, by a flock of chickens.

Striding deeper into the barn, the creature tears into a heap of grain sacks. He finds one filled with a yellowish powdery substance that he scoops into his mouth for a taste. "He growled with pleasure at the taste, at the warmth it imparted to his complaining stomach."

But the famished beast's meal is interrupted when Carlo creeps into the barn, barking and snarling. The dog rushes forward and leaps onto the creature, intent on sinking its teeth into the monster's neck.

On film, the battle is shown in silhouette to lessen the brutality of the short-lived battle. In print, the poor dog is flung into a corner of the barn, broken and bleeding. Onscreen, we simply cut to Vittorio emerging from his home to investigate.

The farmer lights his way with a lantern while calling for his dog. When he finds Carlo's body, his concern mounts. He hears a rustle and is about advance, when suddenly Calder's hand grabs his shoulder, advising, "Dont' move. Back out very slowly."

On film, Vittorio is armed with a rifle he picks up just inside the barn, but in print, he is unarmed.

Both men watch the creature, now in the shadows of the loft above them. When Vittorio is safely at the entrance of the barn with Calder, Dr. Uhl, and the Italian police, Calder tells the men he wants the creature alive. He orders them to bring the wagon he saw in the yard and a long wooden pole—in print, a sharp one.

Also in print, Calder tells Uhl there were hundreds, perhaps thousands of these creatures on Venus. They were only hostile when provoked. He guesses "that poor dog attacked first."

Uhl speculates Venus is going through its prehistorical period, just as Earth once did. He notes a resemblance between the creature and a tyrannosaurus.

Armed with a long wooden pole, Calder attempts to prod the creature toward the wagon, which on film looks like a wooden cage on wheels. He repeats to the police, "No shooting, I want it alive."

Calder nearly maneuvers the creature into place, but when Dr. Uhl tries to push it into the wagon using the cage's gate, the creature is too strong. It hurls the doctor back and then wrests the pole from Calder's grasp.

In the commotion, Vittorio drops his lantern and grabs a pitchfork as the creature ambles past him. The farmer stabs the creature in its back as it yells in pain. It dislodges the fork's tines and turns to Vittorio. The old farmer is thrown to the ground and bitten repeatedly as the others look on in stunned horror.

It's Calder who springs into action, bashing at the creature with a shovel. This momentarily distracts the thing, but once it swats the weapon out of Calder's hands, it returns to its attack on Vittorio.

On film, it's Calder who first grabs a rifle and begins shooting, but in print, it's the police who open fire. They can no longer stand by and allow a man to be killed by the creature. Unfortunately, it seems impervious to bullets and keeps shambling toward them. They fall back to the barn's entrance and quickly close its doors, trapping the creature inside.

At first it rages against the doors, but then things grow quiet inside, and they realize it's tearing into the side. By the time they rush to investigate, the creature has escaped into the woods. It's torn a hole in the side of the old barn. All that's left inside is Vittorio's injured or dead body.

Having lost the creature, the group returns to Dr. Leonardo's trailer, still parked where they'd left it.

Marisa approaches Calder, who is lost to the world in his own thoughts. "I hate to intrude on your precious private thoughts," she growls. "But I'd like to change the bandages on your arm."

For seemingly the first time, he looks down and realizes his old wound has reopened, his blood staining the bandages. This appears to jar him back to the present. He adopts a more congenial tone as he accompanies Marisa into the trailer where she redresses his wound.

By the time she's finished, he's apologized for his brusk behavior and asks her out to dinner—once this is all over. On film, the redressing takes place outside the tailer.

In print, their conversation continues, with Calder verifying the creature really is from Venus, a planet they must return to. "Oh, I don't mean just for the minerals and precious metals—they have importance, sure. But just to do it. Just to make the journey!"

She finds his lust for exploration confusing. "With such an imperfect world here—what gives us the right to seek others? What can we bring them?"

"You don't understand—"

"I do! You men have given up on this world of ours. That's why you look up at space and have your crazy dreams! You don't know how to live on Earth." Then, "So you want escape, Colonel. That's the real truth isn't it? Escape from yourselves!"

Despite her accusations, Calder calms her in an embrace before he returns to the others.

Dr. Uhl has been studying Dr. Sharman's notebook. The creature's basic diet is raw sulfur! Calder concurs, but doesn't quite grasp its significance. Dr. Leonardo tells them there is a rich sulfur bed not many kilometers from where they are, at the base of Mount Etna. It's determined, that's where they'll find the creature. They'll head there in the morning. Leonardo offers the services of the Gardino Zoologica in Roma, but the Commissario disagrees. Now that the creature has become a dangerous threat to the citizens of Italy, they will no longer seek to capture it. It must be killed.

The Commassario boards his jeep and departs. As the second vehicle is about to leave, Calder hijacks it and drives off with Dr. Uhl.

Terror Brought to Bay

Slesar adds a few pages here to allow Calder and his now frienemies a little time to regroup to the Commune di Gerra.

Inside the home of Theresa and Ignacio, a familiar squabble erupts over a dinner barely touched and a belly full of too much Marsala. The spat progresses on cue with Ignacio thrown out and heading for Louisa's tavern for more wine and boasting.

However, tonight his meandering stroll is interrupted by a growl from the woods. The inebriated buffoon quickly incorporates the sound into the private narrative of his muddled mind as the growl becomes a roar.

With his drunken spell breached, he suddenly sees the creature. "He leaped into the air and turned his back on the creature. Then his legs, which had not moved with such speed since he was a boy, now remembered how to travel."

He dashes back home, yanks open the door, and bolts it behind him. Theresa looks up from her dinner in surprise. News of a dragon sprang from his lips. A beast fifty feet high, breathing flames—he saw it with his own eyes!

Theresa dismisses his claims with a snort, chalking it up to so much wine on an empty stomach. But Ignacio surprises her. He grabs the bottle of Marsala and pours it down the washbasin's drain, declaring, "Never again!"

Theresa is overjoyed. Clapping her hands together, she asks, "Ignacio—you mean this?"

"Yes! I mean it, Theresa! Never again buy such cheap wine. From now on—only the best!"

As the novel and film align, we are now back at the Commune di Gerra. The Commissario insists to the General and Contino that it is his duty to destroy the creature before it kills someone. He knows he may be replaced by Contino for taking such a stand, but he must perform the duties of his position.

The Contino has no intention of replacing him.

Then Calder arrives and pleads for preserving the creature's life. He has a plan, if only he's allowed to track it and take it alive. Contino asks, "How do you propose to do this?"

Recalling his experience on Venus, Calder explains the creatures are extremely susceptible to electric shock. If two helicopters were made available, Calder believes they could drop an electrically charged wire net on the beast and paralyze it.

Contino agrees as long as no human life is threatened. Calder will have his 'copters in the morning.

A giant whirlybird hovers eight feet off the ground as the crew below attaches a huge steel net to the undercarriage of the helicopter. (The film requires only a single man to the do the job.)

The hook works fine, releasing the net right on target on the test drop, as Calder and Dr. Uhl observe from the ground. Calder orders the support crew to load bags of sulfur onto the second 'copter. The nonmetallic element will feed the creature once it's been captured. If only they can trap it before the Commissario and his men destroy the beast.

In print, Caulder and Uhl discuss further test drops, but Calder insists there's no time to lose. The crew boards the 'copters, loading a generator alongside the sulfur as Calder hops in beside the pilot of the second, and gives the order to take off.

On the ground, the Commissario and his Carbinieri are already on the road, armed with pistols, carbines, M-3s and flame-throwers. Their German Shepards hot on the creature's trail.

In print, the Carbinieri discuss their mission. An officer named Enrico has heard their weapons will have no effect. The response: "Then we will use fire. Fermati! [Halt!]" They have spotted the creature drinking from the river below them.

On film, the scene begins with the creature beside the river. The baying of the dogs alerts the beast. It roars as it strides across the rocky shore, back to the shelter of the forest.

The 'copters are airborne, searching for the creature. But the Carbinieri spot it first. Backed up against a waterfall, the creature turns to face his attackers.

In print, the dogs break away from their handlers and scare the creature into climbing a tree-lined incline, as the Carbinieri fire their weapons. On film, the creature scales the rocky cliff beside the waterfall as a hail of bullets pepper its impervious, scaly hide.

The police follow the creature, continuing their assault. Now the creature stops to face its attackers. As it advances, a torrent erupts from a flamethrower, and the beast immediately retreats from the scorching blast. As the creature flees, the nearby dry brush bursts into flame, sending a plume of smoke into the clear skies. In print, the smoke is thick enough to blind the crew, slowing their advance.

Meanwhile, the 'copters are closing in on the area. Calder spots a bubbling pool of sulfur and radio-phones Dr. Uhl that, "I think we've spotted the animal. It looks like it's after the sulfur pits. We're going in."

The creature is now larger than ever, roaring in defiance at the sound of the approaching rotors. But it's not in the clear. As Calder scouts the landscape for a clear spot, the second 'bird approaches, the net dangling below its fuselage.

Calder drops a bag of sulfur into a clear spot to lure the creature into the open. A second soon follows to ensure success.

It works. The creature emerges from its cover while the second 'copter stands by. As the creature eats, Calder's bird lands, and the crew disembarks carrying the generator. Calder talks to Dr. Uhl via walkie-talkie and helps guide the net into position.

The heavy net is dropped and lands exactly as planned. In print, the beast is knocked to the ground, but onscreen the creature remains standing, swinging its arms in a futile attempt to break free.

One crew stakes the net to the ground as another sets up the generator and prepares the cable to connect to the steel mesh. By now, Dr. Uhl has landed and stands ready to flip the knife switch. Calder orders the men to jump free as power surges into the net.

Sparks flicker all around the creature as it shutters under the powerful current. It roars in anger and then collapses, paralyzed and unconscious.

On film, Calder silently lights up a cigarette and Dr. Uhl and the soldiers slowly advance on the silent, still beast.

In print, the creature thrashes once more before it succumbs. The Commissario and his men arrive. He regrets they did not arrive sooner to kill the beast.

"It's worth more alive, Commissario," says Calder. "That may be hard for you to understand. But the creature is our ticket back into space."

Probing the Unbelievable

On film, the title "Rome" establishes our new destination. In print, Slesar tees up the opening scene with a few broad strokes on the ancient city, highlighting the excitement in the air,

Illustration from page 53.

before settling in at the American Embassy's anteroom, packed with a flock of reporters.

The attache ushers them into a briefing room. Once assembled, General McIntosh begins his address. He reads from a cablegram signed by the United States Secretary of Defense. The President has authorized release of all information to the press and news agencies. He then reveals the secret mission of the XY-21 spacecraft—its success in collecting specimens from Venus, and its failure to bring all seventeen crewmen home safely.

Colonel Calder, seated on the General's right, will accompany three representatives of the press to view the creature brought back from the planet. The Embassy will provide all the necessary photographs of the creature later.

In print, after the press conference, Dr. Leonardo and Marisa meet with Calder and Dr. Uhl. They ask if they would be allowed to help with the study of the creature. Calder agrees after another "almost a doctor" barb.

The next morning, Calder meets the three selected correspondents outside the Embassy: Maples, an Englishman; Briggs, an American; and Hulda Reynolds, nationality undisclosed.

Calder defers most of their questions to the final summation report coming from Washington, but takes a moment to describe the planet Venus as they ride to the zoo in a limousine: "It's a world out of a madman's dream. Full of yellow dust clouds and desert and fog. You can't see more than a few feet ahead of you, and then all you can see is misty and blurred."

When the newspeople arrive at the zoo, Calder escorts them past the elephant cage and into the elephant house, the only place large enough to house the beast. Inside, the reporters get their first look at the creature laying on a huge 25 foot wooden table with a strong metal band girding its midriff. Its left arm suspended by a chain attached to a massive metal band around its wrist.

Briggs asks about the growth rate, and Calder explains it isn't normal, the scientists believe the atmosphere on Earth has upset its metabolic rate. The more it breathes, the larger it gets.

As the tour continues, Calder introduces Dr. Hans Albert

(Gerhardt Langford onscreen) of Vienna, the world's top expert in anesthesia. Albert keeps the creature unconscious with eighteen hundred volts of electricity coursing through its body, via the wire attached to its wrist.

Dr. Koroku of the University of Tokyo is assisting Dr. Uhl in his research. They've learned the creature's olfactory system is more highly developed than any known creature on Earth.

As the press corp advances up to the platform where the creature lies, Dr. Leonardo and Marisa are administering a compound of sulfur to the beast.

Marisa joins Calder and the two take a moment for a short romantic exchange, while the press corp observes Leonardo and study the creature up close.

Next, Calder introduces them to Dr. Uhl, the civilian scientist in charge of the Venusian project. Uhl explains the creature's respiratory system consists of a complex fibrous filtering system that blocks the poisonous vapors of the Venusian atmosphere. Fortunately, they'll soon be able to duplicate the effect with a synthetic, spongy substance.

The beast has no heart or lungs. Its body is a network of tubes, hence gunfire has little or no effect on it. However, larger weapons such as canons could bring it down.

The news reporters are asked to step back as Dr. Koroku announces a massive electro-dynamometer is coming up to the platform. A cable hoists the giant console overhead, but as it clears the platform it swings into a huge industrial-size lantern. Sparks fly, the lantern breaks free, crashing to the deck of the platform, as Calder yells, "Look out for the cables!"

On the floor, sparks fly as Dr. Albert's electrical board short circuits, losing all power. The elephant house darkens, lit only by the hazy daylight filtering through a skylight. Calder hurriedly ushers everyone out of the makeshift laboratory as Dr. Albert concludes restoring power will not be easy or quick.

Calder finds Marisa and together they exit, as the creature awakens. Straining under its bonds, the creature breaks out of the bands holding its wrists and then prys open the massive band around its midriff. Once free, the creature raises its head defiantly and stands beside the platform in search of escape.

Rampage!

In print, we join General McIntosh at the American Embassy in Rome.

He's visited by Senator Banyon, who just happens to be in town. Beneath a façade of smiles, Banyon, who was outmaneuvered on the first trip to Venus, declares his opposition to a second. Banyon claims public sentiment against another voyage will put an end to the proposition. The loss of sixteen lives sets a miserable precedent.

McIntosh disagrees, the public will support the risks for the benefits a second expedition will provide.

Banyon shifts his argument to the creature that's already killed a man. The General corrects him. It was a dog that was killed. The farmer is still alive, and the creature attacked him only after the old man foolishly provoked it.

Even as the two argue, the creature is under sedation at the zoo. The meeting is over, but the two men's business is not yet finished.

Illustration from page 71.

As the novel joins the movie, a zookeeper guides an elephant out of its cage, away from the chaos outside the elephant house and the shrieks of rage coming from behind its concrete walls. Unfortunately, a moment later those walls crack and crumble under the barrage of the creature's powerful talons.

As the creature clears the wreckage, the elephant trumpets its fury at the alien, and the two giants square off, ready for battle. The creature rushes forward and grabs the pachyderm's head, forcing it back.

A zealous news photographer and the zookeeper rush toward the elephant that topples over them as the creature bears down on it. Screams erupt from the crowd of onlookers, as Calder orders everyone to clear the area. At his request, Dr. Leonardo directs him to the nearest phone.

The battle continues as the combatants spill out of the confines of the zoo, onto the streets of Rome itself. From a phone booth, Calder alerts the General to the situation. McIntosh springs into action. And Segnore Contino calls for immediate assistance from the Italian military.

In print, the elephant suffers horrible gashes, blood pouring from its wounds. The creature is clearly winning the battle, driving its foe backward. With every slash of its talons, the pachyderm loses more of its strength. Closing in for the kill, the creature drives for the elephant's throat, sinking its fangs into the leathery flesh.

On film, the battle still rages as Calder races through the zoo to the car. Once behind the wheel, he drives toward the action. The creature upends the elephant a second time, crushing a parked car under its weight.

For the first time, the elephant gains the upper hand, driving the Venusian to the ground as the creature's arms flail, searching for a grip on its enemy. As the creature regains its feet, the battle continues. The elephant decks the Venusian a second time, but weakens as the film catches up with the novel, and the creature's jaws clamp onto the

Illustration from page 111.

downed pachyderm's neck.

By the time Calder arrives, the elephant lies on its side, still breathing, but perhaps fatally wounded. Marisa, Dr. Leonardo, and Dr. Uhl greet him. Calder tells them help is on the way. He instructs Uhl to escort the others to the Embassy, and to tell McIntosh he's going to track the beast as best he can.

Calder follows the roars of the beast and finds it in the classic pose depicted on the cover of the novel and movie stills: "Its arm lashed out, and its taloned hand closed around a nearby street lamp. The lamp buckled and glass showered into the gutter. Its enormous tail swished menacingly, and then its other hand reached down to grasp one of the running figures in the street."

On impulse, Calder rams the car into the thing's leg at full velocity. The impact topples the beast; it screams in pain or rage, but then clambers back onto its feet. While its down, Calder escapes to safety, hiding behind a column. In print, the creature tips the

car over on its side in retaliation, then moves on.

Calder follows its likely route. In print, he hears the splashing of water. On film, he concludes it's jumped into the Tiber River, which he relays to McIntosh from a conveniently placed phone booth.

Also in print, the pesky Senator Banyon has returned to needle the General. He'd been to the zoo and saw the creature "kill four people—two of them women." He wonders aloud what public opinion will be now.

Soldiers, armed with grenades, and tanks have been dispatched, some have already arrived at the Tiber.

In print, two soldiers, Emilio and Guido toss grenades into the river, ducking down as gushes of water rain down from the explosions. At first, they scoff at their orders, but momentarily, the great beast appears and they alert their commander via walkie-talkie.

On film, Calder joins a group of soldiers on a bridge heaving grenades into the river. At first, there is no sign of the creature, but soon its head rears up to tower over the concrete railing. The men flee as the creature works its way below the bridge and begins breaking through. When the bridge is destroyed, the creature moves on.

In print, Emilio and Guido report their location and soon McIntosh, Contino, and Calder are on their way to Ponte St. Angelo. The General can't stop himself from thinking about Banyon every time another casualty is reported.

When they arrive, Calder learns that one man—Emilio or Guido—remains on the opposite side of the bridge. The soldier tells Calder, via walkie-talkie, that the creature is headed toward the Colosseum.

On film, Calder gives the Ponte St. Angelo location to McIntosh via walkie-talkie, and when the General and

Illustration from pages 80–81.

Contino arrive, he joins them, telling the driver to head for the Colosseum.

Of Death and Love

The novel's final chapter opens with Pepe outfitted in a new suit. It was Verrico's doing; he insisted on it as befitting a boy of such great wealth. At the village general store, Pietre, the shopkeeper tries to tempt the lad with another cowboy hat, wooly pants, or spurs for a horse. But Pepe is no longer interested in cowboy games, they are for children. Now he has chosen to be a spaceman who will travel to the Moon, to Mars, perhaps to Venus.

As for Verrico, he returns to the cave by the beach where the boy hid the cylinder. There, he finds the jacket of one crewman from the spacecraft. He takes it to Mondello and together they bury it in the graveyard. A tribute and dedication to the brave men who lost their lives off the shores of Gerra.

At the American Embassy in Rome, Dr. Leonardo tries to comfort his granddaughter. Soon the creature will be destroyed and Marisa will return to America to complete her education and become a doctor of medicine.

But he understands she is thinking about Colonel Calder. He's seen the look in her eyes, the same look he's observed from the Colonel himself.

"But can a man have two loves, grandfather?" she asks. Space travel is Calder's real love, there isn't room for anything else.

But a man can have two loves, Leonardo explains. He loves the study of birds and animals, yet he also loved Marisa's grandmother. She waits for him in heaven, where their love will bloom again one day.

Their discussion is interrupted by an Italian Major who informs them the creature is headed for the Colosseum, aligning the novel with the film.

The Italian army has already arrived as the creature ambles into the Temple of Saturn ruins. Infantrymen fire upon the beast, trying for a shot at its brain. A flamethrower joins the fray, scorching the hide of the alien beast, causing it to collide with a row of ancient columns that collapse, raining huge blocks of stone down on the troops.

As the creature lumbers off, Calder, McIntosh, and Contino arrive on scene. Calder races into the Colosseum, followed by a unit of infantrymen. The creature enters the Colosseum by scaling its walls, but is momentarily hidden from view.

An eerie quiet hangs over the famous ruins as soldiers deploy on every level. Suddenly, a pair of limestone blocks crash down, barely missing a couple of infantrymen. The creature stands high on one of the upper tiers of the Colo-

Illustration from page 99.

seum, roaring at its enemies.

Calder takes command of a bazooka from one of the men and charges up a flight of stone stairs to get closer to his quarry. He sets himself, takes careful aim and fires, striking the creature in its shoulder. It spins about, screaming in pain and rage.

Seeking to escape the men rushing toward it, the creature scales the side of the amphitheatre to its highest point. It stands atop the great structure, roaring at the men and tanks on the street below. Among them, General McIntosh and Senore Contino.

On film, the creature hurls a massive block of limestone, crushing a trio of soldiers below. Calder rushes to the fallen men, but they are beyond his help. He retrieves a bazooka and continues racing toward the creature.

From the street below, a tank's cannon blasts the beast. (On film, its an artillery gun.) By now Calder has reached an ideal position. He aims and fires the bazooka, dealing the beast a deadly blow. It collapses onto the top

of the wall, barely able to grasp it for support. Again, the tank's cannon (artillery gun) roars, blasting a section of the wall into fragments. With nothing left to cling to, the creature falls over 150 feet to the ground, its body lifeless amid the rubble from the wall.

In print, Calder is both weary and relieved. His shoulders slump as he walks past McIntosh, Contino, Uhl, Leonardo, and Marisa, in silence.

On film, Calder and Marisa walk toward each other silently, slowing making their way to the car.

Uhl says to the General, "Why is it always—always so costly—for man to move from the present to the future?"

This is the end of the film, but the novel includes one final sequence. We join Calder and Marisa at their long awaited romantic dinner—fit to all specifications. But the couple's moment is interrupted by an urgent message from the General. Calder promises he won't be more than half an hour, if she's willing to wait for him. She is.

Calder takes a short walk from the cafe to the Embassy. The General has just received an envelope from Washington, signed by the Secretary of Defense. It's official orders to begin preparations for a second voyage to Venus. The new breathing equipment has been ordered for manufacture. The new XY-22 will be built during the next eighteen months. Even Senator Banyon, can't stand in the way with backing from the White House.

The pilot and commander of the mission will be Calder. The two officers shake hands in congratulations.

Buoyed by the good news, Calder returns to Marisa. The couple talk over dinner and wine for two hours. Before their candle finally flickers out, Calder asks for Marisa's hand in marriage.

"What? Marry a man who'll disappear for months into the void? Who'll never be sure that he can come home?

Illustration from pages 116–117.

Who'll spend half his years in a spaceship or on some terrible alien planet? Who loves space better than his own life? Yes," Marisa replies.

The Players

The final nine pages of the digest are biographies of the movie's stars. William Hopper (1915–1970) not only starred as Colonel Robert "Bob" Calder in *20 Million*, 1957 was the start of TV's *Perry Mason* in which he played detective Paul Drake, the role he is most remembered for. He also starred in *The Deadly Mantis*, that was released in 1957.

Hopper was the son of De Wolf Hopper, an actor, and Hedda Hopper, an actress who later became a syndicated columnist. After high school, Hopper began his acting career in summer stock and then in small parts on Broadway. His movie appearances include *The Fighting 69th*, *High Sierra*, and *The Maltese Falcon*.

He served in the Navy during World War II and was awarded the Bronze Medal and numerous others for his heroic actions. After the war he returned to acting and played Robert Mitchum's brother in *Track of the Cat*, and Natalie Wood's father in *Rebel Without a Cause*.

In 1940, he married actress Jane Gilbert. The couple had a daughter, Joan, in 1947.

Joan Taylor (1929–2012) stars as Marisa in *20 Million*. Even as a child, she always wanted to be an actress. As a youngster and teen, she studied dance and ballet, practicing up to eight hours a day. After high school in 1956, she enrolled at the Pasadena Playhouse, and appeared on stage in over 50 productions during her three years at the famed acting school.

Her first role in film, sharing lead credits with Randolph Scott in Victor Jory's *Fighting Man of the Plains*. Later she played a recurring role in 18 episodes of *The Rifleman* (1960–1962) with Chuck Connors.

John Zaremba (1908–1986) played Dr. Judson Uhl. "Although acting has always been his first choice for a career, circumstances have forced John to try his hand at such jobs as a bandleader, musician, singer, journalist, forest ranger, salesman and publicist, along with his acting."

Zaremba's roles increased when he moved to Hollywood, where he appeared on television's *Arm Chair Detective*, *Favorite Story*, *Dragnet*, *Ford Theater*, *Navy Log*, and *Playhouse 90*. Much later, he was cast in regular roles on the series *Ben Casey* and *The Time Tunnel*.

Thomas Brown Henry (1907–1980) played General McIntosh. He grew up in Los Angeles and attended Stanford University, where he devoted much of his time to drama and speech. After college, his acting career took off with his first major part in 1947's *Joan of Arc*. In addition to *20 Million*, Henry also appeared in Columbia Pictures' *Earth Vs. The Flying Saucers*.

Bart Bradley (1946–) played Pepe. Son of Herb and Chuckie Braverman, Bart first appeared on the *Ed Wynn* TV program at the age of five. He subsequently appeared under his proper name, Bart Braverman in *Cell 2455, Death Row* (1955) and *Somebody Up There Likes Me* (1956).

Henry Slesar (1927–2002) was a prolific author, scriptwriter, and copywriter, famous for his twist endings. His story, "M is for the Many" (*Ellery Queen's Mystery Magazine* March 1957) caught the attention of Alfred Hitchcock, who had it adapted as "Heart of Gold" by James P. Cavanagh for *Alfred Hitchcock Presents*.

He is credited for coining the phrase "coffee break" during his early years as an advertising copywriter. His first fiction sale was "The Brat" (*Imagina-tive Tales* Sept. 1955). Slesar wrote hundreds of stories—mystery, thriller, suspense, fantasy, and science fiction. His pseudonyms include Sley Harson (writing with Harlan Ellison), O.H. Leslie, John Murray, Lee Saber, and Jay Street.

An original copy of *Amazing Stories Science Fiction Novel* in solid condition will likely set you back $100 or more today (2021). At some point, a replica reprint was published, enlarging the digest-size pages to letter-size loose pages, bound with three heavy-duty staples. The reprint makes a great reader copy and is priced at a fraction ($25) the original fetches.

References

<dailymotion.com>
Galctic Central
<IMDB.com>
<sf-encyclopedia.com>
<wikipedia.org>

Paul D. Marks' latest novel: *The Blues Don't Care* published by Down & Out Books 2020.

This issue is dedicated to **Paul D. Marks** (1953–2021). Paul's interview is featured in *TDE11*.

To view a virtual remembrance of Paul visit <youtube.com/watch?v=8prmuLosjfE>

PULPFEST

Celebrating...

MYSTERY, ADVENTURE, SCIENCE FICTION, AND MORE

LOVE IN THE SHADOWS

AT THE **DOUBLETREE** BY **HILTON**
PITTSBURGH-CRANBERRY
IN **MARS, PA**
AUG. 19-22, 2021

Artwork by GEORGE ROZEN for *THE SHADOW* (Nov. 1, 1938)

The End of Wonder

Cogitation by Ward Smith and Vince Nowell, Sr.

"Wonder Stories ended as a digest."
"No! It ended as a 'slick.'"

Two collectors discuss many things about a science-fiction magazine that is over sixty years old.

Background

Vince begins, "The Hugo Gernsback revolutionary all-science-fiction magazine *Amazing Stories* and a host of companion publications about science, electricity, and that fairly new gadget—radio—were all snatched away from him in 1929 in a bankruptcy rigged by a competing publisher.

"Despite those losses, Gernsback quickly started new magazines, including the science-fiction trio: *Air Wonder Stories*, *Science Wonder Stories*, and *Science Wonder Stories Quarterly* (later just *Wonder Stories Quarterly*). After his initial successes (particularly after merging *Air* and *Science Wonder* to become simply *Wonder Stories*), he experienced a gradual downhill run until, after April 1936, Gernsback abandoned this field and sold *Wonder Stories* to Standard Magazines.

"That publisher (Ned L. Pines) changed the title to *Thrilling Wonder Stories* (hereafter noted simply as *TWS*) and resumed publishing on a bimonthly basis in August 1936 (Volume 8, Number 1 on a three-issues per volume schedule). *TWS* ran until January 1955 (Vol. 44, No. 3), or whole number 111.

"In 1957, as a sort-of revival, Frank P. Lualdi of the Better Publications 'Popular Library' group (all under Ned Pines) issued *Wonder Stories*. And that is where the subtitled quotes of this article come in. The 'revival' *WS* was issued not once, but twice."

Sequence

Ward continues, "*Wonder Stories—An Anthology of the Best in Science Fiction* was issued in April 1957. It cost 35¢ and if one were counting whole number issues by title alone, this would have been No. 67 (after Gernsback's last *WS* issue in April 1936). But this issue continued the *TWS* sequence, making it Vol. XLV (or 45) / No. 1, or whole number 112. It was issued in digest size!"

Vince says, "In April 1963, Lualdi put out *Wonder Stories—The Best by Science Fiction's Greatest!* [sic] as a small magazine (aka 'slick') priced at 50¢. Early examination shows it to be the same magazine as the one published in 1957, including authors' contents and the front cover. However, inside, it was marked Vol. XLV / No. 2. That made it whole number 113."

Ward says, "Once we had a chance

WONDER STORIES

AN ANTHOLOGY OF THE BEST IN SCIENCE FICTION

FEATURING:

RAY BRADBURY
JOHN D. MACDONALD
ARTHUR C. CLARKE
FREDRIC BROWN
KURT VONNEGUT, JR.
WALT SHELDON
MARGARET ST. CLAIR
ANTHONY BOUCHER

35¢

The 1957 digest-sized edition of *Wonder Stories.*

to compare issues, we realized that there were many differences between the two publications, including their sizes. The digest measured 5-⅜ x 7-⅝ inches. The slick edition was 16.83 cm x 23.8 cm (or about 6-⅝ x 9-⅜ inches). By the way, there are no artists' credits for cover art nor any of the interior b/w illustrations."

Vince says, "Starting with the front cover (FC), things appear to be the same until you examine their detail. The 1957 FC is less precise, i.e., it is more artistic. While I am no expert at artists' identification by their works, I would hazard a guess that the original could have been done by Richard Powers. The 1963 FC is very precise, mechanically 'correct,' and more in keeping with a lot of later artwork, especially as that appearing in SF 'comic' books.

The back-covers (BC) differ radically, the earlier one being an ad for Popular Library and the later one containing an authors' list and a detail from the FC art. The b/w illustrations for individual stories are the same in both issues and may be by Virgil Finlay. (They use the same starry fields background.)"

Ward says, "However the 1963 edition contains full-page inside FC and BC b/w art by Virgil Finlay, or a damned good imitator of same."

Vince says, "Interestingly, the story contents are very much alike. That probably made it quite inexpensive to virtually re-publish the first issue again. The lead-off work in both issues is a reprint from *Thrilling Wonder Stories* (October 1950) of John D. MacDonald's 'long novel' 'Shadow on the Sand.' This aliens-among-us story takes up over 50% of the pages in both issues. You will enjoy it if you are a MacDonald fan." ("His mysteries are better," interjects Ward.)

Ward continues, "Next is one of your favorite Ray Bradbury short stories, Vince, 'A Sound of Thunder,' reprinted from *Collier's Magazine* from June 28, 1952. Somehow it seems more appropriate today." ("Agreed," acknowledges Vince.) "Then Arthur C. Clarke's early work (from this same publisher's *Startling Stories* July 1952) 'All the Time in the World' reveals how the original story varies radically from Rod Serling's *The Twilight Zone* version as telecast in 1959, starring Burgess Meredith."

Vince takes over, "This is followed by Fredric Brown's 'Man of Distinction,' one of Brown's wonderfully quirky stories. Kurt Vonnegut, Jr. is up next with a piece devoted to the meaning of space (back then), 'Thanasphere.' This first appeared in *Collier's*, September 2, 1950.

"An Anthony Boucher contribution—'Star Bride'—from *TWS* December 1951 presents a parallel to post-war GI marriages. (I hope you are old enough to know that I refer to post-WWII.) Next is a cute cartoon signed by A L VIN. (?)"

Ward adds, "There is no cartoon anywhere in the slick issue; it is exclusive to the digest."

In unison, "And at this juncture we meet a big difference. The 1957 issue contains a short story by Walt Sheldon from *TWS* August 1950 entitled 'Spacemate.' It, too, is an aliens-among-us tale. But this was omitted from the 1963 version, which ran instead a Sheldon short-short story 'The Hunters,' copyright 1952 by Better Publications (Ned Pines). This was a well-written tale of space invaders—with a twist!

"While we're looking at differences, the later publication contains an extra story by Evan Hunter called 'Robert,' about robots not-to-order, and copyright 1953 by Standard Magazines (Ned Pines).

"The final contributor was Margaret St. Clair about elder-care to the extreme, entitled 'The Monitor.' It first appeared in *Startling Stories* in January 1954.

"Besides the brief author bios appearing on the inside covers of the first publication, there was a scattering of 'did-you-know?'-type fillers reflecting the status of science and the man-in-space efforts at the time. By 1963 not

WONDER STORIES

RAY BRADBURY   50c
ARTHUR C. CLARKE
JOHN D. MACDONALD
FREDRIC BROWN
EVAN HUNTER
KURT VONNEGUT, JR.
MARGARET ST. CLAIR
WALT SHELDON
ANTHONY BOUCHER

The Best by Science Fiction's Greatest!

The 1963 slick edition of *Wonder Stories*.

that much had changed, but the fillers were omitted.

"The Publisher was listed as Frank Lualdi and the Editor was Jim Hendryx, Jr. Most other staff position names were different. Both issues offer satisfactory (and a bit better) reading, yet for all general intents they are identical."

In conclusion, Vince asks, "Why were there two releases? As old-time SF fans of the 1950s used to say: 'Ghu knows?'" (Ward wonders, "What the hell does that mean?")

75¢
02194

MARVEL
MAGAZINE
GROUP

TALES OF TERROR AND THE MACABRE

THE HAUNT OF HORROR

JUNE 1973

TM

FEATURING:
CONJURE WIFE
BY
FRITZ LEIBER

THE HAUNT OF HORROR
Article by Richard Krauss

"It's not the first of its kind, though we think it may soon lay claim to being the best; rather, it is part of a long tradition of fictional horror, a tradition that extends back through time to Mary Shelley's *Frankenstein*, and forward to the as-yet-unseen fiction of the future."
–Gerard Conway *The Haunt of Horror* Vol. 1 No. 1 June 1973

Marvel Comics Group was a powerhouse publisher in 1973, branching out with comic magazines and even a trial run of a new digest. Grant Thiessen reports in *Science Fiction, Fantasy, and Weird Fiction Magazines*, "Used to the higher and more immediate profits of the comics, he [Stan Lee] was unwilling to make a firm commitment to the magazine, and he gave it no opportunity to establish itself." Unfortunate, because it had an excellent start, and Marvel certainly had all the resources to make it a success.

The Haunt of Horror Vol. 1 No. 1 June 1973

The Unspoken Invitation
by Gerry Conway, art uncredited

Since genre digest magazine readers are primarily interested in stories, their editors are always cautious about the number of pages devoted to nonfiction content. In *Haunt*, the designer elected to present this material with a different look—7.5 pt. sans serif font versus the 9 pt. serif font used for the fiction. The smaller font takes a moment to get used to, but provides more words per precious page and in turn more pages for fiction.

After too much horror fiction history Conway finally gets to the point in his introduction: "In a way, HAUNT OF HORROR is an experiment. For several years the Marvel Magazine Group has been the leading publisher of comic books on this side of the Atlantic; THE HAUNT OF HORROR is our first effort in another field, and admittedly, we're just the littlest bit uneasy." Hence the digest's roster of top-tier authors and artists.

Conjure Wife
by Fritz Leiber, art uncredited

Reprinted over the span of two issues, *Conjure Wife*, was Fritz Leiber's (1910–1992) first novel, first published in the April 1943 issue of *Unknown*. Revised for the Twayne Publishers' hardcover edition in 1953, it's an excellent choice to kick off *Haunt's* debut; in his editorial Conway wrote: "It contains all that we think a novel of horror and the supernatural should contain: mystery, excitement, suspense, believeable [sic] characters in an all-too-believeable [sic] situation. This is our ideal."

Further testimony to the novel's strength is the number of editions that saw print over the years—including one from Award Books in 1968—just five years prior to *Haunt*. The story was also the inspiration for the films *Weird Woman* (1944), *Night of the Eagle* (aka *Burn, Witch, Burn*)(1962), and *Witches' Brew* (aka *Which Witch is Which?*) (1980).

The story opens with Norman Saylor, sociology professor at Hempnell College, drawn to his wife's dressing room, while she's away. Never before a nosy Norman, Saylor surprises himself by uncovering all the accouterments of a witch. He should know, he built his career around rational explanations of phenomena attributed to the supernatural and witchcraft.

When Norman confronts his wife with his discovery, Tansy is both embarrassed and a little afraid. She only began her secretive practice to benefit and protect Norman from his associates at Hempnell. Norman pleads rationality and convinces her to destroy all her charms and artifacts.

A day later, she feels nothing but relief, whereas Norman starts experiencing trouble. First a student threatens

One of many interior illustrations for *Conjure Wife*, uncredited, but looks like Gene Colan.

Advertisement announcing *The Haunt of Horror* from a Marvel comic magazine.

him over poor grades, then another claims sexual harassment. Next, Norman loses an important promotion, and things head downhill from there.

As the wives of Hempnell's elite faculty play for dominance, Leiber slowly increases the pressure, suspense, and peril.

Prior to his writing career, Leiber was an actor and served as a speech and drama instructor at Occidental College during the 1941–1942 academic year. His fictionalization of faculty life at Hempnell in 1943 is fraught with politics and frenemies that feel authentic and claustrophobic.

Lion 179 paperback, 1953.
Cover by Robert McGuire.

Award AN1143 paperback, 1973.
Cover by Jeff Jones.

The First Step by John K. Diomede,
art by Frank Brunner

Continuing characters are the life's
blood of comic books, so it's no wonder
Conway embraced the idea of a series
for *Haunt*. The intro of John Diomede's
story states, "Beginning a new series of
classic horror in the grand tradition."
The story is told in the form of a letter
which begins like this:

"*You may recall my good friend,
Dr. Warm, who for the past several
years has employed me as a general
assistant in his strange ventures. It
has been my privilege to observe
him, to marvel at the feats of detec-
tion performed by his prodigious
intellect, and to report on those
same exploits from time to time.*"

Dr. Warm's nemesis is his brother,
Canfield. Both are schooled in the
study of incarnations, magic, and the
supernatural. But where Warm is daylight, Canfield is darkness. The story
sends Warm and his assistant to the
countryside in search of nothing more

than a holiday of rest and relaxation.
But since conflict is story, it isn't long
before they find themselves at a remote
farmhouse whose inhabitants soon
begin raising hackles and threatening
possession.

Diomede ably captures the flavor of
a classic series like Edward D. Hoch's
Simon Ark in voice and challenge. This
story would also be well at home in today's indie titles *The Occult Detective* or
Tales from the Magician's Skull.

Neon
by Harlan Ellison, art uncredited

Overall, the production of *Haunt* is
top notch. After all, Marvel was well
connected to an army of top illustra-
tors, designers, and production artists.
Still, the magazine was not without
a few rough edges. Numerous typos
plague both issues and the last two
pages of "Neon" were transposed in
pagination, so it appeared again—as
intended—in issue 2.

Loup Garou by A.A. Attanasio,
art by Mike Ploog

Author of nearly a dozen science fiction stories, A(lfred) A(ngelo) Attanasio (1951–) published the first volume of his Radix Tetrad, *Radix*, in 1981.

The bones of all Haitians are believed to hold magical properties. None so powerful as those of a priest, or mambo, if a woman. That is why Robo, youngest son of mambo Syreeta, vows to protect his dead mother's bones. The eldest son, Nappy Head, doesn't hold such concern, but respects his brother's vow. "We are two who are like one. I have no interest in the bones, I tell you up front. But Robo does, so I must take an interest."

So does Houngan Baah, a male Haitian priest whose offer of thirty gold pieces is refused. This angers the priest who transforms himself into a werewolf a few nights later and begins terrorizing the village.

Attanasio's prose transports his readers into the culture and convictions of a remote Haitian village in this suspense-filled story of Voudoun spirits and retribution.

Seeing Stingy Ed
by David R. Bunch

A twisted surprise awaits the craftsman who visits Ed's feed store hoping to sell his wares. Ed is away, he's told by the shop's new helper, who sits on the musty floor ravling twine into a ball. The craftsman agrees to continue his rounds and in time returns to meet with Ed. The two-page delay handily enhances the strangeness of the new helper and Ed's absence. When Ed finally makes his entrance on page three, it's at the end of a rope.

David R. Bunch's (1925–2000) *Moderan* (Avon, 1971), a collection of linked stories, remains his best-known work. He was also a frequent contributor to *Fantastic, Amazing Stories,* and

other fantasy and science fiction magazines.

The Lurker in the Family Room
by Dennis O'Neil

This pontification about how horror fiction reflects the era in which it was written reads like a comic book geek having a two-way conversation with himself. As Marvel's Stan Lee often remarked, "'Nuff said."

Primarily known for his comic book scripts for DC and Marvel, Dennis O'Neil (1939–2020) also wrote the occasional short story for *F&SF, EQMM, Fantastic,* and *Mike Shayne.*

A Nice Home
by Beverly Goldberg, artist's signature looks like "AN"

An exceptionally bright toddler accepts the condemnation of her parents when she eavesdrops on her sitter's phone conversation. It's just validation. She's seen their behavior and felt their neglect first hand. Something must be done about it, but what can a toddler do? As it turns out, plenty.

Beverly Goldberg's only other published story appears to be "Experiment" in *Worlds of If* (May/Jun 1973).

Ghost in the Corn Crib
by R.A. Lafferty, art Dan Green

Jimmy Latterdale the country boy, and Jimmy Johnston the town boy, put it to George to explain the ghost and its victims.

"I don't know his name, but he had the same name as the dirty hired man and the tinker man. He was some kind of harvest hobo. They fired him over at Towners, and they fired him over at Hofmeyers, and they put the dogs on him at Schnitzgers. He was kind of drunk and nutty. When he came here we had a hired man named Smitty then, and he gave him some more

red-eye and told him to go sleep in the room over the corn crib. And at midnight the ghost came with a rope and made him hang himself."

There's plenty victims more, and by the time George's recollections peter out, the two Jimmies are half in and half out on this ghost thing. So they decide to get up there themselves and see what happens round about midnight. Before the night's done, they're all in.

From the author's page: "Like another famed science-fiction writer, Kurt Vonnegut, Jr., Lafferty [1914–2002] uses the form to explore the foibles and glories of mankind—taking occasional side-trips into humorous fantasy as in 'Ghost.'"

Night Beat by Ramsey Campbell, art uncredited

The twist ending in this four-pager may not take your breath away, but Cambell's atmospheric prose makes the journey memorable.

"He had never been afraid of darkness; it had been the moon that he had feared in childhood, never more so that on the night of the party. But now the darkness seemed a mass of weapons, any one of which might mutilate him. His entire body prickled; each nerve felt the imminence of some poised threat."

Campbell (1946–) was only eighteen when his first story was published, the youngest writer ever published by Arkham House.

Boo KReview [sic]
by Baird Searles, art by H.G.

Searles examines two by Robert Silverberg: *Dying Inside* (didn't like it) and *The Book of the Skulls* (liked it slightly better), followed by a rambling

Interior illustration for R. A. Lafferty's *Ghost in the Corn Crib*, by Dan Green.

gush over Michael Moorcock's *Elric: The Stealer of Souls*, *Stormbringer*, *The Dreaming City*, and *The Sleeping Sorceress*.

Author's Page (Bios.)

Brief, but meaty bios of most of the issue's authors.

Usurp the Night by Robert E. Howard, reprinted from *Weirdbook* No. 3 1970, art uncredited

There is more to the frail and reclusive John Stark than appearances. His accursed experiments with the arcane are a danger to himself and the world outside his rambling estate.

"I experimented with the occult as some men experiment with science. I found that by certain grim and ancient arts a wise man could tear aside the Veil between universes and bring unholy shapes into this terrestrial plane."

Unfortunately for Michael Strang and his fiancé Marjory, Stark succeeds. The tragedy of missing neighborhood cats soon gives way to dogs, and escalates from there, until Marjory herself disappears, leaving Strang no choice but to confront his hideous suspicions. An enthralling contribution to the Cthulhu mythos, packed with escalating feelings of impending doom and swashbuckling action. An excellent closing salvo to wrap-up the debut issue of *Haunt*.

The Haunt of Horror Vol. 1 No. 2 August 1973

Conditional Terror by Gerry Conway, art by Walt Simonson

"An odd fact about people: sometimes horrors don't seem quite as horrible when they're happening to someone else." Conway suggests our ability to separate ourselves from news reports of the tragedies of strangers numbs us to threat, but the horrors we experience through the intimacy of fiction helps reset our balance.

Believe it or not, type and fonts are under discussion next. Story type has been dropped a notch to provide more stories per issue, enabling "two more stories than we'd originally intended." And unmentioned, the type on nonfiction pieces is larger, probably because it was too damn small in the first issue.

Dissatisfied with the illustrations last time, Conway says this issue features "a much more open approach." For me, it wasn't a noticeable change, but the addition of art credits was a notable improvement.

Devil Night by Dennis O'Neil, art by John Buscema

The lead story, featured in a beautiful painting by Kelly Freas on the cover, was a disappointment. The son of an ornery dirt-farmer gets hitched to the ugly daughter of Feeley's livery stable owner in 1918. At their best, every character in this story—except the victims—is despicable, racist, and self-possessed. Its prose is well composed, but the story itself remains bleak and bleaker.

Pelican's Claws by Arthur Byron Cover, art by Dan Green

According to Prussian folklore, Yahweh created the old pelicans. Smaller than today's species, the old pelican's plumage was green and yellow, their beaks sharp and pointed. When the birds abandoned their worship of Yahweh to focus entirely on their offspring, their god was angered. In punishment, when a mother attempted to caress her chicks, she found her beak and claws too sharp. The more she tried to comfort her brood, the worse the damage done. The old pelican's path to extinction was swift and certain.

There's something odd about the

Above: *The Haunt of Horror* Vol. 1 No. 2 August 1973. Cover by Kelly Freas.
Right: Interior illustration for Dennis O'Neil's *Devil Night*, by John Buscema.

young couple that arrives in Blackton County. George Raymond is obsessed with antiquated books and their doctrines. "George said he had been trapped by the pelicans . . . He said they represented man in that they too had fallen from grace and had to suffer for their sins."

A strange tale with a tragic ending appropriate for a horror magazine.

Arthur Byron Cover (1950–) has written short stories for *Pulphouse, Eternity,* and *Heavy Metal*. His first novel, *Autumn Angels* was published in 1975.

The Jewel in the Ash by John K. Diomede, art by Walt Simonson

The second story featuring Dr. Warm and his evil brother Canfield, set five years after the first in *Haunt* No. 1. The two brothers disappeared after an epic battle and each had become trapped inside "a large gem, of dusky color, about the size of a walnut."

Through a series of incidents, Dr. Warm's prison is shattered during WWII and he wakes "on the very plot of ground on which had stood the barn of Mr. Lucas Shoreham [from his earlier adventure]."

Like "The First Step," the entire story is written as a letter by the author, John Diomede, to a man named Ernst, whose role is not defined.

John K. Diomede was a pseudonym of George Alec Effinger (1947–2002), who wrote for *Fantasy & Science Fiction, Asimov's, Amazing, Fantastic,* and other magazines.

Conjure Wife by Fritz Leiber, art by Walt Simonson

The conclusion of the novel from issue No. 1. Digests are notorious for claims like "full-length novel" and "novel-length story," but it's rare when it actually occurs. *Haunt* devotes 138 pages in total to "Conjure Wife," which

includes several full-page illustrations and a recap of part one before the conclusion.

Kilbride by Ron Goulart, art by Frank Brunner

A struggling wordsmith conjures up a demon (Kilbride) to feed him surefire ideas for film scripts. The dubious partnership devolves when Kilbride wrests control from his former boss man. Goulart strikes just the right tone in this humorous nightmare.

> *"Otterson rubbed one knobby hand over his head. 'There are a thousand people in Hollywood with writing talent, ten thousand more who think they have it. Most of them are either starving or writing tripe. What gives you an edge is luck, and I'm going to start having luck.'"*

Ron Goulart (1933–) leveraged his knowledge of Hollywood and ad agencies for this story. A prolific author, Goulart's novels include science fiction, adventure, and superheroes. His nonfiction books include the renown *Cheap Thrills: An Informal History of the Pulp Magazines* (1972). Writing as William Shatner, Goulart ghosted the TekWar novel series, reportedly based on outlines created by Shatner.

Finders Keepers by Anne McCaffrey, art by Billy Graham

A gifted young seer with the uncanny ability to find anything or anyone is coerced into helping a shady insurance man locate a cache of stolen furs. The tone is a bit lighter than many of the forays into the supernatural in this issue, but McCaffrey delivers a fine story, good characters, and a satisfying conclusion.

At the time of this publication, Anne McCaffrey (1926–2011) was already a prominent science fiction author. Her best-known works, the Dragonriders

of Pern series, first appeared in *Analog* (Oct. 1967). "Weyr Search" won the 1968 Hugo Award for best novella. The story was selected by Emily Hockaday for *Analog*'s 90th-year anniversary and reprinted in May/Jun 2020.

Digging Up Atlantis by Lin Carter, art uncredited

An informative exploration of the myths and truths about the fabled lost continent. Carter presents evidence on the origins of Atlantis.

> *"The astonishingly brilliant civilization of ancient Crete was very much like the descriptions of ancient Atlantis. Crete was a gigantic naval power, a maritime civilization that dominated the eastern end of the Mediterranean for about two thousand years. It was by far the most sophisticated civilization of the Bronze Age and very much advanced for its time; in fact, only in the last one hundred years or so has Western civilization caught up with certain of its accomplishments."*

Neon by Harlan Ellison, art by Kelly Freas

When Harlan Ellison got hold of the first issue of *Haunt* and saw the final two pages of his story transposed, he called editor Gerry Conway. "At two thirty on a Sunday morning I received Harlan Ellison's reply: it came first as a shriek and then as a sob over a long-distance telephone call from California. Harlan was irate."

Conway made every effort to undo the mistake, reprinting the story (correctly) in issue No. 2, along with a new introduction and artwork by legendary illustrator Kelly Freas.

The seven-page story is heaped with sarcastic humor and bits drawn from the writer's past, such as clerking at a Times Square bookstore "selling paper-

Advertisement for the issue that never appeared: *The Haunt of Horror* No. 3.

backs and souvenirs to tourists and the theater crowd."

Roger Charma survives an accident and his rebirth with "a collapsible metal finger, the little finger of his left hand; a vortex spiral of neon tubing in his chest, it glowed bright red when activated; and a right eye that came equipped with sensors that fed informational load from both the infrared and ultraviolet ends of the spectrum."

Back on his feet, Charma's karma soon descends from overhead in the form of a winking, pulsing 7 Up sign that declares its love for him; the real love he's been waiting for.

Like everything else that happens in this story, the end is unexpected. "Neon" was reprinted in Ellison's collection *Deathbird Stories* (Harper & Row, 1975).

Author's Page (Bios.)

A page-and-a-half worth of background on Dennis O'Neil, Lin Carter, Arthur Byron Cover, Fritz Leiber, Ron Goulart, and Anne McCaffrey.

Mono No Aware by Howard Waldrop, art uncredited

"The phrase he most often found when reading of Hiroshima was mono no aware. The words meant the traditional acceptance of all bad things in the past as inevitabilities, but with sadness tempered by distance in time."

Inoshiro Nowarra attempts to undo the bombing of Hiroshima that he survived as a child, via time travel.

Like "Neon," "Mono" is more science fiction than haunting horror. Alternate histories are a common element of Howard Waldrop's (1946–) fiction. Primarily a short story writer, his work has appeared in *Galaxy, Analog, Asimov's, Amazing Stories*, and many other SF magazines. His short stories have been collected in over a dozen volumes; his novels include *Them Bones* (Ace, 1984) and *The Texas-Israeli War: 1999* (with Jake Saunders) (Ballantine, 1986).

The page, ". . . In The Wind," announced plans for issue No. 3, which

Material announced for *Haunt* No. 3 (and where most eventually saw print).

Fiction
"The Running of Ladyhound" [advertised as "Demonhound"] by John Jakes
   (*Savage Tales* No. 10 May 1975)
"Fire of Spring" by George Zebrowski (*Chillers* July 1981)
"Goldfish" by R.A. Lafferty (*Crank!* No. 7 1996)
"The Night People" by Alan Brennert (misspelled Brennart)
"Writer's Curse" by Ramsey Campbell (*Night Flights* No. 1 1980/81, *Fantasy Tales* No. 17 1987)

Nonfiction
"The New Witchcraft" by Lin Carter (Perhaps retitled as "Neo Witch Craft"
   Tales of the Zombie No. 4 March 1974)
Interview with a werewolf by Denny O'Neil

never appeared. Purportedly, the fiction backlog was repurposed for the full-size comic magazine, also called *The Haunt of Horror*, launched in 1974. However, the only prose story, "Heartstop" by George Alec Effinger, appearing in No. 1 (May 1974), was not among those announced.

References
Galactic Central
MyComicShop.com
Science Fiction, Fantasy, and Weird Fiction Magazines edited by Marshall B. Tymn and Mike Ashley, Greenwood Press, 1985
Wikipedia

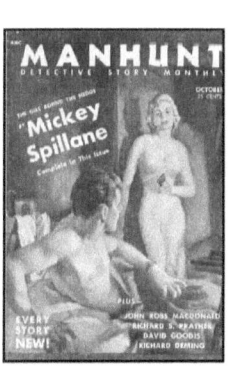

Gnoll Attack

Fantasy fiction by John M. Kuharik

Illustrations by Michael Neno

The super bloom of a sub-tropical fruit, hundreds of miles from Dark City and Buckthorn Burrough, triggered a population boom among local rodents, that

led in turn to a morbid growth in the population of their chief predators, the Gnolls. Eventually the bloom died off, the rodents became scarce, and the Gnolls began to starve. This happened every forty to sixty years, and when it did, the Gnolls did what they always did—headed north by the thousands, eating every warm-blooded animal they could catch.

On a quiet fall day, Dirk and Elvie stood on the back side of their two-room house gazing into their root cellar. He stood short of average for men of the time, seemed to favor his left foot when he walked, and displayed a rough countenance that struggled to smile. His scarred hands, a testimony to outside work and sword fighting, looked older than expected for his twenty-three years.

She moved with the grace of a well-proportioned woman, had an attractive face with a generous mouth that smiled enough for the both of them. Her eyes belied an inner beauty as well, and suggested mystery to those upon whom her gaze chose to linger.

Dirty linen shirts clung to their bodies, stringy hair clung to her face. His hairless head dripped sweat. They'd spent a long morning digging and bagging potatoes.

"Elvie, I think we'll be ok this winter," said Dirk, eyeing what they had already loaded into the root cellar under their cottage, with more to come.

"I believe you this year," she laughed, pulling off her gloves.

"Thanks to your ditch, I don't know how many more bags we can fit in there." She was referring to the new ditch he had dug between the new spring she had found uphill, and the garden. Dirk was sure he had searched every inch of that hill for water, but, well, Elvie had a way of finding things, didn't she?

It had taken a week of digging to bring enough water from the spring to the garden. At first, he worried the ditch he had cut diagonally across the hillside was too long, and had too many leaks. But that eventually proved useful, as the leaks fed a new growth of rich grass for their sheep in the meadow below.

She giggled and looked at her husband's rugged face. "You earned an extra ale with your lunch today."

Of course, he could drink as much ale as he wanted anytime, but this was her way of saying, lovingly, that she appreciated his hard work. "I just might," he said, humoring her. He wouldn't though, because of how ale made him too lazy to work. He gave her side a tickle, and brushed a strand of hair from her always attractive face. "And maybe we *could* knock off early instead, and . . ." But then his body stiffened and he didn't finish his thought. His head jerked sharply right and he held up a hand for quiet.

"What is it?" she asked, grabbing his forearm, alarmed at his abrupt silence.

"Shhh . . . something by the barn."

Suddenly, the two dozen or so sheep grazing contentedly on the new grass in the meadow took off at a run, bleating in fear. Chasing them was a large furry animal that neither Dirk nor Elvie could identify.

"Is that a wolf?" she asked.

"Can't be. Big as that?" He ran after it, grabbing his four-pronged potato spade from the edge of the field. The size of the beast gave Elvie a chill down her spine, but she picked up her shovel and hurried to keep up with her fearless husband.

One can't be sure what sheep are thinking. This group decided to circle the barn as their best chance of escape. Dirk and Elvie watched as the predator, whatever it was, cut the corners, and easily brought down the trailing sheep with one swipe of a paw. With a vicious snarl, it flipped the unfortunate animal over, and began ripping guts out. It slobbered up half the entrails before the victim quit kicking. Focused on sating its hunger, it didn't notice the farm couple approach. The beast yelped in surprise as Dirk lunged and stabbed it in the side with the iron prongs of the spade. It had maybe three seconds to wonder what was happening before Elvie arrived and clubbed its head smartly with her shovel. She hit it again to be sure, and Dirk leaned his full weight on the spade, pinning the animal to the ground. They stepped back as it thrashed its hind legs furiously for a full minute before going still.

"What the hell?" said Elvie, between gasps for breath. "Thing looks a nightmare—like its father was a monster wolf, and its mother a hyena."

Dirk was quiet as he pulled the bloodied spade out from between ribs and watched vital fluids ooze onto the fur.

"I never saw such as this before, but you know, I think it's a Gnoll. Look at the claws," he said, touching a paw with a tine of the spade. "Opposable thumb. You don't see that on any wolf we know of." He looked around nervously. "Certainly, your grandparents told you stories of Gnolls?"

"They died before I was born . . ."

"We've got to hurry, get the sheep into the barn, if we can. Never heard of a single Gnoll. It was always *hordes* of Gnolls the old folks talked about."

Elvie, almost hypnotized by the sight of the bloodied jaws, shivered and missed what he said. "What are we doing?"

"Locking up the sheep. Gnolls come from the south, I don't know why, every other generation or so. They'll kill and eat everything—us too. Got to get everything locked up."

"Why are they coming now?"

"I don't know."

Dirk and Elvie had no luck rounding up any sheep. The terrorized animals had fled beyond reach into the hills, and this fact in itself appeared to rattle Elvie even more than sight of the Gnoll.

The sun was well passed the zenith by the time the couple gave up and headed back to their house. Dirk racked his brain for memories of anything he had heard about attacking Gnolls, but came up with nothing useful. They talked of what kind of onslaught to expect, and how they might block their door and windows. Suddenly, from the entire southern tier of the region, a howling arose that chilled them both.

Elvie saw them first, off to the left, maybe a dozen. "Dirk, they're bigger than the one we killed. We'll never make the front door."

"Head for the root cellar."

The Gnolls saw and smelled them, and went insane. They would have caught the couple had their leader not been diverted by the body of its brethren Dirk and Elvie had killed earlier near the barn. While that group tore into it with their teeth, the farm couple raced to the cellar. They caught another break when the new leader stopped to eat the gloves Elvie had dropped earlier.

Dirk reached the handle of one door and pulled upward, then stepped aside to allow Elvie in first. Feeling the breath of the beast almost on her, she threw down her shovel and leapt past Dirk, landing halfway down the stairs on her rear and bouncing until she sprawled on the dirt floor. Teeth snapped at Dirk's ear as he jumped after her, managing to hold onto the inside handle despite a claw slashing the back of his wrist. He stepped on her hair, and she cried out in pain, as he turned to maneuver the handle of the spade through the inside handles of the door to lock them in.

The Gnolls threw themselves against the doors in a fury of raging bloodlust. The doors sagged and strained against the hinges which emitted worrisome popping sounds. The spade handle rattled with each new assault.

"Quick, pile the potato bags on the stairs to support the doors."

They were tired from the day's labors, and it was dark with the doors shut. Elvie felt like she'd broken her tailbone, but she grabbed the nearest bag she could find, then lugged others to her husband as he stacked them all the way up the steps. Soon, the doorway was completely blocked. Out of breath, they turned toward the sound of each other's breathing and touched each other's faces as they listened to sounds from the floor above their heads. Gnolls had gotten into the house and were running amok.

"They are probably eating our lunch," said Dirk, remembering the pot of lamb stew on the hook over the fireplace embers.

"It won't be enough for them all, that's for sure," said Elvie, intent on a new sound. "Are they trying to scratch through the floor to get to us? Could they get through?"

"I don't know. I guess if they keep at it long enough. It's only pine."

The more she heard wood ripping apart, the more troubled Elvie became. "We've got to do something."

Dirk began to feel around in the dark for something to use as a weapon. Finding nothing he returned to sit by her. "You're quiet," he said.

She didn't reply.

"Elvie," he said, reaching and touching her face. "You ok?"

"Yeah, I guess so. It's just his whole thing took me by surprise. But I'm thinking, don't we have a bag of onions in here somewhere? Let's smash some and rub the juice all over ourselves. Maybe if they can't smell us . . . ."

It was too dark for her to see the confusion on Dirk's face.

His turn to pause. What if Gnolls liked onion-flavored meat? He kept the question to himself, and took a deep breath. He'd trust his experience that things Elvie did usually worked out.

He found the bag and they each took an onion. Elvie bit hers open, he stomped his by foot. Then both rubbed onion juice over themselves until tears streamed from their eyes.

"I'm not putting it in my hair," she said, in what others might have regarded as bit of ill-timed whimsy given the vicious beasts a foot above their heads.

He knew it as her way of buoying his spirits. "Me neither," he said, nervously playing along.

When they finished, they sat back against potato bags. Tears continued to run down their faces as they listened to the Gnolls howl and tear up their house. If anything, the scratching seemed to increase. They felt wood dust, and fragments of wood particles fall through the floorboard cracks and drift down onto their heads. Through the cracks Dirk could see noses moving across the floor above, as well as moving claws. He once caught glimpse of an eye looking at him. That made him jump.

Evie felt drops of liquid on her forehead. "Aww . . . they're drooling on me."

"Maybe they spilled the stew," he offered.

"Maybe worse than that." She paused, "Dirk, I'm not sure we're going to make it."

And that scared him more than anything.

Many miles away, a nomadic fishing clan was camped on the south side of the Little Snake River. Rows of colorful tents were set on a sunny patch of grass at a bend where the shallows were favorable for fish traps. Fish-drying racks dotted the site. Smoke from breakfast fires hung in the air along with the ever-present smell of fish.

As the occupants prepared to start their day, large beasts, unlike any seen before, burst from the sagebrush. Cries of disbelief and terror rang out as ravenous teeth tore into flesh. Even those with weapons ready at hand could do little against the overwhelming num-

bers. The slaughter was over in min-utes.

Meantime, Josh, and his two neph-ews were downriver a quarter mile from the camp, and on the opposite bank. He had built traps there weeks earlier and he was happy with the size of the catches he'd been hauling out of them. As he gutted the current catch, the boys, Birc, eighteen and Dills, eight, speared fish in a deeper pool mid-river. The boys were supposed help him, but Josh, no children of his own, was not the taskmaster their father had been, rest his soul. He was just as happy they had gotten up early to come with him.

Suddenly, they heard the cries of the people being attacked. They couldn't see the camp from where they were, and their first instincts were to run to it. But they stopped when a shadow moving in the low brush near shore stepped into the light, revealing itself as a large-fanged, beast.

"Heyo, look here," Birc said, stum-bling and falling on his backside.

He tried to regain footing on the gravel of the riverbed, as a dozen more came out baring teeth and growling. They launched themselves toward the boy, and he scrambled until finally re-covering his feet. He threw his spear at the attackers before turning to run in knee-deep water back to his Uncle.

"Hurry!" yelled Josh, tightening his grip on his stake-pounding hammer with one hand, yanking Dills onto shore with the other.

The beasts reached the shoreline and began howling, jumping, and tak-ing tentative steps into the water. One pawed an eye where Birc's spear had found its mark.

"They're big," said Dills, rooted in place on the bank, shivering. "Will they come across?"

"Are they afraid of the water?" asked Birc.

"They can't swim," said Josh, "but they watched you wade. Soon as the bravest crosses, the rest will follow. Let's get the horses."

"Come on, run," Birc said, pulling his brother's arm and uprooting him. They scrambled up the river bank on fear-weakened legs, casting fearful glances behind themselves.

"What about Mum and the rest?" asked Dills.

We'll soon see, thought Josh, wondering how he could shield the younger boy from what they would likely find.

Reaching the top of the bank, they ran for the copse of trees, where their horses, having caught the scent of predators, were prancing and pulling against their tethers—so much so that Dills' ran away the moment he untied it. Birc got up on his, as did Uncle Josh, who, drawing on strength he didn't know he still had in his forty-year-old body, pulled Dills up behind him.

"Head for the camp," he yelled, spurring a nervous, and barely controllable horse. Josh reasoned that any camp survivors would be those who had gotten to this side of the river.

When they reached opposite the fish camp, they saw none of their people.

Only red splotches of ground, and more Gnolls gnawing on bones and fighting over scraps of flesh. All the tents had been ripped down and trampled, poles and bedding scattered—a garishly colorful display of death and destruction. Dills began crying for his mother.

Loss and fear combined to grab Josh's head in a vise, blurring his thoughts. How was it possible that his wife and forty people had been killed so quickly? He got his answer, when from his vantage point on the top of the bank, he could see the entirety of the Gnoll horde. Hundreds of Gnolls pressing toward the water, many jumping with pent up energy, some belly deep in the river already. He guessed the first would be scampering across in minutes.

"No one left to save," he said to himself as his fear-crazed horse stomped and struggled to run. His duty now was to save his nephews. He could grieve properly later—if he lived.

An instant before he said to head north, he heard someone call his name.

"Josh, Josh."

A movement off to the left, a flash of white hair and a woman dressed in a leather tunic and leggings emerged from the brush. They recognized her immediately as Nora, the daughter of a distant cousin. That cousin had been an adventurer, returning one day to the camp with Nora's mother—his bride from the City.

Mother and daughter shared the distinction of white hair in the dark-haired clan. But while the mother took to life in a fishing camp with ease, Nora made no secret as a child of hating fish, and all things fishy. So, her father, the adventurer, taught her how to hunt and trap rabbits and find edible plants. The meat she brought back and the natural vegetables she found along the marshy areas upriver were shared with all, and provided a welcomed variety to the diet. The families had long since accepted her difference and regarded her as a valued member.

Grown into a beautiful woman, she attracted numerous suiters. But her inclination to prefer her own company, and her stated intention to move to the City one day, were enough to discourage the sons of fishermen intent on living the life they knew. None had been able to win her over.

She had a crossbow in one hand, two dead rabbits by the ears in the other. Tears ran down her face. She had returned from an early morning hunt, but luckily, had not waded back across to the camp.

"Thank the Fates," she said. "Got room for one more up there boy?" She dropped the rabbits and sprang up onto Birc's horse, settling behind him. "What are we waiting for?"

Despite the deadly situation they were in, Birc was jolted by the fact an attractive woman was pressing against him, with an arm around his chest. His face felt suddenly warm.

"Is there anyone else?" asked Josh.

"They're all dead," she said through tears. "I didn't see anyone get away."

"My mum too?" asked Dills, through tears of his own.

"I think, everybody," she replied. Sorry. Some kind of beasts I've never seen before."

"They're Gnolls," said Josh.

"I only got away because they wouldn't cross the river."

"Oh, that will change," said Birc, showing off his new knowledge of Gnoll behavior.

"I thought we'd head for Hadley Corners. Might be soldiers there," said Josh, as the howling was joined by sounds of splashing.

"Good, let's go," Nora replied, knowing Hadley Corners was too far to reach in a day, but in the right direction for her at the moment.

The horses could see the way, so they let them run full out. They only slowed much later when the howling faded away, then maintained a steady walk for hours.

"The horses need water," Josh said, sometime after noon. "Know of any around here?"

After a few bewildered tries, Nora finally directed them out of the sagebrush to a pond in a depression near some trees. They were all dying of thirst. The people drank first with cupped hands, then let the horses tromp in for their turn. Josh and Birc sat on a log, Dills dropped down next to Nora on a patch of dry grass.

She put an arm around the boy to comfort him and they all sat quietly, contemplating the loss of their families that morning.

Nora broke the silence. "I didn't say this before because it didn't matter, but now it does. Hadley Corners is straight north of here, but too far to reach before dark. My Aunt Elvie's farm is off to the north-east a bit. We could be there in an hour, if you want."

Josh looked up, realizing something for the first time. "Is that the aunt you get the big potatoes from sometimes?"

"The very same."

"She has a real house?"

"Mmm, and a barn."

"Are you suggesting she would take us in?"

"Yeah, with what's happened, I'm sure she would."

"We have to get out of the open. Even her barn . . ."

"Don't worry, she's nice," said Nora, and after a pause, "although a bit odd."

"What do you mean, odd?" asked Birc.

"You'll see."

"No, give me an example."

After thinking, she said. "She always has eggs, but I've never seen chickens. She always has goats' milk, but I've never seen goats.

"So, she goes into town."

"No, I asked her, and she said, get this, 'they come around when I need them.'"

"Also, she has two horses but no corral. You won't see a horse plop anywhere. Now, I did see the horses, and here's my point. She and her husband were loading vegetables on a wagon, and when it came time to hitch up horses, she gives out a low whistle. I'm standing next to her, and I could hardly hear it. A minute later, two horses show up."

"How did you do that?" I asked her.

"Horses can hear long ways off," she said.

"I didn't say it, but I thought, nobody but me heard *that* whistle."

Birc looked like he didn't consider that *too odd*.

"You don't have to believe me. You'll see. She has strange explanations for things that happen."

"And your Uncle?" asked Josh.

"He disappeared years ago. She's on her second husband now. Name's Dirk. Used to be with the soldiers who fought the bandits."

Rooks in the nearby tree tops took off suddenly in a mad racket of croaks and caws. The group leapt to their feet in unison, then looked at each other sheepishly.

"We're kind of jumpy," said Birc.

"Been here too long anyway," said Josh. No one disagreed. Each knew they were set for slaughter in the open like this.

"I'll take Dills this time," said Birc, as he boosted Dills into the saddle. Nora's hugging him on the horse had unnerved the inexperienced young man. Besides, he told himself, he needed to take full responsibility for his brother.

"We'll be to a house soon," he whispered, but the younger boy only let his chin drop to his chest, and resumed to whimpering.

Josh offered Nora his saddle, and he climbed up behind her. "Lead on," he said. The horses were tired, and had to be urged on now. The howling behind grew louder again, and what scared them anew, was a herd of panicked deer racing past.

They plodded on at a slowing pace until Josh said they had to get off and walk, or the horses would die. The howling behind had increased to where they felt like running themselves.

"How much farther," asked Josh, after what seemed like an hour since they had rested at the pond.

"We're here, look."

Dirk and Elvie's farm came into view, and they did break into a run. But the initial wave of happiness that accompanied sighting the house gave way to a stunned dread as they got closer and saw the front door open, no one around, the frame smeared with blood.

"Gnolls have been here already," said Nora, eyeing tracks on the ground and giving voice to all their thoughts. Dills burst out with renewed crying, and nothing anyone in the group said could quiet him.

"How did they get ahead of us?" asked Birc.

"I'd guess a different group crossed the river farther west, where it's narrow like a creek," said Nora.

"And got ahead of the ones chasing us," said Josh. He dismounted and pulled his hammer out of the saddle-bag.

"Right with you," said Birc, getting down, and drawing his filet knife.

Dills and Nora got down too, and handed her reins to Dills. She notched an bolt in her crossbow.

Reaching the door, Josh noticed the blood was dried. Bits of fur swirled underfoot. The howling Gnolls sounded a quarter mile away. Was this to be their sanctuary or a butchery?

He readied himself and stepped inside. Leaning back out a moment later, he said, "No one here, but the place is wrecked."

"I want to see," said Nora, preparing to dismount.

Dills slid off his horse first, dropped the reins and ran into the house. Seeing a bed in the second room, he dove under it.

The horses took off.

"Well, we'll have to make a go of it here now," said Josh, watching them run away. Too bad we didn't get the saddles off."

They all went into the house. Nora's eyes brimmed with tears again. "Aunt Elvie?" she called.

They heard a thumping from under the floor, then Elvie's voice sounding far away, "That you, Nora?"

Dirk and Elvie would explain later what had happened to the them under the house. How they had listened as the growling and scratching eventually stopped. How they'd heard claws clicking across the floor as the beasts first paced around, then slowly wandered away, yelping as if confused.

When later, afternoon winds brought the scent of blood from killed sheep on the hill, the last beasts finally headed that way.

They debated the safety of going out, but Elvie had suggested they give it more time. Exhausted, the couple had dozed off, and slept until the moment Elvie heard Nora calling her name.

While the Aunt and Niece caught up with each other through the cracks in the floor, Dirk pulled bags of potatoes off the stairs to let themselves out. Josh went around back to help.

"You'll keep watch?" he asked Birc.

"You bet."

Before anything else, when he re-entered the house, Dirk removed a board from the wall near the fireplace and pulled out his swords. "Looks like I'll be needing these again."

After handshakes and hugs, it was Nora who asked, "Why do you smell like onions?" And when Elvie answered how onion juice made the Gnolls go away, Nora gave Birc a knowing look.

"Did the Gnolls kill all your sheep," Nora asked.

"I hope not. But they left in a hurry, and we couldn't find them."

"Heyo, Gnolls are here," yelled Birc, a second before the howling made his announcement unnecessary.

They closed the door and braced it with the table. The wood shutters on both windows were already closed and undamaged. The first Gnoll to reach the house threw itself so ferociously against the door that it broke its own neck. Nearby beasts jumped on the body from all directions, ripping it apart, and scarfing it up. Others began clawing at the door, and the sides of the house itself.

Elvie made a show of rubbing her oniony arms against each of them, then leaned against Dirk, and asked for a

chair. Josh looked at his arm doubtfully then up righted the only unbroken chair in the house. They eased Elvie onto the seat. "It's been a long day," she said, with a weak smile.

Sounds of breaking wood came from the bedroom. Birc ran to it. "They broke out the shutters, and one's getting in," he yelled.

The window was small. Only one Gnoll could fit in at a time. This one had an arm and head inside and Birc could hear its hind legs clawing for purchase against the side of the house. Birc saw he could slice at its eyes with his fishing knife, if he was fast and kept to the side opposite its arm. He did that, and the beast howled with pain.

Nora entered, aimed her crossbow, and put a bolt through its throat. Blood spurted, and the beast tried to back out, but was wedged in.

That seemed good, but in no time at all, his pals yanked him out and ate him. Then another tried to climb in. Birc and Nora repeated the process. Dirk stood in reserve.

Dills had come out from under the bed when the shutter was first breeched. He crouched in a corner of the kitchen as far from the action at the window as possible. Through his tears, he observed, "the onion juice isn't working."

Elvie smiled and said kindly, "have patience little boy."

"It'll happen," said Dirk, turning from where he stood next to Nora. And before long, it did. The scratching and battering noise outside fell away, and the chorus of howls diminished to scattered yelps.

When it was totally quiet, they all turned to Elvie, but it was Josh who said, "You're a wizard, aren't you?"

Elvie had slumped in the chair, hardly able to hold her head up. But she nodded.

"She is," said Dirk to them all. "Tries to hide it from the world. It's why we live out here in the middle of nowhere. "But there's no point hiding it from these people, is there?" he said to Elvie.

"None at all," she agreed, softly.

"I knew it," said Nora. "The onion juice is just a cover for the magic."

"You got it."

"And, you don't need that fake whistle to call your horses, or goats, or chickens."

"Right again."

"Finding a new water spring on the hill?"

"Ditto."

"Actually, I'm glad, said Nora, because this means you're not goofy."

"She doesn't look like a wizard," said Dills.

Of course, none of them had ever seen a wizard, but Dills was right. The woman slumped in the chair with dirty clothes, skin splotchy with mud made of potato dust and onion juice, and stringy hair matted with Gnoll drool, looked nothing like any wizard any had imagined.

"I guess I need a bath," Elvie said with a small grin.

"Who doesn't?" they all said at once, cracking up in laughter.

"Thank you for saving us," said Dills, rushing to hug her.

"No problem, little one." She ruffled his hair.

"But there is a problem," Dirk said in a low aside to Josh. "It takes something out of her, the wizardry. The more effort she uses, the more she gets . . . well . . . *drawn down.*"

"Go on."

"Things like finding water, growing big potatoes, summoning her animals are easy for her. But casting a ward protecting six people from an army of Gnolls? Well, see for yourself."

Nora overheard what they said. "So, it seems to me she'll be able to offer us some protection, but we have to do a lot for ourselves."

"I can hear you talking about me," said Elvie. "I'll be all right if anyone wants to get some food started."

I'll wash the cooking pot, said Dirk.

And he directed the others to fetch water, gather vegetables, and bring the ale keg from the cellar. They worked together and put the house in order, discussing how they would handle the next attack, and how to conserve Elvie's power and health.

Over hot soup, Dirk asked if anyone minded it had no meat.

Most said, politely, they didn't mind. Dills said he liked fish better anyway.

"Fish?" said Elvie, somewhat revived after a nap and the meal.

"Maybe if we had a pond . . ."

"Great," said Josh. "Do we dig a fish pond before or after the new entrance to the roof, or the new ladder, or inside opening to the cellar?"

"Or fortifying the house and barn?" added Birc. They all laughed.

Around the fireplace later, amid easy laughs and satisfied sighs, the survivors of the first Gnoll attack of this generation toasted themselves. They had no illusions about life going forward. There would be much hard work, many battles, and more close calls.

But they had hope, they had each other, and they had a wizard.

Born in Binghamton, NY, **John M. Kuharik** is a 1971 Rider College graduate, an Army veteran, and a career public health retiree. He loves alternate universes, and time travel, and spends ridiculous amounts of time playing fantasy MMORG's. His stories, "Brainboy," "Don't See How It Won't Get Worse," and "Suddenly Tired," have appeared in *The Prairie Light Review*. Other Buckthorn Borough adventures appear in *The Digest Enthusiast* No. 2, 4, and 11.

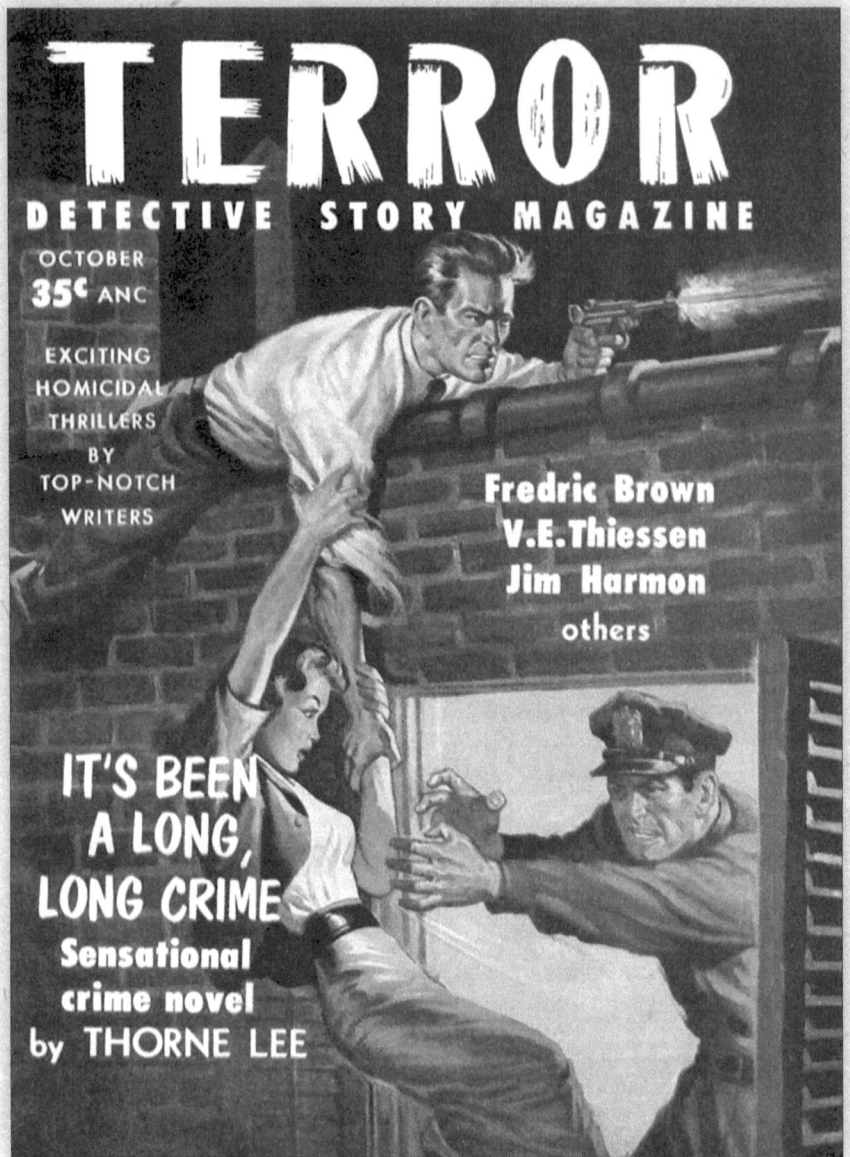

Terror Detective Story Magazine No. 1 October 1956.

"Whether the stories were teenage hoodlumism or gang stories or bedroom fracases, sex was the motivating force. If the reader expected frightening stories of intense dread, he was disappointed."

–*Mystery, Detective, and Espionage Magazines* by Michael L. Cook, Greenwood Press, 1983

Illustration for Thorne Lee's "It's Been a Long, Long Crime," *Terror Detective* No. 1 Oct. 1956.

TERROR DETECTIVE STORY MAGAZINE

Article by Peter Enfantino

"Exciting homicidal thrillers by top-notch writers."

–Cover blurb *Terror Detective Story Magazine* No. 1

As we've come to learn, not all crime digests of the 1950s had long lives. For every *Ellery Queen*, there were several *Homicide Detective* (one and done), and the early death could not always be attributed to the poor quality of the fiction within the covers (one of the best, *Justice*, lasted but four issues). But in the case of *Terror Detective*, a zine that saw only four issues, the generally poor fiction might have been a factor. More than likely, it was due to the sheer amount of reading material available to the public in 1956. Another factor might have been the title, which insinuated a horror-tinged content.

Terror Detective was the brain-child of uber-publisher, Everett "Busy" Arnold, the man responsible for syndicating Will Eisner's "The Spirit" and launching one of the first comic book publishers, Quality Comics, home of such classics as *Plastic Man* and *Blackhawk*. Arnold was not an entrepreneur who was used to failure but, of his four excursions into the crime digest genre (the other three being *Homicide Detective*, *Crime and Justice*, and *Killers Detective*), *Terror* was the longest-lasting at four issues.

Edited by Edward Grenet, who oversaw all four of the Arnold crime titles,

The Great Radio Heroes by Jim Harmon,
Ace A-27, 1967

as well as several of Arnold's men's magazines (*Gusto*), comics (*Web of Evil*) and digests (*Blazing Guns Western*), *Terror Detective* didn't exactly come out of the gates with a bang. Fully one-half of its premiere issue was reprint material culled from Popular's pulp, *New Detective* (at least the second issue reduced that number to one and the practice was halted thereafter) but, with so much detective and crime fiction for readers to choose from, doubtless no one noticed the familiar material.

No. 1 October 1956
128 pages 35 cents

It's Been a Long, Long Crime
by Thorne Lee (13,000 words) ★½
(Reprinted from *New Detective*,
July 1946)

Ladd Chamberlin is a dumb schmuck in the wrong place at the wrong time. While he's having a beer at his favorite tavern, a gorgeous brunette takes the stool next to him at the bar and begins a strange conversation, climaxing with an invitation to the phone booth at the end of the hall. When he works up the nerve to open the booth door, he finds an envelope stuffed with five grand and a postmark from a local town. Perplexed, Ladd returns to his stool and ponders his situation. A short while later, the girl comes back, excuses her drunkenness and requests the return of her envelope. Ladd plays dumb, tells the girl to meet him later in a different spot, and leaves the bar.

Almost immediately, Chamberlin is dragged into an alley, clocked on the head, and unburdened of his newfound dough. A series of ludicrous events follow, and Ladd discovers he's stumbled onto a dangerous arson organization. Luckily for him, the police pretty much deputize Ladd and he goes undercover to bust the mob of firebugs. Overlong and extremely silly, with a truckload of coincidences and obvious "twists," "It's Been a Long, Long Crime" is not a good way to start off a new crime digest magazine (never mind that it's a reprint!); its only strong point, for me, was its joking tone. Thorne Lee had several appearances in the pulps, including a series featuring detectives Renard and Bannister which appeared in *Doc Savage Magazine*.

The Hooked Crook
by Jim Harmon (5500 words) ★

PI Bryce Keller gets a phone call from a frightened girl, claiming someone is trying to kill her, and hoping the dick will come out to help her. By the time Keller arrives at the drugstore phone booth, the girl is dead, injected with a high dose of heroin. The teenage goons that murdered her have stuck around and when Bryce eyeballs them, they kick the shit of him and leave him

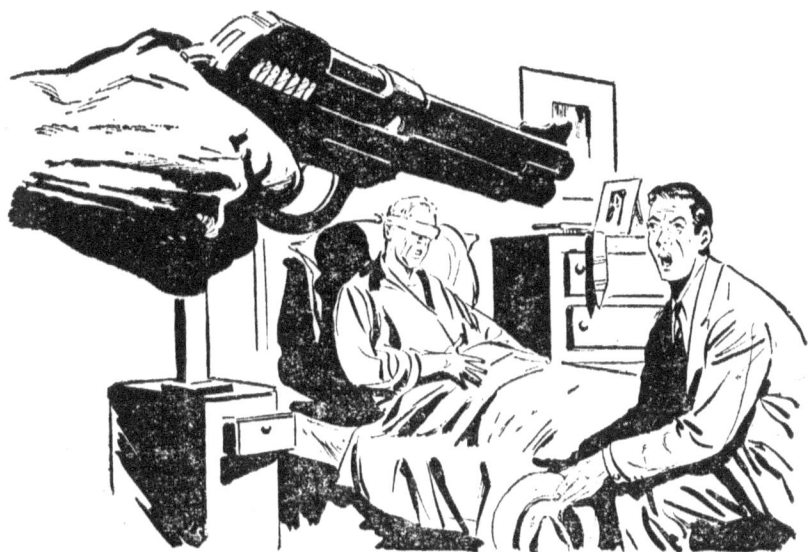

Illustration for Fredric Brown's "See No Murder," *Terror Detective* No. 1 Oct. 1956.

for dead. Not one to abandon a case, even when the client is dead, Keller tracks down the leader of the teen gang and discovers the kid is the son of a man running for Senator and dealing drugs on the side to fund his campaign.

Wrought with cliches, an unremarkable lead character, and badly written dialogue ("Drive you crum bums! It's all our necks!"), "The Hooked Crook" is nothing more than a tired Mike Hammer rip-off. Jim Harmon wrote a handful of short stories for the crime digests but is predominately known for his writing on Old Time Radio (his study, *The Great Radio Heroes*, was one of the first books written on the genre). Harmon later went on to become editor of one of my favorite childhood magazines, Marvel's *Monsters of the Movies*, which in many ways outshone its obvious inspiration.

Bad Medicine by Lawrence Spingarn (2000 words) ★½

Dr. Willis has come to expect the frequent calls from Stella, begging him to come visit the diner and care for her sick husband. Unfortunately, Stella wants her husband's wealth and a life with the good doctor as well. Willis isn't sure he wants to break his oath for a great pair of legs.

Fry by Night by V.E. Thiessen (9000 words) ★★½ (Reprinted from *New Detective*, June 1953)

Louis Ayre, famed painter of risque portraits, has been murdered and the chief suspect is disgraced architect, Mace Fee. The cops think Mace murdered Ayre to recover some dirty pictures the artist bought from Mace's ex-wife, up-and-coming movie star, Patti Louise. But could the truth involve Mace's current squeeze, Melanie, a cigarette girl who works down at Moretti's Forty Nine Club and poses for extra dough? Or is the murderer Moretti, who's been dabbling in blackmail as a side job? The answer may be a bit disappointing but the journey to that revelation is a fun-filled hoot. Author Thiessen, a regular in the pages of *New Detective* and *Detective Tales* during the waning days of the pulp era, jazzes up the proceedings with a fascinating lead character. I was convinced, near the climax, that Thiessen was going to pull off the unthinkable and name his lead hero as the murderer but, alas, the author chose the more predictable path.

Seeds of Death by Arthur Porges
(2400 words) ★★½

Over dinner, Inspector King delights his friends with the story of how a murderer used a bag of rice to upset a mega-ton boulder to pull off what might have been the perfect crime, had it not been for Inspector King and his handy science book. Delightful "cozy" with a charismatic detective who would have made for quite a good series character but, evidently, never made it past this initial case. Arthur Porges was a very prolific science fiction and crime author in the 1950s and 60s, who saw work published in *Ellery Queen*, *Mike Shayne*, and *Alfred Hitchcock* (over 60 stories in *AHMM* alone!) as well as *Fantastic*, *Amazing*, and *The Magazine of Fantasy and Science Fiction*.

Lady in Flight by Rick Daniels
(4500 words) ★ (Reprinted from *New Detective*, February 1946)

Why is everyone in Yermo Beach trying to kill poor pretty Mary? Does it have anything to do with the murder of her friend, Lanny Byrd, or the corpse in the refrigerator? The answer is a bit of both in this utterly ridiculous and overlong "thriller."

See No Murder by Fredric Brown
(8500 words) ★★½ (Reprinted from *New Detective*, June 1953)

Max Easter, temporarily blinded and bedridden, "witnesses" the murder of his good friend, all in the comfortable confines of his own bedroom. But who is the murderer? Could Max Easter be faking his blindness? A detective and his brainy wife think there might be more to Easter than meets the eye but proving it might be impossible. Fun, comfortable "cozy" murder mystery (albeit one with a very wordy expository), written by one of the top crime writers of the 1940s and 50s. The two leads, George and Martha, are very charismatic characters seemingly built for series material but no further adventures materialized.

Dead Right by Jack Bender
(3200 words) ★★

Tension is brewing between a police detective and his wife. The Corby case (man murders wife and dumps her body in front of a subway train) seems to erode what little love they still had and now, as the couple wait for an approaching train, it appears lightning may strike twice. An amiable little crime drama that suffers from a far-fetched twist in its tail.

No. 2 December 1956
128 pages 35 cents

Murderer's Manual by William Vance (15,000 words) ★★

Chuck and June Dillon come to the small Arizona town of Gila, when Chuck is forced to relocate for his job. What they discover there is a hotbed of Peyton Place-like extracurricular activity and back-stabbing, centered around the town's Romeo, the wealthy and powerful Harry Briggs, who seems to have a hold on every man's wife in Gila. Chuck has a hard time settling in to this lifestyle and June only wants a better home to live in, so when Briggs lets her know he can get them a nicer place in exchange for some . . . favors . . . June jumps at the chance. But things don't go well and, very soon, June is hauled in for the murder of Harry Briggs. It's

Terror Detective Story Magazine No. 2 December 1956.

up to Chuck to prove his mousy wife couldn't have stabbed Briggs in the throat.

The first half of "Murderer's Manual" is filled with intrigue and the dynamic of the various couples held my interest completely, but then, alas, there comes the inevitable second half. That's when Chuck dons his Sherlock deerstalker and begins questioning the supporting cast, leading to tedium and a long, drawn-out expository. I was hoping writer Vance was going to throw in a twist and leave June as the murderer, but that was not to be. The reveal is a yawner.

Illustration for William Vance's "Murderer's Manual," *Terror Detective* No. 2 Dec. 1956.

William Vance had several stories published in both the "sleaze detectives" and the "respectables" (*Manhunt, Mike Shayne, The Saint*), and wrote novels such as *Homicide Lost* (Graphic, 1956), *Outlaws Welcome!* (Ace Double, 1958), and *Day of Blood* (Monarch, 1961).

Bleed For Me by John Jakes
(4800 words) ★★★

After a stretch in the army, Leo comes back to town, only to discover his squeeze, Vereen, has moved out without leaving a forwarding address. When he visits his buddy, Detective Ben Clay, the cop tells Leo there's a body in the morgue that might be Vereen. The face is smashed in, identity unknown, but it might be Leo's love. After a few questions are answered, Leo determines the corpse isn't Vereen but one of Leo's old flames, Hilde. Slowly, but surely, the plot thickens right before our main protagonist's eyes and

he tracks Vereen down to her new digs, owned by a rich TV writer. Could Vereen have murdered Hilde to throw Leo off her trail?

The build-up is pulse-quickening, the violence brutal at times, but the denouement is a let-down and almost seems to follow a blueprint for this type of story. Having said that, John Jakes knew how to keep the tension high and his writing is crisp, as in this scene when Leo gets the initial report from Clay:

"I found myself calm, glad quietly that she had been murdered, that at least she might now never remain as some kind of a ghost, haunting me because she existed somewhere in the city or the world."

The Hungry Hound
by Francis S. Battle (1300 words) ★

Stanley wants Karl's property to build an amusement park along the river, but Karl ain't budging. When

Stanley uses the town council to apply even more pressure, Karl kills the man and buries him in his backyard. But Karl's starving hound leads the police right to Stanley's body.

Snapshot of Murder
by Teddy Keller (5200 words) ★½

Ski lodge tour guide Nat Wilson takes the filthy rich (and rude) Charles Meyer and Meyer's new bride, Barbara, up a dangerous slope for a gorgeous view but then watches in horror as Meyer pushes his wife over the edge of a cliff. Meyer cold cocks Nat and then pins the murder on our astonished hero. Can Nat find proof of Meyer's guilt before he's sent up the river? A silly and preposterous thriller with a predictable climax.

Tunnel Kill by Grover Brinkman
(3700 words) ★

When a morbidly obese man jumps in front of a train, Detective Bill Nolan sees beyond the obvious and suspects murder from the start. Turns out he's right; the dead man was smuggling diamonds and his killers wanted the rocks. Like "Snapshot of Murder" before it, "Tunnel Kill" is full of cliched characters, incomprehensible conclusions, and stilted prose. Grover Brinkman was a mainstay of 1950s "low budget" crime digests but contributed mystery stories to the pulps as far back as 1928.

Never Trust a Blonde
by Philip Morgan (4900 words) ★

Lt. Dan Haley finally has the goods on mob boss Lou Costa but the state's witness, hidden in a "safe spot," is gunned down by Costa's assassin. Now it's up to Haley to catch the gunman and use him to put Costa away. A perfectly average crime tale with perfectly average writing ("Take him downtown and grill him!") and a twist ending that's telecast in its title!

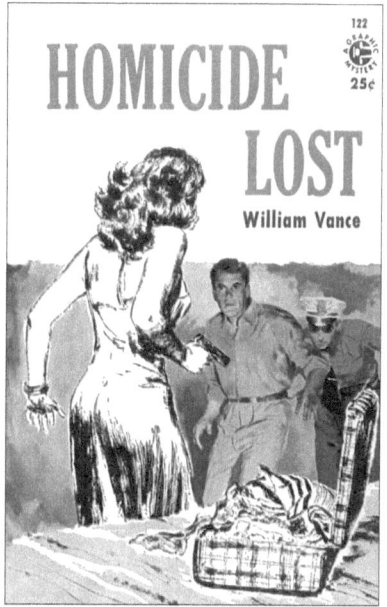

Homicide Lost by William Vance, Graphic 122, 1956.

The Perfect Alibi
by J. M. O'Neil (5700 words) ★★★

Mr. Pesik wants his rich uncle's money, but he doesn't want to wait until the old geezer dies and the will is read, so Pesik plots the perfect crime with the perfect alibi. He rigs all sorts of noises to go off in his apartment while he's traveling to his uncle's house to strangle him. It's all so perfect. The murder goes off without a hitch, and Pesik returns to his apartment for a good night's sleep. The next morning, the police come 'round to ask a series of questions. The man upstairs from Pesik has been murdered and everyone else in the apartment building has an alibi. How will Pesik account for all those noises when he wasn't even home? "The Perfect Alibi" takes its time, setting up its obstacle course in a very entertaining fashion, and then lowers the boom on our protagonist in a deliciously ironic climax.

Illustration for Philip Morgan's "Never Trust a Blonde," *Terror Detective* No. 2 Dec. 1956.

Slow Slay by Robert C. Dennis (5700 words) ★½ (Reprinted from *New Detective,* July 1946)

Talky and boring thriller about a cop investigating a murder at a poker game. Though this issue's cover proudly proclaims "All new stories by the best mystery writers," "Slow Slay" was anything but new; it had, in fact, first appeared a decade earlier in the July 1946 issue of *New Detective* (an issue that also featured stories by David Goodis and Fredric Brown). Robert C. Dennis was not only a prolific contributor to the pulps but also went on to a very successful career as a TV writer (*Alfred Hitchcock Presents, Batman, Outer Limits*), penning over 500 teleplays according to his obituary.

One Case Ala Carte by Steve April (1500 words) ★★

Jack Sands, the private detective, is approached by a man who claims the total of a check sent to a profes-sor working for his firm was lowered when it arrived at its destination. Sands accepts the job but must scramble to get results before the end of his client's lunch break. An amusing PI parody, written by Leonard Zinberg, who also wrote under the more well-known pseudonym of Ed Lacy.

No. 3 February 1957
128 pages 35 cents

Gang Girl
by Harlan Ellison (8400 words) ★½

Very silly juvenile delinquent drama about a straight-laced teenager named Julie who decides she needs a change of pace and becomes the girlfriend of a gang leader named Puff. But don't worry, after Julie watches her Puff knifed to death in a street rumble, she decides being a good girl is all it's cracked up to be. No hint here of the phenomenon that would become Harlan Ellison but, as Harlan explains unapologetically,

Terror Detective Story Magazine No. 3 February 1957.

these "juvie" stories were done to make a living. Still, knowing the author had to put food on the table for him and his young wife doesn't make it any easier to wade through prose as inane as:

> "I nodded my head and he broke into that crinkly smile. Gee, he was cute! I'd known lots of boys in school, but none of them had been as sharp as Puff. He was a real smooth character."

"Gang Girl" was later collected in *The Juvies* (Ace, 1961) but a further reprinting, in *Getting in the Wind* (Kicks, 2012), is the better bargain since *The Juvies* might set you back a couple hundred bucks.

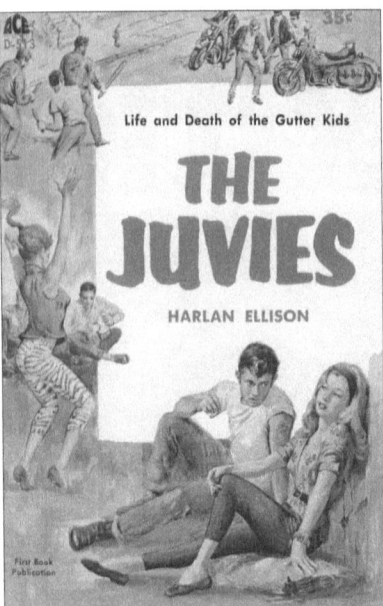

The Juvies by Harlan Ellison, Ace D-513, 1961.

Murder Plays the Mutuels

by Mal Manors (6000 words) ★★

Virtually penniless, Doc Morgan thumbs a ride with a crotchety man driving a horse hauler. The man tells Doc he'll be happy to give him a lift all the way to Jacksonville if Doc will do the driving. Doc happily agrees, and the man lets him know he'll be catching some Z's in the back of the hauler. Several hours later, the vehicle runs out of gas and Doc opens the back to find a dead body and it ain't the guy who was kind enough to give Doc a lift. Wouldn't you know the Highway Patrol would pick that very moment to ride up on the astonished Doc Morgan? What follows is a quick arrest, a hasty escape, and a grisly showdown with the real murderer at an alligator farm. Though it's overlong by several pages, "Murder Plays the Mutuels" does have its fair share of excitement and quite the novel approach to a climax. This was the only short story I could find credited to Mal Manors in any of the crime digests.

Dead Dreams For Sale

by Day Keene (10,400 words) ★★★

Private dick Leo Morley finds his latest client, dress shop owner Mr. Saltzer, has been ventilated in a rather rough manner and now he's out two hundred bucks, but that's not the only problem Leo has; the cops are fingering him for Saltzer's murder. Leo digs deep and discovers Saltzer is only the latest in what appears to be a string of killings perpetrated by . . . a dead man! Five men testified that John Emerson had held them up in their storefronts and, based on that testimony, Emerson was sent up the river for some serious vacation time. But during an attempted prison break, Emerson was killed, so who's out collecting old debts? With three of the five accusers dead, the survivors hire Leo to track the killer before their tickets are punched. An immensely enjoyable romp with shudder pulp overtones and purple prose galore:

"A flight of B-29s roared over and through my head and the bombardier of one of them dropped a sulphur flare that flooded the room with light and revealed a tall, gray-haired, man with a lined face dancing in a daisy chain of a dozen identical Iris'. I remember wondering who the old goat was. Then I realized it was me and the identical girls and the flare faded out and all I was was cold."

I can't say the reveal was startling but, again, it brought to mind the kind of twists that would populate the stories found in *Terror Tales* or *Spicy Mystery*. Since Day Keene got his start in the pulps, the constant exclamation points and dishy dames are no surprise but I've read a handful of the author's novels and I don't remember them being as goofy as "Dead Dreams" (*Home is the Sailor* is a standout). It's the longest story this issue, but it was the fastest read.

Handcuffed Slayer

by Henry Slesar (2500 words) ★★½

Police Captain Al Collier must investigate the murder of successful businessman Jonathan Grenfell, but at least both suspects are still in the room . . . handcuffed to each other! Funny and very witty, "Handcuffed Slayer" is a quick bite to eat with a finale that guarantees a smile.

Game of Death by Bram Norton

(5200 words) ★★★

Irv Gilbert is convinced his business partner, Ben, is out to steal his wife and take over the successful advertising business they've built together. When Ben invites Irv out for a hunting trip, Irv knows what's going down so he mails a letter naming Ben as his murderer just before they hit the forest. Usually, by the third or fourth page, we know (just like Irv) where this narrative is going to take us as we've been down that road more than once or twice, but author Bram Norton (who also wrote for *Sure-Fire* and *Pursuit*) slyly changes gears at least three times on his way to concocting a surprising climax. There's a blink-and-you'll-miss-it subtle hint as to pal Ben's sexuality in an exchange Irv has with his therapist:

> "When Ben got out of the service, he was a different person. Outwardly, he was the same but there was an inner force driving him. First he stole an account called Andromeda Cosmetics, the President of which is a character called Laddie Fairchild."
>
> "That's not the blond, wavy haired Fairchild who's always getting his picture in the paper, and goes around advocating perfume for men?"
>
> "That's the boy. I'd hate to tell you how Ben lined him up."

Home Is the Sailor by Day Keene, Gold Medal 225, 1952.

Get Yourself Killed by Raymond Drennen (5200 words) ★½

Dorothy Meribel, co-owner and number one star of Public Piks, has become something of a diva but, still, it surprises professional bodyguard Kelley Blake when he gets a call from Dorothy, claiming someone wants to murder her. Once he gets to the studio and grills the fading star, he discovers it wasn't Dorothy who called for his help. Who was the mystery caller? Nothing much of interest here, as "Get Yourself Killed" is pretty much interchangeable with dozens of other low-budget "PI" fiction of the 1950s. Shade is thrown on just about every character, and there's a two-page expository at the climax which fools absolutely no one.

Blood in the Stands by Edward D. Hoch (3200 words) ★★

Simon Ark, investigator of the odd,

Terror Detective Story Magazine No. 4 April 1957. Cover by Norman Saunders.

takes in a ballgame with a friend in Miami, but the game is called due to murder. A seemingly impossible crime is solved with ease by the unstoppable Simon Ark. Edward D. Hoch's ages-old detective had previously starred in six strange tales (all appearing in the pulp/digest *Famous Detective*, edited by Robert A. W. Lowndes), but "Blood in the Stands" was a change of pace for Ark, since no supernatural force was responsible for the murder of entrepreneur Ben Hopton (it was the home plate ump!). Ark would get right back in the occult saddle that same month with "The Judge of Hades" for *Crack Detective* (retitled from *Famous Detective*) and deliver another fifty or so

Illustration for Carl Milton's "Blood on My Hands" *Terror Detective* No. 4 April 1957.

supernatural nemeses to justice until Hoch's death in 2008. I must say that, without the occult hook, Ark is simply a poor man's Ellery Queen.

Dog Walk to a Murderer
by Francis C. Battle (2000 words) ★
The Hitch-Hiker by George H. Dammann (1500 words) ★
Lifeless Lover by Jack Sword (2500 words) ★★

"Dog Walk" is a silly short-short about a police detective who uses a dog to sniff out its master's murderer, while "Hitch-Hiker" stars Professor Davis, a kindly soul, who stops to give a wounded vet a lift and quickly regrets it. "Lifeless Lover," about a con man who uses his girlfriend as a pawn in a big payday, starts out promisingly but disappoints in the end.

None of the three short-shorts that close issue No. 3 will make a reader hunt down other stories by the writers, but Jack Sword managed to bust

out of the "sleaze detective" market and place two stories with *Manhunt*, so there might be some hope for quality attached to his name. Francis Battle placed eight stories with such lower-tiers as *Trapped*, *Guilty*, and *Double-Action*, while George C. Dammann, as far as my research tells me, saw only "The Hitch-Hiker" published in the crime digests.

No. 4 April 1957
128 pages 35 cents
Cover by Norman Saunders

Blood on My Hands
by Carl Milton (7600 words) ★★½

Eddie's had a real good day. He sold a boat for his boss and is on his way to drop off the three Gs when a nightclub called the Hi-De-Ho catches his eye. Why not? While he's there, he makes small talk with a babe named Shirl and they head to her place in his convertible. When they get into the car, a man rises from the back seat and tries to take Eddie out with a sap. Unsuccessful, the hood makes good his getaway. Being that he's not the world's smartest guy, Eddie doesn't suspect that Shirl might be in on the ambush and he takes her home. There, after a few drinks, Eddie has his head bashed in and awakens hours later to find Shirl in a pool of blood and his money belt missing. How can he convince the cops he didn't kill the babe?

"Blood on My Hands" is a breezy little shocker, told in a conversational style; we get to know and like Eddie even as we shake our heads in disbelief at all the dumb moves he makes. It's only the outlandish climax that knocks the story down a peg or two.

Bedroom Blonde by Robert Silverberg (2500 words) ★★

Lloyd Harker hires Reeseman and Paula to help him get that divorce he's been itching for. The idea is that Paula will pose with Harker in a hotel bed and Harker's wife will receive a couple of unsavory candids to prove her husband's infidelity. That's the plan, at least, until Paula's husband shows up at the hotel. The only contribution to *Terror Detective* by one of the most prolific authors of the 1950s, "Bedroom Blonde" is a quick fix with a funny final scene.

Death's Lovely Mistress by Matt Christopher (4100 words) ★★½

Walt gets a big surprise when he takes Jean to the drive-in and a man jumps into the backseat just as things are heating up. Turns out Jean has a husband and Walt is the target of a little con game involving her and her hubby. "Death's Lovely Mistress" is an odd tale revolving around office politics, attempted murder, and the unlikely motive of a better-paying job (an extra six grand a year!). The whole scheme goes belly-up and Walt comes out on top, if a little bent and bloodied.

Touchdown for Murder by Robert Turner (3700 words) ★★★

After the girl he loves casts him aside for the high school football star, 14-year-old Leo climbs to the roof of a school building with a rifle and a plan to make headlines. A decade before Charles Whitman and *Targets*, pulp veteran Robert Turner created the misunderstood, mentally ill, and sociopathic Leo, who kills the rival of his affections (although there's a subtle hint that the jealousy *may* be directed at the female in the triangle) with a single bullet and then calmly climbs down and heads home for bed. There's some clumsy psychology in one passage that visits a conversation between Leo's worrying mom and his uncaring father, but the problem may be due to the fact that we've grown numb to the "bad childhood" excuse. Still, warts and all, "Touchdown for Murder" (a really awful title) is a tense and gripping shocker.

Killer Cop by Irwin Booth (6600 words) ★½

Gorgeous Jerri Casala is waiting on a bus when a grizzled bum starts harassing her. Along comes beat cop Russ Jordan to shoo away the vagrant, but the confrontation turns deadly when the stranger pops Russ in the kisser and the cop shoots the man twice. A few weeks later, Russ is on trial and he's got a new girl in the grateful Jerri, but something keeps nagging at Jerri's best friend, Ziggy: the amateur detective work he's done points to a prior connection between the cop and the dead man. Unfortunately, that's where "Killer Cop" turns ludicrous. Irwin Booth is a pseudonym used by Edward D. Hoch.

Illustration for Koller Ernest's "Arsenic Love Potion," *Terror Detective* No. 4 April 1957.

Arsenic Love Potion by Koller Ernst (3600 words) ★★★½

Even an awful title can't diminish the horrors of Koller Ernst's "Arsenic Love Potion," about Arthur and Nannine Matson, the ideal couple who hide a strange existence behind closed doors. Avoiding sex or even close contact, the two seem to percolate inside until the lid blows in a night of violence. Ernst's prose is subtle when it comes to describing Arthur's growing disdain for his wife; all around him are less-polite men who seem to be having a more fulfilling relationship with their "woman." Ernst was a frequent contributor to the "low-budget" crime digests, but did crack through to the "big leagues" now and then. "Arsenic Love Potion" (with a more subtle title) would have been perfect fodder for the pages of *Alfred Hitchcock's Mystery Magazine*.

Crater of Fear by Jimmy Walker (4500 words) ★★½

Laird and Peggy are enjoying their climb up a massive volcano in the snow until danger, in the form of Peggy's husband, rears its head below them. John is not a forgiving husband, and he's determined that both adulterers will find their final resting place atop this dormant volcano. An exciting and unpredictable adventure.

Execution at Eleven P.M. by Jonathan Craig (1400 words) ★

A predictable short-short about a man and his son having their last conversation on death row. But which one is the sentenced man? It would seem a very short amount of space would work against a writer, but "Execution at Eleven P.M." is like an extended one-liner. We all know where it's going, but it's taking quite a lot of time to get there. Jonathan Craig, of course, was responsible for so many more quality short stories over the course of his long career, including several appearances in *Manhunt*, *Alfred Hitchcock's*, and *Mike Shayne*. He also created the

6th Precinct series of novels, featuring detective Pete Selby and Stan Rayder.

Gun for Hire
by Jack Sword (3300 words) ★

A hitman hires on to do away with a businessman's two partners. The first kill goes smooth but, upon shooting the second man, the assassin gets a rude surprise. There's a whale of a co-incidence and a climax that makes very little sense. Those two detriments make "Gun for Hire" almost unreadable.

Laugh Till You Die
by Frank Anmar (7200 words) ★½

Screenwriter Alan Cole gets a call from his old buddy, Paul, who desper-ately needs to talk to him at his place of business, the old amusement park fun house. Alan is a little suspicious since Paul promised to kill him when Alan stole pretty Jessica away from him, but decides he'll let the man have his say. When Alan gets to the fun house, the lights are out and Paul is definitely playing games. Alan laughs it off until the lights go on and he sees Jessica, hanging from the ceiling by her own nylons. Paul has lost his mind! A pure pulp plot disintegrates into a ludicrous laugh-fest.

A Job for Jerecki by Gilbert Schechtman (2000 words) ★★

Jerecki's got a real good thing going. He's partnered with a pal and opened a business aimed at "divorce evidence." In other words, Jerecki opens hotel doors at just the right time and takes a couple pics for an estranged husband or wife. Jerecki got into this high-paying racket because his wife, a good looker named Marilyn, has expensive tastes and it takes a big payroll to keep her happy. But, when Jerecki opens the door to Room 1218 that night, he discovers that Marilyn wants more than just furs and caviar. "A Job for Jerecki" isn't a bad short-short, but it's formulaic and it telecasts its "shock ending" only a few paragraphs into the narrative.

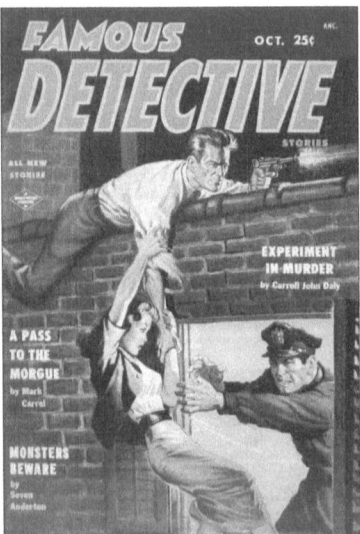

Famous Detective Stories Oct. 1954.

Two of *Terror Detective's* cover paintings ap-peared earlier on issues of *Famous Detective Stories*, a pulp magazine that changed its title numerous times from its start in 1938 as *Detective Yarns*.

Repurposed covers from pulp to digest include:
- *Crack Detective* Sept. 1949 to *Crime and Justice Detective Story Magazine* Jan. 1957.
- *Famous Detective* Nov. 1949 to *Killers Mystery Story Magazine* Jan. 1957.
- *Famous Detective* April 1954 to *Killers Mystery Story Magazine* Nov. 1956
- *Famous Detective Stories* May 1953 to *Terror Detective Story Magazine* Dec. 1956.
- *Famous Detective Stories* Oct. 1954 to *Terror Detective Story Magazine* Oct. 1956.

Opening Lines
Selections from the digests featured in this edition

"It began with a sound, a faint sliding of feet in the deep pile of the rug, and a touch, the sharp bright pain of a knife point thrust against the back of his neck."
"Fry By Night" by V.E. Thiessen *Terror Detective Story Magazine* October 1956.

"Daisy and I were enjoying one of our usual quarrels."
"House of the Hatchet" by Robert Bloch *Startling Mystery Stories* No. 1 Summer 1966.

"Jassie thought about her little white neck, and he thought about the course, rough hemp of the hangman's noose coiling fatally around the soft, smooth, creamy-pale skin of it."
"You Can't Kill Her" by C.B. Gilford *Manhunt Detective Story Monthly* July 1955.

"The great Beldini, feeling not so great, and aware of a faster than usual thumping in his chest, stared into the mirror and lathered the part of his face not covered with sideburns, beard, and mustache."
"Moon Heat" by Ernst Taves *Galaxy* Aug/Sep 1970.

"Hell must be easily as beautiful as heaven, John Ward thought."
"The Strad Effect" by Raymond F. Jones *Vanguard Science Fiction* June 1958.

"Before the war, they used to say the Eisel family had a devil, and considering all that happened, it must have been true."
"Devil Night" by Dennis O'Neil *The Haunt of Horror* No. 2 August 1973.

"When Sebastian gifted Millie a phrenology bust detailing the study of crania for her thirtieth birthday, Millie decided she'd had just about enough of him"
"Phrenology" by Natalie Harris-Spencer *The Dark City* October 2020.

"This was a party which Cholly Knickerbocker, in tomorrow's Los Angeles *Examiner*, would describe as 'a gathering of the Smart Set,' and if this was the Smart Set I was glad I belonged to the Stupid Set."
"Nudists Die Naked" by Richard S. Prather *Manhunt Detective Story Monthly* August 1955.

"I guess I stepped into the sucker category the minute I hauled the well-padded wallet from my hip pocket to pay for my drink."
"Blood on My Hands by Karl Milton *Terror Detective Story Magazine* April 1957.

"There's the gun, Padre. You want to be a hero, use it."
"Sacrifice" by Warren Frost *Ed McBain's Mystery Book* No. 3.

"Nobody but John Hillary Dane would even have considered trying to build a major conservatory in the snow-rimmed crater of Coropuna, and nobody—unless you counted government as somebody—but Dane could actually have done it."
"The City that was the World" by James Blish *Galaxy* July 1969.

"To say my dad didn't have much luck with wives is like saying the Minnesota Vikings didn't have much luck in Super Bowls."
"Killer Advice" by Michael Cahlin *Down & Out: The Magazine* Vol. 2 No. 2 December 2020.